Praise for An Altar By The River

"*An Altar by the River* skillfully blends elements of mystery, horror, and detective fiction in a suspenseful clash of good and evil that will keep readers turning pages to the end." ~Christopher Valen, author of *White Tombs* and *The Black Minute.*

"Another riveting look at what happens when true evil meets "good guy" detectives Corky Aleckson and Smoke Dawes. Husom's colorful characters and small town Minnesota setting are the perfect backdrop for her compelling mysteries, Christine is an expert at weaving in details and clues in just the right doses to keep you wondering until the very last moment." ~Sherrie Hansen, author of *Night and Day*, *Stormy Weather*, and *Water Lily.*

"Convincing police dialog, scary murder scenes, a likeable and skillful female protagonist, and a pleasing cast of coworkers and friends characterize Christine Husom's Winnebago County mysteries--I just wish there were more of them. *An Altar by the River* is third in the series and, like the others, gives readers intriguing glimpses into evil-doers' minds while following Sergeant Corinne Aleckson's investigation.

"Darker and more haunting than the earlier two mysteries, with overtones of real life secret fears, this novel's a thoroughly enjoyable read, a scary investigation, and a pleasing example of how the author creates both bad characters and good, with deep insights, clever plotting, and smart switches in point of view. I definitely enjoyed this, and I really hope there might be more to come." ~Sheila Deeth, author.

Also by Christine Husom

AN
ALTAR
BY THE
RIVER

Third in the Winnebago County Mystery Series

Christine Husom

The wRight Press

The wRight Press edition published 2018.

Cover art by Richard Haskin, Minneapolis, Minnesota
Cover layout by Precision Prints, Buffalo, Minnesota

The wRight Press
804 Circle Drive
Buffalo, Minnesota, 55313

Printed in the United States of America

ISBN 978-1-948068-04-8

Written with compassion for those who have suffered through abuse, and with gratitude for the people who are dedicated to helping them heal.

Acknowledgements

Thank you, family and friends for your continued support. It means more to me than words can express. Also, thank you to a team of helpers for your expertise, advice, ideas, and proofreading: Dan Husom, Scott Bernstein, April Carlson, Ed Dubois, Judy Lewis, Lisa Kamrath, Tia Larson, Elizabeth Husom, Morynn Marx, and Adrienne Murray. I greatly appreciate everything.

1

The laptop computer mounted next to the steering wheel in my squad car beeped, and a message appeared on the screen.

Phone Gregory Trippen @ 802-555-4243.

I was near the southwest border of the county, driving past rolling acres of plowed fields readied for planting in the upcoming weeks. I took a right onto the next road, a bumpy gravel leading into a small Finnish Lutheran cemetery at the rise of a hill. I stopped my car, flanked on both sides by headstones adorned with names full of double vowels and consonants.

It was an unfamiliar area code. I punched in the ten digits. It barely rang when a panicked "Hello?" came from the other end.

"Gregory Trippen, please."

"That's me."

"Sergeant Corinne Aleckson, Winnebago County Sheriff's Department. I had a message to call—"

"It's my brother. He's on his way to Winnebago County to sacrifice himself on Satan's altar." His words tumbled out with urgency.

I pulled the memo pad from my breast pocket and tried to digest what he said. "Mr. Trippen, could you repeat that?"

"Jeff phoned a few minutes ago to tell me. He even sent me a picture of the dagger he's going to use to my cell phone. I tried to talk to him, find out where he is, but all he would say is he's on his way to Winnebago County to sacrifice himself on Satan's altar. I don't know what to do."

Sacrifice himself on Satan's altar? In Winnebago County?

"Mr. Trippen, does that make any sense to you? Is your brother suffering from a mental illness?

"Yes. To both questions."

"Okay, let me get some information and we'll take it from there. You said you don't know where your brother is, but he's on his way here to Winnebago County. Where are you? I don't recognize the eight oh two area code."

"It's Vermont, but I'm in upstate New York right now. I'm an over-the-road truck driver. Just dropped off a load and was on my way home when Jeff called."

"Okay. I'll need your full name and date of birth to start the report."

"Gregory Patrick Trippen, December thirteenth, nineteen eighty."

"Address?" It was in Vermont. "And your commercial license was issued there?" I asked.

"Yes."

I sent a message to Winnebago County Communications requesting an out-of-state search on Trippen.

"But what about my brother?"

"What's his full name, date of birth, address?"

"Jeffrey Leon Trippen. Ah, born April thirtieth, ah, nineteen eighty-two." He paused. "I only have his post office box number and latest cell phone number, which he's probably thrown away by now."

While Trippen continued, I typed in the vital statistics and sent a second message to Communications. "He's moved around a lot, landed in New York last year. He gets P.O. boxes so I can send him money, but I never really know where he's staying. Poor Jeff went off the deep end years ago. I don't know what else to do to help him except send him money. I never expected this." His voice cracked.

Communications found Gregory Trippen at the address he gave and as the holder of a commercial driver's license. They found an identification-only license for Jeffrey Trippen, issued in Vermont two years prior.

"Mr. Trippen, what's your brother's connection to Winnebago County?"

"We grew up there, in Wellspring. My mother got us out of there when we were still kids, but it was too late for Jeff."

"What do you mean?"

"Our mother married a man when we were little, after our dad died. It turned out he was a hard-core Satanist. When I got older I started to believe that monster killed my dad so he could have my mom and her boys."

One thing at a time.

Was Gregory Trippen a rational man? It was difficult to determine in a few-minute phone conversation packed with wild claims of what his brother was planning, their involvement with a cult, and that his stepfather had likely killed his father to marry his mother and gain control of her sons. "Mr. Trippen, we need to meet in person. When can you get to Oak Lea, to the sheriff's department?"

Trippen's voice was trembling and sounded like he was struggling to hold in his tears. "I hadn't thought that far. I about lost it getting that call and seeing the picture of the dagger on top of it all. I did the only thing I could think of. Call you guys."

His end of the phone went silent. "Mr. Trippen?"

"Yeah, I guess I'll have to come to Winnebago County. I never wanted to go back there, but I gotta do all I can to save my brother. I'll get this rig back. I'm four hours from home. I don't like to fly. My brother won't fly, so if I drive, hopefully I'll still make it there before he does."

"It's a long drive from Vermont."

"About thirteen hundred miles. Twenty hours or so in a car."

"You'll need to sleep before you start off on another long drive."

"My friend is out of work. I'll hire him to go with me, and he can take the first leg."

"What about your mother? Where is she?"

"In Vermont, but I don't want to tell her about this yet. She feels she's responsible for Jeff's illness, and worries all the time. I want to leave her out of it for now."

"All right. I'll give you my cell number so you can call me when you have an idea of when you'll get here."

"I can trust you, right?"

"Trust me?"

"A few years ago when I thought *they* had finally given up on us, I phoned a lieutenant there to ask about my father's case. He was one of the deputies who was involved with it."

"What happened to your father, exactly?"

"He was deer hunting with three other guys, and they all said they mistook him for a deer. They all shot their shotguns, and two hit him. They didn't know which two it was. *All* of them mistook him for a deer? I was hoping they'd reopen the case, but the lieutenant said the detective had determined that it was an accident."

"Do you remember the lieutenant's name?"

"Armstrong. Alden Armstrong."

Alden Armstrong. A veteran of many years with the department.

"And your father's name?"

"Harlan Manthes."

"Not Trippen?"

"No, my mother legally changed our names after we got to Vermont, for protection from *them*."

"I will never give you a reason not to trust me, Mr. Trippen. At least not intentionally."

His voice was hesitant. "I need to believe you." A pause, then, "I wasn't trying to offend you or anything, but I've learned to protect myself from people who you think are one way and then they turn out to be the opposite."

"I understand. To let you know, I had Communications send me a physical description of your brother. According to this he's five ten, one hundred and sixty pounds, brown hair, blue eyes. I'll pull up his photo when I get back to the station. He has an identification card, not a driver's license. Is that correct, from what you know?"

"Yeah. He had a license, but he lost it—a drunk driving offense—and never tried to get it back. He might weigh less than one sixty."

"What's his style in clothing? How does he wear his hair?"

"I haven't seen him in two years. He was looking pretty unkempt at that time. Long scraggly hair pulled back in a ponytail, long beard. He wears jeans and whatever shirt or jacket he picks up at places like the Salvation Army."

With a photo to match Trippen's description of his brother, he'd be fairly easy to spot. There weren't many transients in the county. They tended to pass through Winnebago in search of counties better equipped to handle their needs.

"Where is your brother headed to? Where is the altar located?"

"I don't know for sure. We were always blindfolded on the way there and back, plus it was dark out. You know, nighttime. It's in a wooded area, and by either a river or a creek. I know that much. I'd say within fifteen minutes of Wellspring."

"Wellspring is near the western border of the county. If you were blindfolded, how can you be sure it was in Winnebago County?"

"I guess I can't swear to it, but I know we never drove over a bridge, which we'd have to, right, to leave the county?"

Good observation for a blindfolded kid. "From Wellspring?" I mentally visualized a map of western Winnebago County. "Yes, you're right. So you think the altar might be somewhere on the southern bank of the Mississippi River, or the eastern bank of the North Fork of the Raven River? Or was it more like a creek?"

There were many creeks throughout the county. When rainfall was scarce, the Raven was more like a creek than a river in some areas.

"I'd say it seemed more like the Raven, or even a creek, than like the Mississippi. It was a little ways from the altar area, and I never actually saw it. But I could hear moving water not too far away."

"If you were blindfolded, how do you suppose your brother expects to find it? Do you have reason to believe he has been in contact with your stepfather?"

"No, not unless the creep found Jeff somehow. But Jeff would have told me that, I think, but I guess I don't know for sure. Maybe Jeff wasn't always blindfolded. That monster took Jeff to the altar a lot more times than he took me, poor guy."

"Are you clear to write down my number?"

"Is it the one you're calling on?"

"It is."

"I got it on Caller ID. As soon as I get to a rest station I'll pull off and send you the dagger photo."

"Good. Thanks. I'll put out an attempt to locate on your brother."

"Thank you, Sergeant. I'm really scared for Jeff, and I believe I can trust you. I have to tell you, I didn't feel that way about Lieutenant Armstrong. It was like he was hiding something."

Armstrong was arrogant, but I had never had reason not to trust him. Did Trippen know something I didn't?

2

The Coven

Cyril Bishop stepped into the semi-sanctuary of his office and closed the door behind him. He longed for a break from needy people. It was his job and he did it well, but their demands were often pointless.

"He always carried a hundred dollar bill in his pocket. Here, put this in his right front pocket."

"She asked to be buried with her favorite shoes. She went square dancing every week, and these were her favorites."

"Here's her confirmation Bible to take with her."

"He was never without his rosary beads. We want him to keep them with him for all eternity."

Pointless. The unpleasant part of his job was to keep the families of the deceased happy, and they paid him well. His Lord and Master had provided him with an established business, the one Cyril's uncle had started and he had expanded. People came from miles around, entrusting the bodies of their loved ones to him. His makeup artistry was unmatched by any other mortician in Winnebago County, and word had spread.

Cyril was restless. There were important dates around the corner, and he needed assurance things were in place. He paused to pray. "Hail Satan, king of hell and ruler of this world, give me continued strength and wisdom to defeat your enemies."

He pulled out his cell phone and dialed the first number. No answer. The message he left was simple. "The meeting is on for tonight." He left the same message on two more phones. The men would need no other information. Tuesday was the night they kept their calendars clear in case a meeting was called. They would all be there at the appointed hour and location. Their high priest had ordered it.

3

I looked around the cemetery as I thought about my conversation with Gregory Trippen, then opened my phone and dialed Detective Elton "Smoke" Dawes' cell phone number. When I'd started with Winnebago County, Smoke was my training officer and had become my mentor and best friend in the department. I believed our relationship would have become more intimate if there were fewer obstacles.

"What's up, Corky?"

I heard a dog barking nearby.

"Are you in the middle of something?"

"No, I'm home."

"Oh, sorry, I didn't hear you go off-duty."

"Just pulled up to my garage. Hang on. Three forty, Winnebago County."

"Go ahead, Three forty."

"I'm ten-seven."

"You're ten-seven at eighteen oh two. Goodnight."

"Okay, Corky." I heard his door "ding ding ding" when he opened it. He slammed it shut.

"I got a strange one for you. One I doubt you've heard before."

"Hey, Rex, buddy, you miss me?" It sounded like his dog was panting into the phone, and I envisioned Smoke bent over, petting him. "With all my years in, you think so, huh?"

"A man is on his way to Winnebago County to sacrifice himself on Satan's altar."

"Come again?" I repeated the implausible sentence. "Okay, I'll give you that. Never heard that one before. Give me the particulars."

I summed up Trippen's phone conversation. "I put in an ATL on Jeffrey Trippen. Communications should have it up any minute. And there was something else he talked about. Do you remember the hunting accident where a man named Harlan Manthes was mistaken for a deer and shot and killed?"

"No, don't recall hearing about that one. Must have been when I was serving with Lake, or Cook County, before I came back to Winnebago."

"I'll look up the report later."

"Winnebago County, Six oh eight?" Communications Officer Robin's voice came over the radio.

I told Smoke goodbye, shut my phone, and depressed my radio button to reply. "Go ahead, Winnebago County."

"A domestic in progress at Twenty-seven Forty-five Pleasant Avenue Southwest, Kadoka. Female party called nine-one-one, line got disconnected, no answer on call back."

"Ten-four. Who's in the area for backup?"

"Seven ten," Deputy Brian Carlson answered.

"Seven fourteen will head that way. I'm about seven miles out," Deputy Vince Weber added.

"Copy."

The call information appeared on my screen. "Collin and Nichole Jasper residence. Unidentified female called, cried 'Help' into the phone. Male voice in the background yelled 'You,' then the line went dead. Return calls not picked up."

My heart rate kept pace with my car's speed as I pushed the accelerator down. I activated the lights, but kept the sirens silent. I was within a few miles of the residence and didn't want to alert the male offender. Domestics were often volatile and carried a high potential for danger. Countless officers had been injured or killed responding to those calls. I typed Carlson and Weber a reminder, "no sirens."

I passed through the city of Kadoka, drove another mile to Pleasant Avenue Southwest, and took a right. The Jaspers' home was the first on the left. A grove of thick pines hid the house from the road. I parked, sent Communications the message I had arrived, and got out.

I was walking across the road toward the house when Carlson's squad car pulled in behind me. Weber came from the other direction a few seconds later. We gathered together, pushed through a space between the trees, and raced to the side of the house. Weber won. We crouched below the level of the windows and quickly crept to the front door.

Yelling and banging noises were coming from inside the residence. In exigent—emergency—circumstances when officers believe a person is in danger, the law allows them to enter a building or dwelling without either the owners' permission or an official search warrant.

Vince Weber was a compact body mass of strength. I appreciated his ability to break open a door, ramming bar or not. Without a word, he jammed his elbows into his waist, pulled his shoulders up to stabilize his head and neck, and rapidly sidestepped his way into the closed door. The simple deadbolt did not keep him out. The door swung open so hard that it hit the wall and bounced back.

The perpetrator didn't have time to react. Weber drew his gun and was in the house in one movement. Carlson and I had already drawn and followed him in, a hair behind. Weber went right, Carlson went left, and I took center. We had our weapons trained on a young man wearing nothing but an astounded expression. His arm stopped mid-swing, a foot or so from a woman's face.

"Drop to your knees. Now!" Carlson ordered.

The man continued to stare. "On your knees *now*," he repeated.

The man finally understood the order and complied.

"Put your hands on your head and interlock your fingers."

Weber holstered his Glock, moved in, and handcuffed the naked man in under ten seconds. When he was restrained, Carlson and I holstered our weapons.

I looked at the young woman who was shaking and hugging herself tightly, like she was trying to still her body's movements.

"Is there anyone else in the house?" I asked.

She looked around the living room, her eyes darting from one out-of-place item to the next. A coffee table lay on its side and magazines were strewn on the floor. A lamp lay on the couch, its shade pushed to an unusual angle.

She shook her head. "No, just us."

"Okay. Carlson, Weber, get his information. I'll be with her in the next room." I waved the young woman toward the kitchen area.

Her voice was weak, tentative. "Should I get him some pants?"

"Good idea." To ensure security, I followed her into the bedroom and watched her pull a pair of sweatpants out of a drawer. "Why don't you grab some socks, shoes, and a shirt. He'll need them when he gets out of jail."

She crumbled halfway to the ground. "He's going to *jail?*"

"Yes." Of course.

"I don't want him to go to jail. I'm not pressing charges."

"Ma'am, three deputies witnessed him committing assault. It's not up to you. We're the ones charging him."

I reached for the pants, and she handed them over. "Get the rest of his clothes, and we'll talk about it." She pulled out underwear, socks, and a shirt and gave them to me without a word.

"Let's go talk in the kitchen."

She weakly nodded and headed that direction. I handed the man's clothes to Weber and Carlson on my way by. "Probably good to get his pants on, at least."

The deputies guided him to his feet. The man was crying and babbled incoherently while Weber told him to lift first one foot, then the other. He helped him dress while Carlson steadied him.

The young woman sank onto a chair at the table. Her head was bent, her face near the table. Tears dropped onto her folded, trembling hands.

"Your full name and date of birth?" I pulled out my memo pad and found a clean page.

She identified herself as Nichole Ann Jasper. Collin James Jasper, the man in the next room, was her husband. They were twenty-five and twenty-six years old, respectively.

"Nichole, tell me what happened tonight."

"All I can say is, sometimes my husband has these flashbacks. He gets a little crazy, but he's never acted like this before, yelling at me, coming after me."

"And tonight?"

"He didn't hit me or anything. I think he might have, though, and then you deputies came in."

"You called nine-one-one."

"I was scared for him. He commutes to work with a friend. Tonight they stopped for a drink. Collin just can't drink. He can't handle it. He got home and had this scary look in his eyes, took off his clothes, and started yelling at me, accusing me of hiding his boxers and tee shirt—that's what he sleeps in at night. I thought maybe he took some kind of drug. I mean, he doesn't take any, but maybe someone slipped something in his drink. I don't know."

"We'll check him out, run a drug scan. What did you mean when you said he has flashbacks?"

"It's a long story, and I can't really go into it. Let's just say he suffered a lot of abuse as a kid. Alcohol can trigger those old memories. More than memories. I think his mind goes back to the time when he was powerless against some very bad people. Only now, if they tried to hurt him, he said he would fight back. When he was young, he couldn't."

"You sound like you know your husband very well. Are you afraid of him?"

"I'm not afraid of him, I'm afraid *for* him. I worry they still have a hold on him."

"They?"

Nichole shook her head. She wasn't going to tell me who *they* were.

"His mother, father, another relative?"

She shrugged and remained silent.

"Okay, we'll take him to the hospital, get him checked out. He'll spend the night in jail, hopefully make his first appearance in court in the morning."

Nichole visibly shrank, her shoulders dropping several inches. She looked frightened and fragile, more like a young girl than a woman in her mid-twenties.

I spoke softly. "Minnesota law says we have to make an arrest for fifth degree domestic assault under the circumstances. Hopefully your husband can get the help he needs with his flashbacks."

Nichole nodded. "He's working on it. We both are."

"Good. That's a start. Will you be okay here tonight? You want to call anyone to come and stay with you, or maybe go to a relative's or a friend's house?"

Nichole inhaled deeply and straightened, lifting her head and shoulders. Her spine went rigid. "No. I'll be all right."

Collin Jasper's head was extended down as far as his neck would allow. He closed his eyes when the deputies led him out the door and down the length of the driveway.

Carlson followed Weber and Collin Jasper to the hospital. Carlson phoned an hour later to inform me Jasper's check had revealed he was clear for drugs and his blood alcohol level was .02 percent—a negligible amount.

Something had triggered his outburst, his flashback. His wife said he couldn't drink, and if that small amount of alcohol had sent him into fight mode, he should never drink.

"Weber's taking him to the jail. He'll be there in a few minutes," Carlson said.

"Thanks Brian."

4

The Coven

As night closed around them, the four men formed a close circle. The waxing crescent moon offered little light through the trees, but it didn't matter. They were at home in the dark.

"The abduction and preparation must take place between the twenty-first and the twenty-third, in keeping with our calendar. The sacrifice for Saint Mark's Eve is the twenty-fourth," High Priest Cyril said.

"I'm scheduled to drive the volunteer van for Harbor Shelter on Friday night, the twenty-third. It works out well. The streets are filled with homeless drunks and addicts," Roman said.

Noris nodded. "And we know the cops don't have the time or the resources to try to track them down when they go missing."

"It's our duty to eliminate those people, purge them from the earth. Human sacrifice furthers the work of our Master."

"Try to find a female this time," Noris said.

"It will be the one our Master provides, female or male. We will take who he sends. Hail Satan!" Cyril said as he lifted a wooden rod. Its handle was in the shape of a goat's head.

"Hail Satan!" The others chanted in unison.

"We'll have the young female sacrifice on Walpurgisnacht, Beltane's Eve."

Dieter looked up. "Younger ones' spirits send out much more energy when they leave."

"We will not vary from our plan. Roman will secure our sacrificial victim on the twenty-third. The room, the drugs, all in order?" Cyril looked at Dieter's shadowed face.

"All in order."

"Good. Let's offer our thanks before leaving."

The high priest began, a guttural sound erupting from deep in his throat, "Dark angel, archangel, your power gives us power and brings heaven to our sight. Rise up, Lucifer, bring us your light . . ."

5

My phone beeped, alerting me I had a message. I picked it up and flipped it open. It was the dagger photo from Gregory Trippen. There was no wonder he was concerned. The blade looked to be about nine inches long. It tapered to a sharp point and was silver in color. Stainless steel? The handle appeared to be sterling with ornate designs tooled into the metal. Six red stones formed a line down the center.

An elaborately decorated work of art obtained for self-destruction. Self-sacrifice. I sent the dagger photo to Communications and requested they print it on the color copier.

A number of calls the next few hours prevented me from returning to the sheriff's department until late. A waxing moon lit the clear night skies and threw crescent-shaped slices on the surfaces of lakes and ponds I passed along the way.

Todd Mason, a good friend of mine, was the only deputy in the squad room. He stood when I entered. "All yours," he said.

"I heard your call. Have fun with that noise complaint."

"Second one at that apartment this month. Have to write a citation if it keeps up. Hopefully I'll be back to finish my reports before the end of our shift."

"I'll tell you all about a phone call I got when you get back."

"All righty." And he was out the door.

I went into out-of-state records and pulled up photos of both Gregory and Jeffrey Trippen. Gregory resembled Vince Weber from the shoulders up: husky, no neck, which gave the appearance his head rested directly on his shoulders. But unlike Weber, he had a full head of brown hair. Weber kept his head shaved. Gregory's expression was serious, bordering on pained. The image looked like a mug shot, not a driver's license photo.

Jeffrey's features reminded me of John Lennon from photos taken in his later years, when his hair was long and he sported a beard. But their eyes were different. Lennon's revealed intelligence, hinting at defiance. Jeffrey's eyes conveyed a cross between wistful and fearful. The eyes of a tormented man that still had hope. What look would they hold now that he had given up and planned to end it all?

Jeffrey Trippen was out there somewhere, headed for Winnebago County, carrying a very dangerous weapon. We had to find him before he, or someone else, got hurt.

Robin swung her slight, bony body around in her swivel chair when I entered Communications. "Oh, Corky, I meant to get that copy to your box, but it's been too busy."

"No problem. You guys have been getting a ton of calls all night." I picked up the dagger image printout lying next to the copier. Every pore in my body prickled. The larger version was far more fearsome than the miniature one on my phone.

"One nasty blade on that thing," Jerry called over from his seat in front of the communication panel's hundreds of buttons and switches. The ends of his squint lines touched his graying sideburns. The 911 phone receiver lit up, and he redirected his attention.

Robin stood and stretched. "What's this all about? When the reporting person called, first he asked for the sheriff. I told him it was after business hours, so I could put him through to the sheriff's voicemail. He seemed frantic and asked to speak to the next in command. Instead of explaining how admin was gone for the day, I told him I'd have you call as soon as possible."

I nodded.

"So what's the deal?" she persisted.

"Gregory Trippen is worried about his brother, Jeffrey, who said he is on his way to Winnebago County. Gregory believes he is carrying that dagger and intends to hurt himself."

"We got that in the ATL. Officer extreme caution. That's scary."

I nodded. "I saw the ATL when you sent it out, and you got it right. We look for him 'til we find him."

I wanted to do some investigating and talk to the sheriff before I revealed the sacrifice on Satan's altar detail to everyone in the department. I told Robin and Jerry "thanks," made my way back to the still deserted squad room, and set to work searching old files listed in the computer records.

Manthes, Harlan. There were a few calls attached to his name. In 1984, he had reported a burglary at his residence. In 1985, harassing phone calls. Also in 1985, a fender bender.

1986, a small fire in his detached garage. I jotted them down in my memo book.

Case number 19881104. Accidental shooting death while hunting.

I headed to the records room where the files from the beginning of time were stored in mammoth, horizontal file cabinets. I unlocked the door, stepped in, and visually scanned the letters on the drawers as I walked. The M drawers started at the end of the north wall and continued around to the east wall. Manthes was in the third drawer from the bottom. I stood on tiptoes while I pushed one Man-file after the next until I found Manthes. Harlan was the fifth or sixth one alphabetically.

I pushed more files backward and forward curious if either Gregory or Jeffrey was in there for any reason. Neither one was. Back to Harlan. I pulled his file and plopped onto a nearby chair, prepared to read several reports, but the only report in his file was the 1985 minimal damage crash. No other reports, no photos.

I grabbed a three-step ladder and set it in front of the open drawer for a better vantage point while I looked. I pulled files of the others with the same surname: Bruce, Catherine, Eugene, Theodore, William. Harlan's reports were not wrongly filed in any of them. I searched one nearby file after the next. Nothing. I opened the N drawer, but there was no Harlan Manthes in the Na section either. It was rare, but occasionally a missing sheet or two turned up accidentally misfiled.

Three reports, including the investigation of his death, were nowhere to be found in my thirty-minute search. Very odd.

Gregory Trippen had talked to Alden Armstrong regarding his father's death a few years before. There should be a report on that. I found the Tra-Tri drawer and fingered through the back files. Tripp, Triton. No Trippen. What in the world?

I headed back to the squad room and searched the computer for Gregory Trippen. There was one entry. On July second, three years earlier, he had called with a request to speak to an officer. Alden Armstrong made the entry: "Spoke with Gregory Trippen regarding a question he had on a case involving his father. Question answered. NRN." NRN. No report needed. When a citizen called with a legitimate concern about an investigation, it required a report.

It was time to talk to Alden Armstrong.

6

The Coven

Dieter Munden returned home from the outdoor temple meeting and went downstairs. He stepped into the small temple in his basement and turned on the light. The black walls absorbed much of the illumination. The room was dimly lit and cast in shadows. He bowed at the image of the pentagram painted on the floor, then made his way to the small altar and lit the black candles on it. The Black Book lay between the candleholders. Dieter picked it up and drew it to his forehead, grateful once again for the position of power and authority he had been granted when Royce Sparrow left the coven to start a new one in Saint Cloud.

Dieter had been a lonely child, raised in the countryside of Germany outside of Bonn, the birthplace of Beethoven. His parents worked long hours in their gift shop, and Dieter was left to his own devices most of the time. He loved science, especially chemistry, and spent hours with the chemistry set he had gotten as a birthday gift. Eventually, that had led to his decision to pursue a career in pharmacy. Studying drugs and their families, their purpose, contraindications, and potential side effects appealed to Dieter.

He had explored potential universities in Germany, other European countries, and the United States. The educational opportunities in the United States seemed endless. Dieter was intrigued by the vast opportunities in America.

He had researched the geography and climate of the upper Midwest in the United States and found it was similar to his homeland. He found a suitable college. The School of Pharmacy at the University of Wisconsin in Madison had been around for over a century. It was established in 1883 and the first of its kind to offer a baccalaureate degree in pharmacy. It was also the first in the nation to offer doctoral degrees in pharmaceutical chemistry, pharmaceutics, the history of pharmacy, and social studies of pharmacy.

After a year of deliberation, he had applied at the University of Wisconsin in Madison. His parents weren't thrilled with the idea of Dieter going all the way to the United States for college when there were so many fine ones in Germany, but they weren't opposed to it either.

He had met Cyril Bishop in biology class the first day at school. Something about Cyril drew him in immediately. His confidence, his charisma. They differed in personality and looks. Cyril was six four, lean and muscular, with dark hair and eyes. His roman nose was his most prominent facial feature.

Dieter was six inches shorter than Cyril, but weighed more. He had shied away from athletics and physical activities as a teen and had accumulated rolls around his middle. His eyes were a light hazel shade, and he controlled his brown curly hair by keeping it short. His best facial feature was his winning smile.

Cyril had chosen Dieter as his lab partner that first day. Dieter was not a loner when Cyril was around, because Cyril didn't allow it. Dieter thought back to their first conversation, when they had walked out of biology class together.

"Dieter, huh? Any idea what your name means?"

"Ruler of the people."

"I like it. Not too different from the meaning of my name. Cyril means lordly. My parents chose it for a reason."

"What is that?"

"I'll tell you all about it someday. I don't want to sound like a big bragger when we barely know each other."

Dieter had wondered if Cyril had descended from royal ancestry.

Most students at the university were from Wisconsin and often went home on weekends. Dieter could not go to Germany at the drop of a hat and spent weekends on the deserted campus, hanging out in his dorm room or at the library. Cyril's family lived an hour outside of Madison, and the second time he had gone home for a weekend, he'd invited Dieter. He had gladly accepted, eager to meet his new friend's family.

Cyril's mother was quiet and serious, and Dieter had noted that Cyril had a similar personality to his father. Friday night, about an hour after they had gone to bed, Cyril's father had come into his room and told him it was time to go. Dieter had made some noises about time for what, but Cyril's father had told him to go back to sleep. Cyril had left with his father.

Dieter was curious and a little jealous that Cyril would be called in the middle of the night to go somewhere with his father. When he'd asked him about it the next day, Cyril had told him it was a power-renewing mission and he would give him the details later. Dieter had imagined it was some sort of magical mission. Cyril had seemed more energetic after the outing, which made him all the more curious.

"Someday I will take you with me, but you need to be prepared. You must be willing to give your all. But by giving your all, you will be greatly rewarded."

Dieter remembered feeling excited at the possibility of being more like Cyril.

7

Todd Mason returned to the squad room twenty minutes before our shift ended. He threw his memo pad on the table then sat down. "Two young guys sharing a place. Like to play their music really loud. They'll be deaf by the time they get to be my age."

"Ah, yes, the ripe old age of thirty-two. How young are they anyway?"

He flipped open his memo pad and looked at a sheet. "Twenty-one. Both of them. I told them it was their final verbal warning. Next time it's a citation. You put out an ATL, huh?"

"Yeah, look at this." I pulled the dagger image from my pile and handed it over.

"What the hell?"

"Speaking of which, the guy we're looking for is on his way to Winnebago County to sacrifice himself on Satan's altar using this." I handed him the printout of Jeffrey Trippen's identification photo.

"Whoa." Brian Carlson came into the room and dropped his briefcase on a chair. "What are you saying?"

Mason handed both photos over.

"Dungeons and dragons? What's this about a sacrifice?" Carlson asked.

"That guy looks lost, sad," Mason said.

I filled the deputies in on the details Gregory Trippen had shared regarding his brother and their involvement in a cult, and the belief his stepfather had killed his father to marry his mother. I didn't tell them about the missing reports. Mason's hazel eyes were intense and didn't leave my face. Carlson's big blue eyes stared at the dagger photo.

"What's your take on all that?" Carlson asked.

I shrugged. "I don't know. Keep the satanic part quiet until I talk to the sheriff. You know how the rumor mill blows things out of proportion."

They both agreed.

After a minute of silence and another look at the printouts of the dagger and Jeffrey Trippen, Carlson pointed at the training-schedule bulletin board hanging on the squad room wall. "You guys see they finally got the details posted for our annual team-building?"

"No. I haven't looked yet," I said as I hung the sheets of Trippen and the dagger images—with explanations—on the postings board next to photos of a few criminals who were on the loose. Fugitives from justice.

"Finally. They've had 'save the dates' up for a month at least," Mason said.

We gathered in front of the bulletin board. Carlson and Mason stood behind me, reading silently over my shoulders.

The memo read: "All members of the sheriff's department, probation services, and county attorney's office are required to participate in a team-building exercise April 22nd, 23rd or 24th. Your group assignments are listed below. The first step is to contact the other members of your group and pick a date that works for all of you. Meet in Room 130 at your scheduled date and time. Wear casual and weather appropriate dress. Sign up by April 19th."

"We have to pull our teams together to decide on a date. That's an odd way of doing things," Todd said, glancing at his watch.

"No kidding. And why are we with probation and the county attorneys anyway?" Brian said.

I turned toward the deputies, making them take a comfort-zone step back. "A new twist this year, I guess. We work with the same criminals, different aspects. It'll give us a chance to get to know those guys outside of the courtroom."

"By getting down and dirty? I hope it's not what we did last time. It took me a whole day to recover," Todd complained.

The previous year we had been divided into teams of varying abilities and had to run a seven-mile, hilly course through Lake Pearl State Park, following directing signs. We were required to start together as a team, stay together as a team, and finish together as a team. Hopefully in first place. Todd Mason and I were on the same team. He was a faster and stronger runner than me and had pulled me, literally, up a few of the higher hills so I could keep up. Our group had managed to finish first in spite of my lagging.

"That was a tough one. If you hadn't dragged me half the way, we never would have done so well. No question I was the weak link on that team," I said.

He patted my shoulder. "Nah. You were the motivator—you just had shorter legs than the rest of us."

I touched the top of my head. "True, my five five to your six one. Which is close to what all you guys were, I think."

"I was in a slow group. We had Edberg, who's getting up there in years. And Weber. For being so stocky, Weber's a surprisingly fast sprinter, but you can't sprint for seven miles. At least we didn't come in last," Carlson said.

"I doubt it will be an endurance course this year since we have the other departments with us," I countered.

"Yeah, one or two of those guys would drop dead for sure. Can you imagine Collinwood—" Mason was referring to our rotund county attorney.

I interrupted, "Be nice, Mason." I studied the assignments. "So I got Mandy Zubinski, Vince Weber, Donny Nickles from probation, and Eric Stueman from the attorneys." I thought for a moment. "He doesn't much care for me. Stueman."

Carlson crossed his arms and rested them on his chest. "He just got here a few months ago. What'd you do to turn him off that fast?"

"Who knows? We haven't had much contact, actually. I testified at a couple of DUI cases he handled, and he was very stand-offish. I tried to make small talk, and he wouldn't even answer me."

"Been pretty friendly to me. Seems like an okay guy."

"Like I said, I don't think he likes me."

Carlson stepped closer to the board and pointed with his pen. "I see a pattern here. Look at the people on my team, and Mason's. It's like people on every team have problems with at least one other. Doesn't seem like the groups were chosen by eeny meeny miny moe, does it?"

"You could be right, Brian. People go to the chief deputy from time to time with complaints about other deputies, if it's something they can't seem to resolve themselves. He'd have the inside information if anyone would," Mason said.

Looking at my team members, I had an issue, or ten, with Zubinski, and Zubinski had a personality conflict with Weber. I wasn't sure where Nickles and Stueman fit in. From my end, Nickles and I got along fine. Maybe Weber had something against him. Did Stueman have something against me, as I suspected?

Mason looked up and rolled his eyes back. "I hope we don't have some weird session where we all have to confess how we feel about each other personally. We don't need to know that. And we could end up with harder feelings than we got now."

"We don't have a lot of hard feelings in the department— we've got a good group around here. We can't all be best friends, can we? We're just speculating, anyway. Have to wait and see," I said.

"You sergeants weren't in on the planning?" Brian asked.

"No, admin figures that stuff out."

Mandy Zubinski and I were on the same schedule of days on and days off. She was still on duty, so I phoned her.

"Mandy, it's Corky."

"Hi, Sergeant. What's up?"

"Have you been to the squad room yet, seen the memo on the team-building exercise?"

"No, why? I do have the dates for it penciled in my calendar, though."

I paraphrased the memo for her.

"No offense, but team-building with other departments seems a little strange," she said.

I didn't disagree. "They're expanding the range of our mandatory training requirements, that's for sure."

"We don't have to run like a hundred miles through the state park again, I am hoping against hope. Not with Weber on our team. He burned out faster than me last year."

A corporate concern.

"Nah, I don't think they could expect probation and the attorneys to do that. They count on us, not them, to chase and physically battle the bad guys."

"Adding those two departments has got me a little curious, anyway."

She couldn't see me nod. "Our first day off is Saturday, the twenty-fourth, so that's the best day for us. Unless you want to do it on the Thursday or Friday morning before our evening shift."

"I think we better go with Saturday."

"We can go with oh eight hundred to noon, or thirteen hundred to seventeen hundred. Any preference?"

"Let's take the early shift."

"Agreed. You want to call Weber, Nickles, or Stueman?"

"Your call."

"Okay, you take Stueman, I'll talk to the other two. Let me know if he has a conflict with the date, and I'll do the same."

"Will do."

7

The Coven

Roman Jenkins was exhausted. His family medicine practice had grown along with the population increases of the Wellspring area. He started early in the morning and worked until dinner time nearly every night. Cyril was calling late night meetings of the coven with increased frequency, cutting further into his already shortened sleep schedule. The meetings and rituals used to give Roman renewed energy and strength. Now they seemed to zap him more and more. He was exhausted and weary.

The words of the last paragraph of the Hippocratic Oath played through his mind. "While I continue to keep this Oath unviolated, may it be granted to me to enjoy life and the practice of the art and science of medicine with the blessing of the Almighty and respected by my peers and society, but should I trespass and violate this Oath, may the reverse be my lot."

He had recited the words with his graduating class. His Almighty was Satan, and the left-handed path was his birthright, passed down to him from one generation to the next as far back as his family could trace. There were the chosen and the unchosen. That was never to be questioned or doubted. Roman was chosen, as was one of his sisters. She had attained the honor of High Priestess in the northern Michigan coven where they were raised. Their other siblings had been offered as sacrifices.

Roman had attended the University of Minnesota and was accepted into its medical school. He discovered like-minded followers of Satan, and they found a spot in a wooded area on the Mississippi River in Saint Paul to hold rituals. There were homeless drunks and drug addicts in abundance when they needed them, and human sacrifice earned the worshippers places of honor in hell.

A few members of Roman's extended family had relocated from Michigan to Winnebago County in Minnesota fifty or sixty years before. They had a strong presence there, with miles of areas suitable for outdoor temple locations. They were chosen and did Satan's bidding.

Coven members had helped him establish a practice in Wellspring and introduced him to the beauty who became his wife. She understood all they must do in service to the Master. The leaders had let the Jenkins keep their firstborn, but not their second. Roman had determined there would be no more children, and his wife had agreed.

Roman served well and had been appointed as deacon years before. His family had no material wants. Satan had given to them in abundance.

Roman crept upstairs, opened his son's bedroom door, and listened to the quiet sounds of his rhythmic breathing for a few minutes. Did he want for his son what his parents had expected of him: to attain a position of authority in a coven? He was surprised by his question and closed the door.

He went to his bedroom, undressed, and climbed into bed beside his wife. She turned to him, but he did not respond. He needed to conserve what little energy he had for the weekend, from securing the victim through the sacrificial ritual and ensuing orgy. He prayed for the fortitude to get through it all.

9

I struggled to find my ringing cell phone that was somewhere in my bed with me. No idea how it got there. It was my Nextel, my work cell. I located it on the fourth ring and pushed the button.

"Sergeant Aleckson."

"Sergeant, it's Greg Trippen. Did I wake you?"

"I'm fine. Are you on the road?" I stretched my left arm.

"Yes, and it looks like we'll get to Winnebago County about seven o'clock tonight."

"All right. Good. To let you know, I sent the attempt to locate on your brother to all eighty-seven counties in the state."

"Was that necessary?" His voice was strained.

"We don't know where your brother was when he phoned you. He could have been in Canada for all we know. Another county may find him before he has the chance to get here."

"I didn't think about that. Okay."

"Call me when you get close, and we'll arrange a meeting."

"Thank you."

"Drive safe."

It was only seven a.m., but there was no point in trying to get back to sleep. I was wide awake thinking about the Trippen case with its disturbing overtones and missing files. I dialed Smoke's number.

"Isn't it a little early for Sleeping Beauty?" he said in place of hello.

"Oh, I thought you'd be up before now," I threw back.

"Woke up witty, huh? What's up?"

"You have any time to meet this morning? I have some things to run by you."

"Must be important if it has you up this early. About the satanic altar case?"

"It is."

"I got court at nine, unless they plead. I'm about to leave and could stop by on my way. That work for you?"

"That works. I'll start the coffee."

I rolled to the side of the bed and decided my flannel pajama bottoms were decent. Not unlike what a number of people wore in public. I pulled a rose-colored hooded sweatshirt over my sleeveless tee, stretching my arms and neck in the process.

My bedroom was on the second floor of my country home. I took the stairs down to the main level more slowly than usual. My body protested being awake and moving that early in the morning.

While the coffee brewed, I splashed water on my face and brushed my teeth and hair. Smoke knocked on the garage side door before I had time to pull it into a ponytail. I hurried over and flipped the deadbolt. He gently pushed as I pulled the door open. I turned and headed to the counter, where the coffee pot had finished its task and was silent again. I felt Smoke at my heels.

"Pajamas or running outfit?"

"I didn't take the time to dress."

"Cute little lambies on your jammies. And your toenails match your hoodie."

I glanced down to see if that was true. It was. "I do my best to coordinate my sleepwear and nail polish."

Smoke was striking in a tailored black suit with thin, light gray pinstripes, a gray shirt, and a checked tie a shade darker. He leaned back against the counter and extended his long legs. His graying, short, thick hair matched his outfit. I took a second to admire what my mother called his rugged good looks: an angular face, with long dimples in his lean cheeks, a strong chin, and full lips. But my favorite feature was his bright, sky-blue eyes.

"How come you're so dressed up?"

"My brother bulked up and can't wear most of his clothes anymore. Gave me six suits." He flicked a small speck of lint from his sleeve.

"Very nice." I reached into the cupboard for cups, poured coffee in them, and handed him one.

"Thanks." He accepted the cup and took a sip. "I decided to wear them on court days and such. What'd you want to talk about?"

I set my cup down and reached into my briefcase that rested on a barstool at the counter. I withdrew printouts of Jeffrey Trippen and the dagger he intended to use on himself.

Smoke half-whistled and reached for the photos with his free hand. He set his cup next to mine on the counter. "You could do some serious damage with that. Long blade, sharp point. Ornate, jeweled, expensive looking. Apparently a simple dagger won't do when you're sacrificing yourself on an altar. For Satan. Trippen has a vacant look. Kinda like he left a long time ago."

"I can't imagine him traveling across the country with that weapon."

"You said last night his brother thinks he was living in New York, but he hasn't seen him in two years, so he doesn't know for sure."

"That's right. Jeffrey could be in Winnebago County now for all we know. Gregory Trippen figures that he'll get here around seven tonight."

"Good." Smoke set down the papers, picked up his coffee cup and took a sip.

"What I wanted to ask you is, how well do you know Alden Armstrong?"

"Outside of work?" Smoke lifted his eyebrows like it was the first time he had ever considered it. "Huh. I know he was a little older when he got married. Close to forty, I think. Had three kids in pretty close succession. Must be teenagers about now. His wife works for the newspaper in Little Mountain. At least she did. He's not a guy that talks about his family much around the office. Like most of us, I guess. Not unusual. Most guys don't say much unless you go on break with them."

"That's true. Ever get the impression he would do something unethical, illegal even?"

"What are you getting at, Corky?"

"I didn't have a chance to tell you last night, but when Gregory and Jeffrey Trippen were little boys, their father was killed in a hunting accident. Gregory suspected his stepfather—whom he calls a hardcore Satanist—was responsible for the death."

Smoke frowned. "What's his name?"

"I didn't get it yet. When I talked to Gregory last night, I was mainly focused on Jeffrey's plight, the case at hand. This morning I wasn't quite awake and didn't think of it.

"Anyway, Gregory called the sheriff's department three years ago and talked to Armstrong, who was the deputy who handled the case back when. Armstrong told Trippen it was an accident. There were three guys with Harlan Manthes. They supposedly all mistook him for a deer and shot. Not sure who hit him, but he was killed."

"When did this happen?"

"Twenty some years ago."

"Obviously, the guy would not be wearing a deer costume in the woods during hunting season, unless he wanted to die. Sounds fishy, does it not?"

"It does."

"So the three guys shoot. No rifle season for deer in Winnebago County, so they'd have shotguns. Slugs." He rubbed his freshly-shaven chin, considering. "That part of the story is believable, depending on where the victim and shooters were standing. Three hunting buddies with another hunting buddy who becomes the victim and the three give the same story. We'll review the files."

I swallowed the sip of coffee in my mouth. "That's the problem I wanted to talk to you about. There are no files to review."

"Whadaya mean?" His eyebrows came together.

"The reports are missing from the Manthes file. No reports. No photos. Nada."

Smoke looked up at the ceiling and sucked in a lungful of air while he listened.

"I checked all calls attached to his name, and the only report in his file is a rather benign one—a fender bender he had. I looked for quite a while last night." I reached over and tapped his arm. "And when Gregory Trippen talked to Armstrong a few years back?"

His eyes fixed on mine again. "Yeah?"

"I don't exactly know what went down, but Armstrong wrote 'no report needed.'"

"Seems to me a discussion like that constitutes a report unless the evidence compellingly proved it was an accident. Even then, a kid who lost his father and wants a good explanation deserves more than that." He paused in apparent thought. "I'll be done with court by noon, I'm guessing. Armstrong should be in his office today, as far as I know. You're on duty at three?"

I nodded.

"Track me down, and we'll have a little chat with the good lieutenant." Smoke set his cup down and lifted a shoulder. "It's possible he pulled the files when the Trippen boy called him then put them in a desk drawer and they got forgot."

Smoke knocked on Alden Armstrong's door frame to alert him. He stepped in first, and I was a close second.

Alden Armstrong's name suited him well. His large, strong arms extended from broad shoulders. He was a big guy. Well over six feet, perhaps two hundred and fifty pounds. Brown hair sprinkled with gray, cut military style. Armstrong was seated at his desk. He looked up and seemed to take us both in with one glance.

"Lieutenant, got a minute?" Smoke asked.

He raised his right hand then waved. "Sure, have a seat."

Smoke and I sat down across from Armstrong "Question on a case?" he asked.

"Good guess. An old case. Harlan Manthes."

A storm cloud crossed Armstrong's face and forced his eyes partially closed. He stood, nearly brushing me as he passed by, and closed his office door. I hazarded a quick peek at Smoke. His expression was unreadable.

Armstrong sunk back into his chair, failing to mask his agitation. "That is an old case."

"Tell us about it." Smoke slipped into his interview mode. I was the appointed note taker.

"Not much to tell. Tragic accident. Four friends deer hunting, and Manthes got in the line of fire."

"From three different guys?"

Armstrong shrugged. "They were trying to flush out deer. According to the men who were with Manthes, they said he got ahead of them and they didn't realize it. He stepped into a clearing, and they shot."

"That's why God invented blaze orange," Smoke said.

"I was the first one on the scene. Manthes was not wearing orange. I asked the others about it, and they said he had an orange hat on, but must have lost it when he got separated from the group. They seemed pretty upset, shooting their friend in the back."

"The back?" I asked.

"Two big, twelve-gauge-shotgun-slug holes."

"They all have twelve-gauge shotguns?"

"As I recall."

Smoke studied Armstrong for some seconds. "Anything else?"

"Not that I can think of. Pretty cut and dried." Armstrong grabbed onto the arms of his chair, and his knuckles whitened.

Smoke slid to the edge of his chair. "What are you *not* telling us?"

"I don't know—"

"Alden, you got up and shut the damn door when we asked about the case. Why would you do that? It's an old case. A closed case. Look at you. You look like you're ready to jump out of your skin. What are you hiding?"

Armstrong's face flushed. "Nothing—"

Smoke leaned forward and laid his arm on the desk, not far from Armstrong's chest. "Even a rookie can tell you're lying, Armstrong. Spill it."

"Really—"

"Damn it!"

"No, I—"

"If you are so forthcoming, maybe you can tell us where you hid the report on this so-called accident." Smoke's complexion darkened to a brown tone of red.

"Nowhere."

"Sergeant, do I look like I'm playing games here?" Smoke didn't give me time to answer. "Where did you put the damn reports?" He half-stood, grabbed a piece of Armstrong's shirt, and tugged.

As shocked as I was seeing Smoke manhandling a superior officer, my fleeting thought was, *Armstrong is going to cry.*

"Let go. I'll tell you everything."

10

The Coven

Noris stood in the squad room staring at the photos of the man and the dagger attached to the bulletin boards and wondered what exactly was going on. The man was close to his age and looked familiar, but he didn't recognize his name. He'd seen that dagger before, or one like it. How many could there be in the world?

No other department personnel were around. He took the photos down, made four copies, and stuck them at the bottom of his report pile. He quickly replaced the originals on the board without being discovered. It wouldn't matter if he was. He had been hiding in plain sight there for years. As his uncle had before him, and another would after he had gone to his reward.

Noris chose to work the three-to-eleven shift because he could glean the most information and take the appropriate actions most easily. And still make it to the temple services on time.

The sheriff's administration personnel were in their offices until four thirty or five. He gathered the important facts floating around when he walked through or was in the squad room listening to other deputies. He kept track of the calls the other deputies had and made enough small talk to find out what reports he needed to read. It was usually easy enough to decide which ones to trash.

There was one female in particular he managed to get a lot of useful information from. She was ignorant of how much she helped the coven and their Lord and Master. Her time of service was winding down and would come to a triumphant end soon. He smiled. Satan would be very pleased with the offering of her sacrifice.

Noris was a faithful servant and addicted to his position of power. The pleasures he enjoyed on earth—and they were many—were nothing compared to the ones he would have in hell. His work here was earning him a place as an immortal ruler. For all eternity.

As far as Noris knew, his family had worshipped Satan since the world began. A branch had moved to Minnesota in the early territorial days. They were as well-connected as anyone, in any coven, anywhere in the world.

To members of the coven, outside of the leaders, he was known only as Noris, his middle name. Like any other person that went by one name. If his full name and real identity was revealed, the coven would be compromised. He would be arrested, and the coven would lose their connection in the sheriff's department. They couldn't afford that. They needed him there, watchful and vigilant.

11

Armstrong brushed Smoke's grip-induced wrinkles out of his shirt. "It may not be safe to talk here," he said quietly.

"Spill it, Lieutenant."

Armstrong nodded once in resignation. "I was first on the scene, responsible for the main report. Edberg was second. He took photos of the body, collected each guy's weapon, and put them into evidence until we sorted it all out. I got statements from each witness/shooter. Miles Walden was the investigator. Did you know him?"

I shook my head, Smoke shook his. "Heard of him. He was gone before I started. Didn't he die right after he retired?"

Armstrong thought a moment then nodded. "The shootings appeared to be a tragic end to a day of deer hunting. A few other deputies showed up, like always at a major scene. Detective Walden got there pretty quickly and talked to each guy again. He stood where the hunters said they'd been when they shot Manthes. I walked to where Manthes' body lay. Walden determined that if Manthes was not wearing blaze orange, he could easily have been mistaken for a deer from that distance.

"Some things didn't wash, in my opinion, and I wanted to charge the men with manslaughter two for negligently believing that Manthes was a deer and shooting him."

"Why's that?" Smoke askcd.

"I didn't think murder one would stick."

Smoke lifted his eyebrows. "Explain."

"All three of them had twelve-gauge shotguns loaded with slugs. From where they said they stood, it was sixty yards away."

"Fairly tough shot. Hell, they weren't even slug guns. No sights, like a slug barrel would have. Not very accurate at sixty yards."

Armstrong nodded. "And I could see Walden just fine at sixty yards. Certainly could tell he wasn't a deer. The capper? No spent shells around the sixty-yard line. Of course they fly, but I looked for a while, and nothing. I asked the guys about it, and the undertaker said he'd picked 'em up when he was waiting for us to get there. He reloads them at home."

"He what? I have never heard of anyone reloading a shotgun slug."

"Me either."

"Even if he did, why would that even remotely cross his mind when he had just shot his friend?"

He shook his head and shrugged.

"Undertaker, you said?"

"Mortician, yes."

"You collect the empty shell casings from him?" Smoke asked.

"All three of them. Not that it did any good after he'd tampered with the scene like that. Idiot. The coroner examined Manthes' body, but his wife—widow—wouldn't let us do an autopsy. Manthes took two hits. One shooter missed. Either shot would have killed him. Two big holes in his back."

"You said you wanted to charge them. But you didn't?"

"No, you could say I met with strong resistance on that."

"From whom?"

"First, it was Detective Walden. He said there was no reason to charge them. It was clearly an accident. Why tie up the courts for no reason? I talked to the sheriff. Hooper was in office then. The three shooters in question were all professionals, pillars of the community, no criminal histories."

"But your gut was telling you something different."

"After the phone call, I knew I was right."

"What phone call?" Smoke leaned in.

"That night, the night of the shooting, I got a phone call at home. Didn't have Caller ID back then. And I had an unlisted phone number. Male caller, obviously disguised voice—muffled, sounded like Boris Karloff, menacing—told me to quit trying to make something out of nothing. Told me if I didn't keep my mouth shut about the case, my family would disappear and I would never see them again. He named them each by name."

Armstrong shuddered. "There was no doubt in my mind he meant it. Evil words, evil voice. It came across the phone lines, and every hair on my body stood up. All I said was, 'understood.' It's haunted me ever since."

"You report that to anyone?"

Armstrong looked down and shook his head. "I didn't know who to talk to, who to trust. It was the first time in my life I experienced real fear. Can you believe it? The kind of terror you can actually taste? He threatened my wife, my kids. He knew my phone number. Only work, of course, and friends and family members knew it. I had the phone company trace his number, and it came back to a pay phone. I had our phone number changed the next day. A year later, on the same date, I got a phone call from the same guy reminding me to keep my mouth shut. Changed my number again. Didn't matter. Got another call the next year and every year since. Finally quit changing my number the third year."

"You suspected someone in the department was involved in some sort of cover-up?"

"Hate to say it, but yeah, what else could it be? Unless he threatened another deputy into providing my phone number, and that didn't make sense. Never could figure out who it was, though. Walden? Edberg? One of the other deputies who was at the scene or in the squad room when I was writing the report and spouting off about the shooting seeming suspicious?"

Armstrong's confession seemed to ease the stress lines that years of secrecy had etched in his face.

"Ever think about contacting the FBI? Or about moving? Changing jobs?"

"They all crossed my mind for about a minute. I frankly didn't think it would help. The FBI, who knows? And whoever it was threatening me wouldn't give up 'cause I moved. Maybe he'd even think I'd have the investigation reopened if I felt safe, away from the department. If I stayed here I could be on the lookout for any sign of who he was.

"And the main reason is, Molly and I grew up here. Our ancestors homesteaded here. We didn't want to leave." He glanced at Smoke, then me. "Yeah, I told her so she'd be aware. I kept my word, and so did Boris Karloff. My big regret is that a crime went unpunished. If it was just me who was threatened, that would be one thing. I would have pushed 'til I found the rat. But my wife? My kids? I did what I did to protect them."

Smoke nodded.

What would I have done under the same circumstances? Or if someone had threatened my mother, my brother?

Armstrong continued, "I kept a veiled watch, here and there, on the three Wellspring community pillars for a couple of years. Aside from the fact that one of them, a surgeon named Royce Sparrow, married the victim's widow—"

Smoke blinked. "Royce Sparrow? Big-name surgeon in Saint Cloud?"

I jotted the name down. Gregory Trippen's stepfather.

Armstrong raised his eyebrows in affirmation. "Coincidence? I don't know. They basically went to their jobs during the day and back home at night. I quit looking. My prime suspect was Sparrow. But if he wanted Manthes dead, how did he convince the others to go along with it? Who in our department was in his pocket?" He paused. "You asked about the missing files?"

Smoke and I both nodded.

"A few years ago, I got a call from a young man, Harlan Manthes' son. Gave a different last name. Trippen. He was looking into his father's death."

"That's what brought us here."

Armstrong looked momentarily puzzled then inclined his head to the left. "Ah. Trippen asking for another investigation?"

"Have you been to the squad room? Seen the ATL?" Smoke asked.

"No, I was off this morning for personal appointments. Been playing catch-up in my office so far this afternoon."

I explained. "Gregory Trippen called last night to report his brother Jeffrey is on his way to our county to sacrifice himself—"

"Sacrifice himself?"

"On Satan's altar."

Armstrong's chest rose and fell at a fast pace, and his face flushed.

"Satan's altar? What are you talking about?"

"According to Trippen, Sparrow was a hardcore Satanist. Introduced the boys to the cult. Screwed them up big time."

"Dear God!" He stood and walked to window and stared at something, or nothing, outside. "Back to the missing files. When I got the call from Trippen, I told him I'd go through the records on his father's death and call him back. That's when I discovered the files had gone missing. I have no idea when they disappeared. Probably shortly after the incident. I just don't know. That's when I knew they—whoever *they* are— meant business.

"Trippen didn't say anything about his stepfather being a Satanist, or about any cult activity. That makes me particularly relieved I did what I did. I told Trippen it was ruled an accident and there was no evidence to support anything else. The reason I didn't write a report when he called was to protect him."

"How so?" Smoke again.

"I believed Manthes' death was no accident. My family was threatened when I made that known. I didn't think Gregory Trippen would be safe if he came back here and started asking to have the case reopened. Someone in this department took those files, and I didn't want a new report to fall into the same, wrong hands. There are a number of personnel who read them—detectives, brass, sergeants. A bunch of them were here twenty years ago when this all went down."

"No idea who the dirty cop is?"

Armstrong shook his head. "There are fifteen who were here then and are still here now."

"You keep track?"

"Damn straight. As long as I work here and get that annual phone call, it's the least I can do."

"No hint at all over the years?"

"I read every report and each staff member's annual review, and I have no idea."

"Why haven't you talked to the sheriff?" I asked.

"He's one of the fifteen."

My heart sped up at that.

"Gregory Trippen will be arriving here about seven o'clock tonight to help look for his brother," I said.

Armstrong squared his shoulders. "For his sake, the further I stay away from him, the better. But keep me in the loop. Discreetly. This place has eyes and ears."

A sensation, an electrical zing, shot through my body. Was there a set of evil eyes and ears, watching and listening, at the Winnebago County Sheriff's Department?

12

I followed Smoke to his desk in the pool of detectives' cubicles. We were the only ones in the area. Smoke sat down at his desk, plopped one elbow on the top, and lowered his head into his raised hand. He rested his thumb against his temple and rubbed his four fingers into his forehead.

I broke the silence, speaking softly. "Do you think we have a dirty cop working here?"

Smoke continued his head massage. "Armstrong's convinced there is. We both know anything's possible. I've been running every old-timer I can think of through my brain, and there's not a one I would suspect. But I never had reason to before."

"When Armstrong made the comment about the sheriff being one of the fifteen, I had a moment of panic. He's the only man my mother has dated in almost thirty years of widowhood. What if it's him?"

"Don't jump to any conclusions. I don't believe it is Denny Twardy." He straightened his shoulders and dropped his hands on his desk. "Remember that training we had a few years ago? The morning session was on gangs, the afternoon was on cults?"

"Sure."

"The thing that stuck in my brain about people in cults is they act in secret, keep what they are doing hidden. Occult means dark, hidden, clandestine. Only one reason for that— they are up to no good."

Another electrical zing ran through me. "It's about time for shift change. I'd better get to the squad room for any pass-on info from Hughes."

"Call me when Trippen gets into town?"

"You want to be in on my meeting with him?"

Smoke nodded. "Not that I'm as paranoid as Armstrong, but we can interview him here at my desk. Detectives should all be home by then, unless something big goes down, that is."

"Sounds good. Later then."

My time on duty usually passed quickly, responding to calls, answering deputies' questions about policies and procedures, or assisting them at scenes. But waiting for Gregory Trippen's call sent everything into slow motion.

I thought about my encounters with the officers who had been with the department the longest. The seniority list hung on the squad room wall. When I got back to the office, I snatched down the list, made a copy, and returned it to its place. Most of the oldest employees had been promoted to administrative, or other positions, but a few were still on the road, on patrol.

Sheriff Twardy, Deputy Scofield, Lieutenant Randolph, Sergeant Miller, Captain Brinkmann, Deputy Edberg, Detective Conley, Sergeant Winston, Bailiff Jansen, Deputy

Brooks, Deputy Maple, Bailiff Olgilvey, Detective Harrison, Chief Deputy Kenner, Lieutenant Armstrong. Three were females. Did that eliminate them from the pool of suspects?

My head was swimming with images: cases I'd worked with the officers, conversations I'd had, training experiences, reprimands I'd gotten as a rookie deputy, and the occasional time I'd gotten called on the carpet by admin for a decision I'd made as a sergeant. I trusted each one of them professionally.

Personally? I'd been to retirement parties or other department events with most of them. One went to my church. Two had children I went to school with. I'd been to their homes as a teenager and remembered nothing sinister about either of them.

My ringing cell phone startled me. It was a little after six. Trippen's number. "Sergeant Aleckson."

"Hi, it's Greg Trippen. We just got into town—made better time than I thought. I'm dropping my friend off at the Oak Lea Motel. Are you able to meet me somewhere?"

"Sure. Can you find your way to the county courthouse?"

"I should be able to. The town has grown a lot in twenty years. The courthouse is still by Bison Lake?"

"It is. Come to the south side, the lake side, of the building. You'll see the outside entrance to the sheriff's department. I'll meet you there."

I phoned Smoke, who was still working at his desk. "Are you free?"

"No, but I'm cheap."

I smiled and rolled my eyes. "That's true. Trippen is on his way here. I'm going to meet him at the south entrance."

"I'll be right there."

I stepped outside to wait. The early evening air was cool and fresh. I drew in a few cleansing breaths. A green Forester pulled into the parking lot, and a husky man of medium height climbed out and stretched, then shook his arms and legs. It had likely been some time since his last stop. He spotted me when he looked up. I had the advantage of knowing what Gregory looked like and waved. He nodded and climbed the steps to meet me. We shook hands.

"Before we go inside, are you carrying any weapons of any kind?" I asked.

"I got a multi-tool. It's got a small jackknife on it."

"Do you mind handing it over? I'll give it back when you leave."

He shrugged, reached in his pocket, withdrew the tool, and gave it to me.

"Thanks. For safety's sake, I need to do a quick pat-down, unless you'd rather have a male officer do it."

"It's all right."

I pat searched him and found nothing but his wallet.

Smoke opened the door as I lifted my entry card to the scanner. "Sorry, detained by a phone call."

Gregory Trippen took a step back.

"No problem," I assured him.

Smoke extended his arm. "Detective Dawes."

Trippen accepted his offer and shook his hand. He lifted his eyes to the mounted security camera in the entrance, then focused on Smoke's back when Smoke turned around and headed into the office. He led the way to his desk.

Smoke gestured for Gregory to take a seat, but he remained standing, looking around the vast space, divided into smaller office areas for each investigator. "How do I know I'm safe here?"

"You're safe. You have my word. It's after office hours, and there is no one on duty who was with the department twenty years ago."

Trippen's agitation was evident. "Is there somewhere more private we can go? You know, soundproof, no windows?"

Smoke took the extra step whenever possible to ensure comfort for victims and families of victims. He thought before answering. "Sure. There's a small meeting room in the courthouse. We'll head there."

Smoke once again led the way with Trippen close behind, looking right and left obsessively as we headed down one hallway, then the next. I brought up the rear. Meeting Room C wasn't soundproof, but there was no one around to hear us.

We all sat down. Gregory studied his folded hands. "Do you know anything about those people, what they do, the Satan worshippers?"

Smoke stretched his arms. "I've had a few training courses in my career."

"I took a course two years ago on gangs and cults," I said.

"How about with the cult members, the Satan worshippers themselves?"

I shook my head, and Smoke said, "I haven't had any direct dealings with them."

"You have, you just didn't know it because they don't tell you who they are. You've probably investigated crimes they've committed."

"Meaning?"

"I don't know who's all in the local coven now—and I'm sure it's still active—but when I was a kid there was a doctor. My doctor, the one my mother took us to. She didn't know his connection to them. At that time there was an undertaker. He was one of the ones who killed my father, and the same one who handled his funeral. The drugstore owner was another. And others from Wellspring. I'd see them around town but didn't know their names.

"During the rituals they wore capes with hoods and they looked different, especially in the dark, but I knew who they were. When they were by the fire, performing the rituals, their faces were distorted, but their voices always gave their identities away to me. I know a deputy with the sheriff's department was there one night, maybe more than one night, but I don't know who he was."

Smoke's eyes narrowed. "How do you know he was a deputy?"

"Because that night we were at the altar and I was close enough to hear the undertaker say something like, 'Trusted deputy, you are doing well, watching carefully for any reports at the sheriff's department that might be incriminating to our coven.' The deputy said, 'Yes, High Priest, I am very vigilant.' I wasn't sure what *incriminating* and *vigilant* meant, but I had close to a photographic memory when I was a kid and looked up the words in the dictionary at school the next day."

"Photographic memory. Comes in pretty handy, huh?"

"It's not the same as it was when I was young. And it was good, like for school, but there's a lot of other stuff I'd like to forget."

Smoke nodded. "Tell me about the deputy."

"He was turned so his hood covered most of his profile. His voice was low, like a smoker's. I was just a kid and didn't think about people's ages then. Every adult was old to me. Hearing his voice in my mind now, I'd say he was in his late thirties, early forties, but that's only a guess."

If it were somehow possible to hear the recording of that voice from Trippen's memory, it might have provided a piece of the puzzle.

"Greg, you told Sergeant Aleckson your brother is planning to sacrifice himself on Satan's altar. Why?"

"Jeff lost his ability to cope a long time ago. I guess he finally lost all hope of fighting his demons. They destroyed his life, his basic self. It should have happened to me too. I don't know why it didn't. I hate to use this phrase, but for Jeff it must be, if you can't beat 'em, join 'em."

"By killing himself?"

He nodded. "They are evil, evil people. They control by terror, do horrible things to you, make you do horrible things you can't talk about."

"What kinds of things?"

"I can't get into that right now. I haven't slept for two nights, and if I start dredging it all up, I won't sleep tonight either. I'm here to find Jeff. I can tell you a year's worth of my personal experiences, and I'd love to expose them, but they have been at it for centuries and are very, very good at keeping their crimes well hidden. Like most victims of SRA, I've kept my mouth shut about it."

"What's SRA?" I asked.

"Satanic ritual abuse." He paused. "They marked me so I wouldn't forget."

"How?" Smoke asked.

"I'll show you."

Gregory shifted forward. His belly covered his belt and settled on his thighs. He lifted his leg partway, then reached down, grabbed the bottom of his pant leg, and pulled his foot across his knee. He untied his shoe, dropped it to the floor, and pulled off a white sock that had brown leather insole stains on the bottom. He turned his foot upward as best he could, revealing his sole and its mark.

"It's an upside down cross. They burned one into each of my feet on my tenth birthday."

Smoke coughed. A cold wave, followed by a hot wave, washed over me. I winced involuntarily and hoped Trippen didn't notice. Neither of us was a parent, but we both had great difficulty dealing with violence against children.

Smoke kept his eyes leveled on Trippen. "Why did they do that?"

"So I would walk on Jesus's cross every day of my life."

Smoke and I escorted Gregory Trippen out of the building. When we passed by the squad room, two deputies looked up from their report writing and eyed our makeshift parade. When we reached Trippen's car, he turned to face us.

"Thanks, both of you. I think I'll be able to sleep tonight, now that I'm here, and knowing you're on the watch for Jeff."

I pulled Trippen's multi-tool out of my pocket and returned it to him. "What are your plans for tomorrow?"

He shrugged.

Smoke took over. "We should get together, talk some more when you're up to it. Never say never about nailing the guys that did that to you and your brother."

His expression revealed a glimmer of hope before it turned wary. "Okay if I call when I wake up?"

"Of course. Here's my card." Smoke handed it to him.

I withdrew a card from my breast pocket and gave it to him. "And here's mine, with more contact information."

Gregory took them, nodded, and climbed in his car. As he drove away, Smoke said, "I'm glad the sheriff will be back in the office tomorrow. A lot has gone down since yesterday."

"That's for sure. And it's been strange having him gone for a whole week."

"The county administrator has been after him for how many years to use up some of his vacation days. He accumulated the max long ago, and he's just losing what he could acquire. After his wife died what, three years ago, I don't think he's taken more than a day off here or there."

I smiled. "At least he and my mother have that in common. Two workaholics. Mom said they were going to paint her shop over the weekend. Some vacation, huh?"

Smoke grinned. "Yeah. Oh, I meant to tell you, but got sidetracked. I got a call from my dog-breeder buddy. Your puppy will be weaned and ready to go in two weeks. If you still have your heart set on an English setter?"

"I do. I loved my grandpa's setters when I was a kid."

"You said you wanted a dog who likes to go on long runs, and you're about to get your wish."

"I just hope I can keep her happy and content in between runs. I read they need regular, vigorous exercise. I don't remember my grandpa doing anything special. His dogs pretty much ran around the farm and seemed fine."

"You've got acres around you. She'll be fine. Sure you don't want a male? They're bigger."

"I fell in love with Queenie."

"Queenie?"

"I sort of copied you. You have Rex. King. I thought Queenie was kind of cute."

"A watchdog is not supposed to have a cute name." He feigned annoyance.

"All right. She'll have a regal name. Queen. I'll call her Queenie when there are no bad guys around."

Smoke chuckled melodiously.

"Winnebago County, Six oh eight?" Robin's voice on the police radio interrupted.

I depressed the call button. "Go ahead."

"Report of a two-vehicle crash with injuries on Highway Fifty-five and Albert Avenue."

I ran to my squad as I said, "Ten-four. En route from the station." I yelled over my shoulder at Smoke, "Meet you at the sheriff's office at oh eight hundred tomorrow?"

"Copy that."

13

The Coven

Noris drove his squad car to a county park and stopped. He got out and walked a short distance away. He wasn't supposed to leave his car without letting Communications know and needed to stay close in case he got a call for service. He pulled out his personal cell phone and dialed Cyril's number. No answer by the third ring. Leave a message, or not?

Leave a message. "A business question," was all he said. It was enough to alert Cyril something had happened that he should be aware of.

Their phone conversations were brief and cryptic, never enough to reveal much about their activities in the event they were picked up on a two-way radio or a baby monitor. That happened more than people thought. Cell phones were sophisticated radios, operating on over a thousand channels. Easy to intercept. But people continued to utter private words into them all the time.

Noris waited impatiently by his squad car for ten minutes for a return call, then climbed in behind the wheel and went back out on patrol. An hour passed before Cyril phoned him back. They did not exchange greetings or disclose names.

"First location, your convenience," he said and hung up.

Noris was proud of his position in the coven, but there were times he felt Cyril was taking advantage of him. He had played interception for the coven at the sheriff's department time after time. He was the one taking the personal risk.

He did not like going to the mortuary in uniform, but that was what Cyril was telling him to do. Stop by sometime during business hours. He knew people wouldn't think a thing of seeing a squad car in the mortuary lot. Cops were the escorts for funeral processions in Winnebago County, and there were other official reasons to be there.

But if another deputy or detective or someone in administration happened by, that was something else. They would wonder what department business Noris had there and might bring it up, start asking questions. Cyril and Noris had agreed their cover was that Noris had stopped in during his break as a favor for his aunt. That she had asked him to pick up information on all the services the business provided.

Noris was the youngest in the coven's leadership circle and would be appointed High Priest when Cyril died or stepped aside as the leader. Roman didn't seem interested in the position. And Dieter preferred being Cyril's left-hand man. Of course, that might change if Cyril was out of the picture.

Dieter's whole life was the coven. Noris had a life he enjoyed outside the coven, one he never talked about to the others. The less they knew about that, the more he was able to continue in it.

Wellspring was in Noris's duty cover area. He headed that direction and was in Cyril's office fifteen minutes later. Noris handed Cyril the photos of Jeffrey Trippen and the dagger, which Cyril studied for some minutes.

"That looks like it could be the younger Manthes boy. And Sparrow's dagger."

"I wondered if it was Sparrow's. It looked familiar to me, just like Jeffrey did."

"You were young when the Manthes family disappeared and Sparrow left for Saint Cloud to start a new coven."

"How would Jeffrey get Sparrow's dagger?"

"That's what I'm wondering. Sparrow said he never found the three of them—his wife and her kids. Why would he lie to us if he did?" He stared at an oil painting on his wall. "We'll need to meet to show the others what you have. Eleven o'clock tomorrow night, Deacon?" Cyril said.

"Yes, High Priest."

14

The sheriff's office was a good place to talk. The walls had an extra layer of insulation to keep conversations private, unless people were yelling loudly. Smoke and I sat down opposite Twardy.

The sheriff listened to every word I gave him on Jeffrey Trippen, Gregory Trippen, Harlan Manthes, and the missing files. His face grew more and more somber the longer I spoke. Smoke had talked to Alden Armstrong earlier that morning, alerting him about our meeting with the sheriff. When I finished my account, Smoke called Armstrong in to join us.

Armstrong looked like he either hadn't slept a wink the night before or was in mourning. His green irises were surrounded by pinkish scleras, and dark circles bagged beneath his eyes.

"For godsakes, Alden, you tie one on last night?"

His mouth turned downward, but he didn't answer.

"Aleckson brought me up to speed on her case. Dawes said you can shed some light about the missing files."

Armstrong took a chair next to me. His words tumbled out quietly as he briefed the sheriff, providing details regarding his suspicions about Harlan Manthes' death, the threats against his family, and Gregory Trippen's questions several years before.

Sheriff Twardy's face grew a shade redder each minute Armstrong spoke. "For godsakes, Alden, what in the Sam Hill got into you, keeping something like that concealed? Obstruction of justice, in my book."

Armstrong appeared stricken. His shoulders rounded in near collapse, and his voice cracked when he spoke. "Sheriff, I couldn't talk to anybody. I'm sorry, but I didn't have a choice. These people are serious, dangerous. Come to find out they're even more dangerous than I thought. And connected. They obtained my unlisted phone number as soon as I got a new one. I thought I'd figure out who the dirty cop was around here, but I never could."

The sheriff studied Armstrong intently during his confession. "All right, enough said. For now. We'll take this investigation one step at a time. The number one priority is finding this younger Trippen boy before he hurts himself or someone else in the process. I see no reason to mention any satanic connection. Our residents would go into a panic if word of cults and altars leaks out."

"I'd like to reopen the Harlan Manthes case," Smoke said.

The sheriff didn't hesitate. "Done. We need to take a closer look at that. The shooting, the missing reports. Of course I remember the shooting, but I couldn't tell you who was involved after all these years. You have the hunters' names, Alden?"

Armstrong glumly nodded. "Names, dates of birth, addresses. Memorized. With a written copy of them locked in my home safe. In case something suspicious ever happened to me, or my family, I wanted those three men to be at the top of the suspect list. I couldn't figure out who else was working with them, but I had their names."

Twardy glued his eyes on Armstrong and lowered his voice. "You think we got a Benedict Arnold among us?"

Armstrong solemnly nodded.

Sheriff Twardy's frowned expression reflected the gravity of the situation. "We'll flush him out. We have to."

Armstrong dropped his face into his hands and kneaded his head.

"Dawes will start poking around. We'll keep you out of it, Alden. I don't want to involve internal affairs just yet. The fewer people who know about this, the better. Write those names, dates of birth, and addresses down and give them to Dawes."

Sheriff Twardy flipped a page on the notepad that lay on his desk and handed it to Armstrong. Armstrong ripped out a sheet, jotted the information down, and gave it to Smoke.

Smoke read for a moment. "I'll get on it."

"Sheriff, the night I got the call, Carlson and Mason were in the squad room and I told them about the satanic part, but I asked them not to say anything."

"Next time you see them, tell them to stick to that until further notice."

"I will."

The sheriff stood, indicating the meeting was over. "I'm due at an interview in five minutes." He fixed his eyes on Armstrong once more. "Alden, now would be a good time to take your family on that vacation you've been planning. Get in the car and disappear for a week. That's an order. Don't tell even your best friend where you're going.

"Fill out a vacation request and backdate it for sometime in February. If anyone asks me where you went, I'll tell them the truth. 'Armstrong keeps his private life private and I didn't ask.' What is this world coming to? For godsakes!"

We filed out of the sheriff's office in silence. I headed toward the outside entrance, and Smoke followed. We stepped outside onto the veranda. I closed my eyes and turned my face toward the sun to soak in a few rays, hoping it would brighten my spirits.

"The last job I wanted around here is Internal Affairs," Smoke said.

"I don't blame you. I wouldn't want it either, but at least no one will know that's what you're doing."

"I hope Denny doesn't stroke out before Jeffrey Trippen turns up, and we flush out the malevolent scumbag."

"No kidding. He has us all worried when he gets upset. I envision his blood pressure numbers skyrocketing. I mean really, how can my hyper mother and our hyper sheriff have a calm relationship? I don't get it, but they actually seem relaxed when they're together."

"That is interesting. I wouldn't exactly call either one of them hyper. Denny's excitable when it comes to cases and his staff. Otherwise, he's pretty calm. Your mother? She's hyper-vigilant when it comes to family. You and your brother mostly. And she has lots of projects going, but . . . yeah well, I guess she is pretty hyper." He waved his arm gently. "She has a calming aura about her, though."

I snickered. "Seriously? So what do you know about calming auras?"

"Maybe it's motherly instincts radiating from her. She gives the impression she's keeping close watch and has everything under control."

"You've known her longer than I have. She is very capable, running her business, taking care of Gramps and his house, her own house—"

"Trying to keep track of you and John Carl," Smoke added.

"Yes, and that."

"Being left a widow with two babies at age, what, twenty-one—"

"Twenty."

"That's a lot to cope with."

"I can't even imagine. As weird as it is, her dating the sheriff, I'm glad she has someone in her life after all these years."

"Thirty years, from age twenty to age fifty, is a long time between romantic relationships. You think they'll get married?"

"I don't know. Mother says they're taking one day at a time. Between Gramps' failing health and John Carl's failing marriage, there's a lot up in the air right now."

"John Carl still thinking about moving back to Oak Lea?"

"He doesn't come right out and say it, but I think he has his hopes set on Emily changing her mind and taking him back. He's in denial his marriage tanked. I feel so bad for him, but he'll have to make a decision one of these days."

"Been there, done that, and it's not an easy one to make. 'Course, I wasn't married. So it was a little less complicated to walk away."

"But you wanted to be married."

"I did. She didn't. Broke my heart, but I moved on."

"Except for one day a year?"

Smoke squeezed his face into an uncomfortable looking expression. "Probably not a good topic right now, or ever."

I had stopped at Smoke's house one evening the past summer. He'd been drinking, and told me it was the anniversary of his leaving the woman who would not commit to an exclusive relationship with him. Between his near-inebriated state and our unspoken mutual attraction, we had found ourselves in one another's arms for an intense few moments. Smoke had managed to break away before we got to the point of no return.

There were times I longed to be back in those moments, to find out what it would be like if Smoke hadn't stopped us. We maintained our close working relationship and remained good friends, but the threat—or promise—of an even closer connection loomed nearby.

I pulled my car keys from my jeans pocket. "I've got an appointment with my shrink, so I best get moving."

"Making good progress?"

"We are. Maybe one or two more sessions. Doctor Kearns is pleased. And so am I, of course."

"I'm glad you finally went. A couple of traumatic incidents like you went through, you need someone to help you deal with 'em."

"You were right. You and everybody else who tried to convince me. I honestly—I guess naively—thought it would work itself out in time."

I pulled my red, 1967 classic GTO into a parking space at the Oak Lea Memorial Hospital where Dr. Lester Kearns rented an office space for his private practice. I made my way to his office, greeting people I knew along the way. In my years with the sheriff's department, I had gotten to know many of the doctors and nurses. Even the hospital administrator. Very well. But that was another story.

Dr. Kearns' young, sweet-faced assistant, Grace, smiled when I stepped into the reception area. When she was born, could her parents have known her name would become the self-fulfilling prophesy of her persona and character? I imagined a halo hovering over her head.

Grace stood then closed the space between us. "Corinne. You're looking so well, and that shade of blue is perfect on you. The doctor is ready for you, so I'll tell him you're here." She floated out of the room and soundlessly returned seconds later. "Go right in." Grace was one of the reasons Dr. Kearns had a successful practice and positive feedback from both his patients and the public at large.

Dr. Kearns was standing by his desk when I entered his azure blue office. I had chosen, subconsciously or not, a polo shirt the same shade when I dressed that morning. The color of serenity. The state of being I longed for and strived toward.

Dr. Kearns and I shared our customary handshake. Since the first time we met, I had tried to duplicate his grasp when I shook others' hands. His hands were warm and dry, but not too dry. He had a way of gently sliding his fingers slowly in until his thumb was in place. That's when he squeezed firmly and quickly, passing on the assurance that he was there, confident and competent to help.

"And how are you today, Corinne?" Although most people called me Corky, I seldom corrected those who didn't. As a child, I had thought my given name was embarrassing, but the older I got, the better I liked it.

"I'm feeling well, more like my old self all the time."

"Glad to hear it."

"Thanks to you."

Dr. Kearns smiled, a fairly rare occurrence. He wasn't exactly stingy with his smiles. He kept all facial expressions to a minimum.

"You know this is a team effort. Sit down and bring me up to speed."

I settled into a cordovan-colored leather chair. Dr. Kearns lifted a notebook from his desk then sat down across from me.

My eyes closed for a moment as I sorted my thoughts. "I was lying in bed last night thinking about a case I'm working on, a case involving children who suffered horrific abuse. And for some reason, it put what I had been through in a whole different perspective."

"Oh?"

"Alvie Eisner tried to kill me because I was hampering her criminal intentions. Langley Parker abducted me, apparently because I fit the profile of the women he liked to torture, kill, and dismember."

"Yes."

"Of course those experiences traumatized me, but everything you've been telling me these last few months has finally sunk in. I am strong. I love my job and can't let two crazy . . . sorry . . . people dictate my life. Or my thoughts. Or my feelings.

"After both of those incidents I remembered feeling so grateful to be alive, so grateful I had survived. I kept thinking I was fine. Okay, I wasn't so fine, but I was grateful. That's it. I feel I'm on earth for a reason, and Eisner and Parker are not going to interfere with that."

Dr. Kearns nodded then changed the subject. "How about your personal relationships? Nick? Smoke?"

An equally difficult topic. "I've had to accept that I don't have much control there. I was falling in love with Nick, and he made me choose between him and my career after only a few months of dating. A part of me will always love him, and his daughter, Faith." Dr. Kearns took notes, his head bobbing slightly here and there.

I took a quick breath. "Smoke? He's put too many obstacles in the way, and he's probably right. He's a lot older, and we work together. He was my father's best friend. All good reasons not to get involved personally."

"You mentioned at an earlier session that you wondered if you were looking for a father figure in Smoke."

I mulled that over for a second. "You know, growing up, the important men in my life were my grandfathers. Mother didn't date. I don't necessarily feel like I'm looking for a father figure because I had my grandpas. It could be, since they were forty and fifty years older than me, a man twenty years older than me doesn't seem that old. I don't know. Obviously I'm still confused about men. I sometimes wonder if I'd even know how to have a lasting relationship."

"Your grandparents' marriages provided you with good examples."

"True, but we didn't live with them. Could that be at the heart of John Carl's marriage problems? He didn't have our father as a role model of how to be a husband. According to Emily, and I think it's true, all he does is work."

"Of course I don't have answers about John Carl's marriage. But you've talked about how your mother works so much. He may be modeling his work ethic after hers."

Very possible. Likely.

Dr. Kearns asked more questions about my sleeping, eating, and exercising habits, then addressed some general issues. My mind wandered to Gregory and Jeffrey Trippens' abuse and Jeffrey's mental illness.

"Dr. Kearns, how familiar are you with victims of Satanic ritual abuse?"

He blinked and jerked his head back a fraction. "Where did that come from?"

"The case I referred to earlier. The man I'm working with said his brother is planning to sacrifice himself for Satan. He said they were brought into a cult as children. I'm trying to understand what's going on in that man's mind. I mean, self-sacrifice? I thought maybe you had some insights."

Dr. Kearns shook his head as he processed the implication of my words. "I have had patients come to me with a variety of symptoms, the probable results of being ritually abused, with or without the claim of SRA. Sometimes it takes a number of sessions before they remember, or admit, what's at the core of their mental health problems. When I suspect that's what it is, I refer them to Dr. Marcella Fischer. She's very experienced. I'd say she's an expert in that area."

"Where's her office?"

"Here in Oak Lea. Out in the country. She has a home office. People are less intimidated, it seems, going to appointments there." Dr. Kearns stood, went behind his desk, and opened a drawer. He pulled out a card and offered it to me. "Would you like to talk to her, perhaps meet with her?"

"Yes, I would. Thank you. I'm way out of my league with this one."

"It's not something you can wrap your mind around very easily. Shall I give her a call, see what she has for openings?"

"That'd be great."

Dr. Kearns spoke into the phone seconds after punching in ten numbers. "Marcella, Les here . . . Good, good. Say, I have a Winnebago County sergeant here who's working on a case involving a probable victim of SRA . . . That's right. She'd like to meet with you. Do you have some time to talk to her? . . . Right, thanks." Dr. Kearns handed me the phone.

"Dr. Fischer? It's Sergeant Aleckson. Thanks for talking to me."

"Certainly, Sergeant. How can I help you?" Her voice was low and smooth.

"I'm working on a case involving a couple of brothers who were allegedly involved in a cult as children, and one is planning to kill himself as a sacrifice to Satan."

"Oh, dear."

"If you can fit me in sometime soon, I'd greatly appreciate it. I've had training on cults, but nothing like this. I'm concerned about his behavior, how he might react when we find him."

"Certainly." I heard her shuffling papers or turning pages. "I have two openings today, in fact. A one o'clock or a four o'clock."

"I'll take the one o'clock."

"Certainly. You know my location?"

I glanced at the address on her card. "I do. See you at one."

I thanked Dr. Kearns, then Grace, and headed down a hospital corridor. I spotted Nicholas Bradshaw, the hospital administrator and my former love interest, coming toward me. There was no delicate way to avoid him short of disappearing into thin air, and as many times in my life as I had willed that to happen, it never had.

His scent reached me before he did and reminded me of inhaling it with my face against his neck. I felt weak, vulnerable, confused. Was my career more important than Nick and his precious daughter, whom I missed every day? With a large amount of guilt, I knew if I had to think about it, even momentarily, the answer was yes.

"Corky! It's been a long time." Nick stepped in close and pulled me against his body for a half-hug.

"Hi, Nick. How's Faith?"

"She's great, as always. She asks about you all the time." He eased his grip, and I took a step back.

"I wish I could see her, but I'm told that will just complicate things for her."

"Change of mind, heart?" he implored.

I searched his classically-handsome face. "I guess we're at a standstill."

"Until you retire?"

I realized I was holding my breath and forced the air out of my nose. "Someone will snatch you up long before then."

"And you, I guess. Someone with nerves of steel who can actually watch you get into that squad car day after day."

I shrugged. "Say 'hi' to Faith for me. Good to see you, Nick."

He gently took my forearm in his hand, nodded, dropped my arm, and walked away.

My legs were shaky all the way to my car. After I sat in the seat for a minute, I phoned Smoke on his cell phone. "What are you up to?"

I heard the verbal exchange coming from his police radio.

"On my way to a drive-through to pick up some lunch."

"Which one?"

"I haven't decided yet, Arby's or Culver's."

"Where are you now?"

"A block from the office. Why?"

"Meet me in the parking lot of Culver's? I'm near there."

"Ten-four."

I was waiting when Smoke drove in. He pulled up so we could talk, driver's side window to driver's side window.

"What's up?"

"I have an appointment with a psychologist who has worked with a lot of people who have supposedly been involved with cults. I'm hoping she can give me some insights into what Jeffrey Trippen may be like, you know, his behavior. We've been in enough situations with unpredictable behaviors."

"Yeah, we've had plenty of those deals go south in a hurry."

We both thought a moment, envisioning scenarios.

I recalled a memorable one. "Remember that burglary a few years ago? The one where the guy broke into a house where the woman was home alone with a baby? He was all wild-eyed and scared the living daylights out of her."

"Yeah. Sure. She managed to get into the baby's room and locked the door. Good thing. In the few seconds it took her to dial nine-one-one, the guy was outside howling at the moon." Smoke threw his head back and imitated the suspect.

I grinned at his silly action. "That was a long night. Weber was first on the scene, got him in a body lock and had enough strength to hold him until Carlson arrived. I got there a minute later. It seemed like hours before the ambulance got there so we could backboard him and get him to the hospital. It took a hefty dose of sedatives to bring him down. We all thought he was on meth. He certainly acted like it, but he was having some type of psychotic episode instead."

"I think it's a good idea, meeting with someone who works with cult victims, possibly getting some insights on how to deal with Trippen before we find him. Good thinking, little lady."

I smiled and nodded. "Mind if I tag along? I need a break from looking through the personnel files of our old-timers."

"I don't mind, and I doubt if the doctor will either. She sounded hospitable enough on the phone.

15

I rode with Smoke in his squad car to Dr. Fischer's home office, four miles from downtown Oak Lea. The maple trees bordering her driveway were leafing out and would completely block the view of her house from the road in another week.

"Nice digs," Smoke admired as he put the car in park.

"Not bad."

Dr. Fischer's home was a two-story Tudor-style, sided with stucco and decorative timbers. We walked to the front entry, and Smoke rang the bell. Dr. Fischer opened the door and smiled warmly. She stepped back, allowing us entrance into the foyer.

"Sergeant Corky Aleckson." I extended my hand, and Dr. Fischer shook it firmly.

"Nice to meet you, Sergeant. And . . . ." She turned to Smoke.

"Elton Dawes, detective. I kind of invited myself. I hope it's all right if I sit in on the meeting," Smoke said as he took her right hand into his.

Dr. Fischer's pupils widened a tad when she looked into Smoke's eyes. His eyebrows rose, as if he was surprised by her reaction and hint of attraction. I had witnessed the effect he had on women of all ages over the years and wasn't surprised.

Dr. Fischer looked like a model. She was around five-foot-nine, maybe one hundred and thirty pounds. Her breasts sat high on her chest, so there was a long expanse between them and her waist. Her hips curved slightly, evidenced by the slim, fitted skirt outlining them. Her beige silk blouse was a couple of shades lighter than her taupe skirt. Light brown hair, cut an inch above her shoulders, flipped up at the ends and provided a nice frame for her violet-blue eyes. She was classy from head to toe.

"Thanks for taking time from your busy schedule, Dr. Fischer," I said, breaking the spell between her and Smoke.

Her eyes flicked over to me. "Certainly. Please come in. My office is right over here." She lifted her arm, indicating the door on our right. Smoke and I followed her in.

"Sit down. Please." Dr. Fischer pointed at a sitting area with a loveseat and two stuffed armchairs. Smoke and I both went for the loveseat, but I shifted to an armchair before we wedged in together.

"May I offer you something to drink? Bottled water, coffee, tea?"

We both said, "No thanks."

Dr. Fischer lifted a notebook and pen from her desk then sat down in the other chair. She folded her hands around her pen and leveled her eyes on me. "You said you are working with two brothers who were involved in a cult as children. And one is planning to sacrifice himself to Satan."

"That's correct." I gave her a summary of my initial call from Gregory Trippen, his description of Jeffrey, his belief his stepfather had killed his father, our meeting with Gregory, and the inverted crosses burned on the soles of his feet. Dr. Fischer delicately nodded throughout my monologue, occasionally glancing at Smoke.

I summed up by saying, "Dr. Kearns recommends you as the person to talk to. He says you're an expert in the area." I withdrew a memo pad and pen from the back pocket of my jeans.

Dr. Fischer shrugged one shoulder. "I went into this field because I was greatly influenced by a book I read as a teen. The book was called *Sybil*—"

"I saw the movie," Smoke interrupted.

She looked from Smoke to me. "It was about a young woman who was sexually and physically abused from a very young age. When her immature mind and body could not abide what was happening to her, she developed dissociative identity disorder, or DID. She fragmented into many separate personalities."

"Fragmented into separate personalities?" I had heard of split personalities, but the term *fragmented* struck me as a much worse condition.

"Multiple personality disorder?" Smoke asked.

"Yes. Now it's generally known as dissociative identity disorder. The mind is capable of forgetting, or repressing, traumatic experiences. There are a variety of conditions and terms to describe this. Besides dissociative state, there's traumatic amnesia, psychogenic shock. Dissociative amnesia can occur after any type of traumatic event."

I jotted the names down quickly to keep up. "It's not schizophrenia?"

"No, that's often confused by laymen, but schizophrenia is very different. The word is taken from Greek words meaning 'split mind,' so it's no wonder why it's confusing. Schizophrenia is a severe mental illness where the person suffers from delusions and hallucinations—"

"Like hearing voices," Smoke chimed in.

"Correct, but does not have multiple personalities, as the name suggests."

"What is dissociative identity disorder, exactly?" I asked.

"It is quite a remarkable protective device, a coping mechanism. For example, when a child is being abused by a trusted adult such as a parent or caregiver, the child needs to block out awareness—the memory of the event—to survive the relationship. The victim's memories and feelings go into the subconscious and emerge later as a separate personality. When more traumatic things happen to the victim, more personalities can develop. These personas have different memories and different functions."

"The personalities that have split off have different memories?" I said.

Dr. Fischer nodded. "The strongest personality becomes the gatekeeper and tells the others when they need to take over for a while. Sometimes there is actual fighting for control between the personalities. DID is a sad thing, of course, but extremely fascinating at the same time. A subconscious technique that allows people to survive trauma and abuse. It's tragic that a little child, or anyone, would have to resort to it to protect themselves." Dr. Fischer raised her hands a tad. "And it's not just children. Adults enduring torture sometimes fragment to keep from dying. There are a few documented cases where they have found up to a hundred different personalities, all housed in a single person."

"I had no idea." It was beyond my comprehension. There were days I had trouble managing my one personality.

Smoke shifted to the front of the seat. "What kind of numbers, percentages, are we talking here, doc?"

"A small percentage. No one really knows because of all the undiagnosed cases, but most likely somewhere between a tenth of a percent and one percent. Other estimates put it up to seven percent of the population."

"Seven percent is a lot of people."

Dr. Fischer nodded. "Yes, it is."

"How many personalities do you typically see in a client?" I asked.

"There is no 'typical.' I've worked with people who have two to four, mainly. The worst case I treated had thirteen alternates that we identified. She suffered unbelievable abuse as a child on through young adulthood. Her family was heavily involved in cult activities. We worked for years, but hadn't completely integrated her. We were making significant headway when she died suddenly of an apparent heart attack. A fragile, yet strong woman. I think about her every day."

"How long ago was that? I asked.

Dr. Fischer studied her watch, as if looking for the answer. "Just about three years now."

I nodded. "Where did she live?"

Her eyebrows drew together. "Rockwell, but that's not where the abuse happened." Rockwell was the next town southeast of Oak Lea.

Smoke extended his long legs in a stretch then pulled them in again. "Working with these people, you've seen the separate personalities come out at different times?"

"Yes. It's quite astonishing. The alternate personalities actually look different, sound different, have different mannerisms. I work to get each of them to trust me. I'm not always sure who the core person is when we start. It might be that the gatekeeper has sent in the personality who deals best with medical or professional personnel. Fragmented personalities are not fully mature ones."

"By core person, you mean the original personality?" I said.

"Correct."

"And how do you figure that out?" Smoke leaned forward.

"My professional trade secrets?" Dr. Fischer smiled at Smoke in a way that bordered on flirting.

Smoke smiled back.

"You have to understand the magnitude of this condition and all the implications for the patient. Multiples are in the mental health system for an average of seven years before they are diagnosed.

"They usually suffer from depression, anxiety, may have had suicide attempts. Finding out you have multiple personalities is not easy to accept, but it is also something that doesn't always come as a complete shock, either. It helps explain gaps in time, or wearing certain clothes they would never choose, or finding items in their house and wondering how they got there."

My mind wandered, recalling a few suspects over the years who claimed they didn't know how stolen items came to be in their possession, or how they ended up naked at a beach, or why they had driven into a public building. Was it possible they were telling the truth?

"One tool I use is to give my DID clients a notebook. I instruct them keep the notebook in one spot in their living quarters and to write to their alternates, actually addressing them by name. They write and the alternates write back, in different handwritings, no less. Sometimes it's a child who prints like a child and can't spell very well."

"So some of these, what you call alternates, are children?" I asked.

"Yes, that's quite common. They may be of the opposite sex. I've read some have animals as alternates, but I've never dealt with that."

Smoke furrowed his eyebrows in disbelief. "Animals?"

"DID is extremely complex." Dr. Fischer studied Smoke's facial expression. "I've used hypnotherapy to invite the alternates to come out, to talk, while the core person stays. Co-consciousness is important in the healing process. The pain each personality suffers needs to be brought to the surface. Healed."

I tried to envision what that healing process would be like. My own counseling sessions paled in comparison.

"Most of my clients are on meds for depression, anxiety, or both. Many have benefited from art or movement therapy. Painting, drawing, sculpting, all enhance recovery from psychological disorders. Dance therapy strengthens the mind-body connection, based on the concept that movement and emotions are directly connected."

I attended a weekly ballet class. Though I had never thought of it before, I silently agreed with the doctor. Movement and emotions were definitely connected.

"I've given you a very brief snippet of the disorder. Still, I have given you a lot of information to digest. Do you have any questions?"

I was processing her words and couldn't think of a single intelligent question to ask.

Smoke cleared his throat. "This isn't meant to discredit your work, it's meant as a clarifying question. You mentioned that you used hypnotherapy. Some years back there was a big hoopla about implanting false memories in patients."

Dr. Fischer nodded. "Yes, there were a lot of stories to that effect back in the eighties. Assuming psychotherapists can implant false memories in patients is just not plausible, as far as I'm concerned. I've done a great deal of research, and I'm not aware of any studies that proved it is possible to do so."

"Good to know," Smoke said.

I thought of the main reason we were there. "Dr. Fischer, Jeffrey Trippen has mental illness, maybe DID. How do you think he'll react when we find him? Is there a special way we should approach him? Anything we can say that might help keep him calm?"

"I wish there was an easy answer to that, but there isn't. If he does have DID, it could be that one of the alternates purchased the dagger and made the phone call to his brother."

"So you think it's possible Jeffrey may not be coming here, after all?"

"No, I think either Jeffrey or an alternate is very intent on doing exactly what he said. He has a definite plan. I'm sure you've ascertained how complicated this is. The best assurance you—any of you at the sheriff's department—can provide is to calmly and firmly call Jeffrey by name and reassure him he is safe, that you will get him to a safe place, keep him safe, and you will keep the bad people away from him," she said.

I thought of the bad person who was lurking around the sheriff's department. If he was around when Harlan Manthes was killed, had he figured out who Jeffrey was? What if a citizen reported a suspicious guy who fit Jeffrey's description and our dirty deputy got to him first? Could we keep Jeffrey safe?

Dr. Fischer shifted then tugged to readjust her skirt. "You called me an expert in this field, and I do specialize in DID, but that can occur from other abusive situations as well and not be cult-related. There are a number of ministers who work with the spiritual aspects of healing. I'll give you the name and number of a local one. He'd be a good resource. And I think it would be helpful for you to talk with one of my patients, if you're interested."

"Yes," Smoke and I said in unison.

"I have a couple in mind. I'll check with them and get back to you."

"That would be great," I said.

"Thank you," Smoke added.

Dr. Fischer wrote on the back of her business card. She handed it to me and said, "Pastor Daniel Trondholm." I knew who he was. He had a congregation on the north side of Oak Lea.

I gave Dr. Fischer my business card, and Smoke followed suit. "Got one for me?" Smoke held out his hand to her.

"Certainly." She retrieved another from her desk and gave it to him. "I'd like to offer my help when you find Jeffrey. I know your officers are trained to handle critical incidents and hostage situations, which this may very well be. If Jeffrey does have DID, either his core personality or one of the alternates is holding the rest of them hostage. One of them may want to die, sacrifice himself, but it's likely not all of them do. Please don't hesitate to call. I've been working with SRA victims for many years."

"We appreciate that," Smoke said.

As we walked toward the entry door, I said, "What is the cure rate for people with DID who get treated?"

Dr. Fischer blew out a quick breath. "There is no cure, but long-term treatment can be very successful."

"Doesn't it bother you, having clients come to your home?" Smoke asked.

Dr. Fischer's lips pulled to one side. "When my practice took this rather unexpected turn, working almost exclusively with SRA victims, the other psychologists in my group asked me to move out of the building."

"Why's that?" Smoke asked.

"Are you ready for this?" Dr. Fischer quietly said.

Smoke cocked his head to the left. "Sure."

"Things started happening. At first it was mostly an annoyance, but it grew in intensity."

"Things?"

"Spiritual beings work with electrical energy. In this case it was demonic-spiritual beings. The office lights would flicker. That went on for a while. We had electricians in and they couldn't find anything wrong. Then appliances started breaking—the refrigerator, then the microwave in the break room, printers, the fax machine. One very hot day it was the air conditioning."

"Maybe the circuits were overloaded or the appliances were old," Smoke said.

"Frankly, I didn't think much of the flickering lights. I mean, fluorescents do that here and there. It was one of my patients that brought it to my attention. She was very, not psychic, exactly . . . very sensitive. I'd say in tune with the spirit world. She has what they call spiritual discernment."

I jotted the term on my memo pad.

"During one of our sessions she stopped talking, put her hands over her ears, and closed her eyes. I waited for a minute then asked her what was the matter. She looked at me with this very tired, weary expression and said, 'Can't you hear them screaming?' I said, 'Who?' and she said, 'The angels of darkness.'

"I was taken aback and didn't answer right away. She said, 'They're the ones who are doing that with the lights.' As she was talking to me, the lights went crazy for a minute, then my computer made this loud pop. We both jumped, it was that loud. They crashed my computer."

"They, as in the angels of darkness?" Smoke's voice held an edge of sarcasm.

"I realize it sounds bizarre, but after hearing the stories of what these people have been through, I was convinced. The next day, I told the other psychologists in the group what my client had said, and one of them said they couldn't afford to have more computers crash, or have other things break, not to mention the times the lights flickered and drove everyone crazy. I'm not sure if they all believed in the whole evil spirit thing or not, but they voted unanimously that either I drop the cult victims or I leave."

"So you left," I finished.

She lifted her shoulders. "I couldn't desert my clients. We were making headway. Many had the hope of recovery for the first time in their lives. I felt I had been called to work in that specialty, in that special niche. I was a little apprehensive wondering if *they*—" Dr. Fischer sought Smoke's eyes, "—as in the angels of darkness, would bother us here. And they did, of course." I glanced around and listened closely. I didn't detect anything out of the ordinary, but maybe my instincts only worked in the physical world. "What did you do about it?"

"I called the minister I told you about, Pastor Daniel Trondholm, and he did what you might call an exorcism."

Smoke crossed his hands on his chest. "On your house?"

Dr. Fischer nodded. "Yes."

"And how'd that go for you?"

She stared at Smoke. "Detective, you're a skeptic. Do you really want to know?"

Smoke shrugged and dropped his arms to his sides. "Sorry. Yes I do. I want to know."

"First let me say that my clients are followed, tormented, fearful. They feel threatened. Those who have spiritual discernment see the evil spirits. When things started happening here, one of my patients said there were demons surrounding the outside of my house. I knew they wanted me to stop, like I had at my other office."

"But you didn't," Smoke said. Admiration was evident in the intonation of his words. Whether he accepted the demon explanation or not, he had a natural fondness for brave women.

"You're not afraid?" I asked.

She smiled and shook her head, in answer to Smoke's comment and to my question. "Pastor Trondholm came, ordered the demons to leave, and blessed my house. I have nothing to fear. They have no power over me." She nodded at the large wooden cross carved from the wood of an olive tree hanging over the mantel of her fireplace. My grandparents had a small one like it in their bedroom.

"Moving the office to my home turned out to be a good thing. My patients are leery of so many, many things. But they're comfortable here. I've had a number of them ask to see their files, to check to see if everything is there. They've had bad experiences with medical records that have gone missing. Police records that have disappeared. Other psychologists they've consulted with who deny ever meeting them or hearing their stories. The Satanists have been at this for centuries and are very, very good at what they do."

Gregory Trippen had said almost the exact same thing.

"How do people, your clients, find you?" I asked.

"Ministers are my biggest referral source. Other psychologists, psychiatrists, therapists are a close second. Some word of mouth from victims, but not much. They may talk online to other victims, but most don't tell the other people in their lives. Co-workers, friends, sometimes even spouses don't know what they have been through, what they had to do to survive in the cult."

Smoke looked at his watch. "Dr. Fischer, we've taken enough of your time. Thank you very much." Smoke offered his hand, which Dr. Fischer accepted in a gentle handshake.

Dr. Fischer and I shook hands. "Yes, we greatly appreciate it."

"And my offer to help stands. Anytime."

16

Smoke and I were silent on the walk to the car and for the first few minutes of the return drive. I felt heavy, burdened by everything the doctor had told us.

"Can you imagine the patience that woman has? Working for years to—"

"Put Humpty Dumpty together again?"

"Smoke." He had lightened the timbre, so I couldn't resist asking, "You think our guy who was howling at the moon was a multiple personality, one of which was a dog or a wolf?"

"I do not want to go there, little lady."

"We got a ton of information from Dr. Fischer, but until we find Jeffrey Trippen, we still won't really know what we're dealing with."

Smoke nodded. "In this job, what's new?"

"It makes me wonder, though."

"About?"

"You know, the calls where someone is up to something and you get there and the person just gives you an innocent stare, like they don't know what's going on?" I said.

"Yeah, that's happened to me more times than I can count. I figured they were either good actors, mentally out to lunch, or on some kind of drug."

"Or maybe suffering from dissociative identity disorder."

"Don't over think that one. If a person commits a witnessed crime, he is still responsible, whether he remembers or not."

"I know, but it has got me curious about some incidents."

"Curious. Your middle name."

"And yours."

The vehicle in front of us crossed the fog line. Her speed varied between forty-five and fifty in a fifty-five mile an hour zone. I pulled the keyboard of Smoke's laptop closer to me and typed in the license plate number. The 2006 Cutlass was registered to a seventy-five-year-old woman who had a valid driver's license and no violations.

"She likes to hug the shoulder and drive within her speed capabilities," Smoke observed as he pulled out to pass.

I lifted my hand in a half-wave as we sped by. "Oh, I meant to tell you, guess who I ran into at the hospital today?"

"Your former lover?"

"He wasn't my lover, but yes, it was Nick."

Smoke raised his eyebrows in surprise. "Oh, I just assumed— you dated awhile. So how is Mr. Perfect?"

"You and my grandma with your Mr. Perfect stuff. Obviously he isn't perfect, as no one is, but he seems to be doing fine. He asked me to reconsider leaving the sheriff's department."

"He didn't."

"Said he'd have to wait 'til I retire."

"He didn't."

"I told him not to wait."

"You didn't."

"Something like that."

Smoke dropped me off at my car, and I had just enough
time to go home, change into my uniform, and report for duty
at three o'clock. My cell phone rang on the drive back to the
station. The sunbeams dancing around in my vehicle and
bouncing off the metal on my phone made it impossible to
read the dial. I hadn't heard from Gregory Trippen and
figured it would be him.

"Sergeant Aleckson."

"Corky, hi, it's Jean Brenner." Something was wrong.

"Jean, hi. Everything okay?"

"That's why I'm calling. I just got a call from Shakopee
Prison. Alvie Eisner just passed away at the hospital."

"Oh. Wow. Oh. Wow. We knew this was coming—I mean,
she hung on longer than any of us thought she would—but
wow. Rebecca will be so sad her grandma died."

"I know. I was hoping you could be here when I tell her."

"Gosh. Um. Sure. Her bus gets home at three thirty?"

"It does."

"I'll stop by as soon as I can after shift change at three.
Hopefully there won't be any emergency calls between now
and then."

"I'd really appreciate it. Alvie requested cremation, and
no service of any kind. Outside of Rebecca, her brother Henry,
and her newfound mother Elaine, there's no one else that we
know of to contact."

Alvie and her brother, Henry, had been abandoned by their
mother at young ages and suffered severe abuse at the hands of
their uncle. Both Alvie and Henry had mental problems, but

Henry's were more pronounced. He had spent his adult life in institutions and group homes. Did he wonder what had happened to Alvie when she stopped going to visit him?

Rebecca's father had hanged himself while in prison, before Rebecca was born. And her mother had left her on Alvie's doorstep shortly after her birth. Alvie was the only parent Rebecca had. When Rebecca was ten, Alvie had begun a revengeful killing spree that landed her in prison. For life. As it turned out, a brain tumor had meant 'life' was only a few months long.

Alvie's mother had shown up out of the blue during Alvie's trial. But Alvie had wanted nothing to do with her after all those years of separation. It was too little too late, as far as she was concerned.

Ironically, Alvie had asked me to be Rebecca's guardian. Ironically because Alvie had tried to kill me. Despite that, I loved Rebecca and wanted to find her a good, stable home with loving parents, so I agreed. Dale and Jean Brenner, Rebecca's best friend Tina's parents, had welcomed Rebecca into their family with open arms.

I visited often and took the kids on outings. Tina's older brother, Justin, was active in sports, so I arranged fun things for the girls when Dale and Jean were at practices and games with Justin.

"You still have some contact with Alvie's brother? We haven't talked about it for a while," I said.

"I do. When Alvie signed the adoption agreement, she asked if I'd bring Henry his hygiene items to the group home once a month. Rebecca goes with me. Henry seems to appreciate the visit, but he's in his own world most of the time. I'm not sure if he knows who we are or not."

Her end was silent for a second, then she continued. "I'm still bothered by the great-grandma issue. I had to respect Alvie's wishes not to let her see Rebecca, but now that Alvie's dead, I think Rebecca should at least meet her."

"I agree. I have Elaine Van House's contact information, and I'll let her know about Alvie. Today would *not* be a good time to tell Rebecca about her. Give her some time to grieve for one grandma before finding out about another."

"You're right. See you when you get here."

"Okie doke."

I clamped my phone shut, and it rang again.

"Sergeant Aleckson."

"Sergeant, it's Marcella Fischer."

"Oh, hi, Doctor."

"I wanted to let you know I was able to contact one of my clients and talked to her for a while. She's amenable to meeting with you. She knows who you are and will call you today or tomorrow."

"And her name?"

"Forgive me, but I'd rather not say, in case she has a change of heart."

Someone who knew me? "Okay, I can respect that. Thanks, Doctor, for your help, and for all the info you gave us today. I was telling Smoke you must have tremendous patience."

"Smoke?"

"Detective Dawes."

"Smoke. Hmm. Why do you call him that?"

"It's his nickname, one he earned, but that's his story to tell."

"You've piqued my interest."

I bet I did. Up a notch or two, that is. Her interest in Smoke was piqued the moment she locked eyes with him.

"I hope my client talks to you. She has a lot to tell."

"I hope so too, and thanks again."

"My pleasure."

We hung up as I pulled into a space in the sheriff's department parking lot.

"Six oh eight, Winnebago County."

Communications Officer Robin answered. "Go ahead, Six oh eight."

"I'm ten-nineteen." At the station.

"You're ten-nineteen at fourteen forty-five."

I gathered my things and walked into the office, chewing over different thoughts. Rebecca Eisner had known her grandma was dying, but it would be difficult to tell her about it anyway. She was only ten years old and had dealt with many terrible things caused by her grandma's criminal actions.

Then Dr. Fischer's call had gotten me thinking about the Trippen/Manthes cases. Two days before, I had received a call from Gregory Trippen that opened separate investigations. One involved the unsettling discovery that a member of our department was likely involved in covering up a murder years before.

We were looking for Jeffrey Trippen, who was out there somewhere. Did he suffer from dissociative identity disorder, fragmented into many separate personalities? Was he tortured and tormented by demons following him? Did he think dying was the only way to escape?

And why hadn't Gregory Trippen phoned yet?

17

"Sergeant Aleckson, report to my office." The words greeted me from the archaic loud speaker system as I walked through the double doors on the south side of the building.

The sheriff must have heard about Alvie Eisner's death.

I wound my way past deputies and office staff to the sheriff's corner office and poked my head through the open door. "Is this about Eisner?"

Sheriff Twardy stood up from his chair. "Alvie Eisner? No, why? She finally give up the ghost?"

One way to put it, and in keeping with all the talk of spirits so far that day. "Yes. I just got a call from Jean Brenner."

"A relief, I guess."

"I guess. We still need to tell Rebecca."

"A heck of a deal. You're good with kids. You'll do fine. I'll notify the families of her victims, Clarice Moy, the Keltons, and what's her name, Marion McIllvery. I'm sure they'll be glad to know. So how are you feeling?"

"Numb."

He nodded. "It'll take a while to sink in."

"You wanted to see me?"

"This could have waited. I know you need to get to your shift change briefing with Sergeant Roth, so I won't keep you long. This is a far cry from what we discussed this morning, in case you're wondering. I need your help with something."

"What's that?"

"Your mother's birthday is coming up next month, and I don't know what to get her."

My lips curled into a small smile. It was the last thing I'd have guessed the sheriff wanted from me.

"It's been a while since I've bought a gift for a woman, not since my wife died, and I've been wracking my brain trying to come up with something."

"Sheriff, don't feel bad. My mother is not exactly easy to buy for. Since she owns her own dress and accessory shop, she gets everything she needs in those lines, clothing, purses, and jewelry. Well, not fine jewelry, but—"

"That's an idea. Her birthday's in May. Birthstone's an emerald. Maybe an emerald ring or a necklace, something like that."

"That's way too expensive. She'd have a hard time accepting such an extravagant gift."

"Any other ideas?"

"The Villager has some cool things. Funky art deco pieces. A thousand candles in every possible scent."

"What is that expression about a bull in a china shop? That would be me."

I suppressed a laugh. The sheriff was not a large man and far from clumsy.

"You could always get a gift certificate at the gift shop or at one of the restaurants. If you want, I can go shopping with you sometime." *Did I really say that?*

"Oh, mmm, thanks. I'll let you know." He probably couldn't imagine it either.

"Sure. Well, I better catch up with Roth so he can get home."

"Right. Oh, one last thing. I talked to Dawes when he got back from that psychologist visit with you. What was your take on all that?"

"I went into that meeting clueless, that's for sure. I'm going to do some Internet searches about dissociative identity disorder and see what I can find on satanic worship. I'll be meeting with one of Dr. Fischer's clients, and I hope to get more from Gregory Trippen, if he would ever call me."

"Why don't you call him?"

"I will if I don't hear from him by six or so."

Sergeant Roth was tapping his pen on the squad room table when I walked through the door. "We haven't found your missing dude yet." He threw a glance at Jeffrey Trippen's photo. "I sure don't like the looks of that dagger."

"No one does."

"So what's his story? A homeless guy traveling with an ornate dagger?"

I shrugged. Sheriff Twardy didn't want the cult connection mentioned until we had a better handle on the broader implications, like who the spy was in our department. I thought of Armstrong's comment about the place having eyes and ears and looked at the five other deputies in the squad room. They all appeared occupied with their own tasks.

"His brother's worried about him."

"I would be too."

"Hopefully, we'll find him and not his body. It's a helpless feeling when you're looking for a guy and he's nowhere to be found."

"We'll find him."

"Anything special to pass on?"

"Not really. Pretty routine calls all day. I served a couple of warrants. Oh, and I finally found good old Pauly Swanson." Roth smiled.

"Where?"

"Walking home from town. Correction—staggering home from town."

"Pauly intoxicated?" I kidded.

"Currently sleeping it off in a cell is my guess."

"Man. They might as well forget about collecting all the money he owes the county in court fees and fines. It is one vicious circle. We arrest him, he goes to court, the judge fines him, and court fees are attached. He's released. Drinks what money he gets from Social Security so he's in arrears again, and we start the process all over."

"One vicious circle, all right. Eventually they'll either waive the fees or sentence him. Wouldn't be a bad thing to dry him out for a month or two. And get some decent food into him."

I raised my eyebrows and nodded. "I better get on the road. I got some bad news to deliver. Alvie Eisner died, and I need to tell her granddaughter."

"You having a party later to celebrate?"

I shrugged. "Two things make me a little sad. Knowing Rebecca will be hurting, and she'll be the only one grieving. Well, maybe Eisner's mother will. But like you say, people will celebrate, if anything."

"I would if I were you. Celebrate." Roth stood, grabbed his things, and we walked out together.

I needed to tell Smoke, my friend Sara, my mother, my grandparents, my brother, and even Nick about Alvie, but my phone rang on the drive to the Brenner house before I could start. Gregory Trippen. Finally.

"Sergeant Aleckson."

"Hi, it's Greg Trippen."

"I was actually starting to worry about you."

"Sorry. I just woke up. I hoped I would crash, and I really did. Kind of surprised me I could sleep that long. Eighteen hours."

Eighteen hours? "You were awake for a few days. No wonder. How are you feeling—any better?"

"I am. I'm surprised. I didn't expect to, but knowing I'm here for Jeff, whenever he shows up, and having your help has helped me relax somehow."

"I'm glad to hear that."

"So what's next? What should we do now?"

There were many questions and countless issues to resolve.

"Gregory, I'm tied up with some things. Why don't you take tonight to unwind, relax as best you can, and we'll meet tomorrow. Unless your brother makes his appearance before that."

"Are you sure? You'll let me know if you find Jeff?"

"I will phone you immediately."

"Okay. Then I'll help get my buddy on a flight back home. As luck would have it, he got a call about a job interview. They want to see him Monday, so he's anxious to get going."

"That's good news for him. You take it easy, and we'll see you tomorrow."

I pulled in the Brenners' driveway and parked.

"Six oh eight, Winnebago County."

"Six oh eight?"

"I'll be out at Three twenty Farmland Avenue on a follow-up." As I spoke, Jean opened the door and waved me to come in.

"Copy, at fifteen eighteen."

I knew Rebecca would be excited when she got off the bus and saw my squad car. I hoped that would ease the pain of my news a little. I scooted into the Brenners' house and hovered in the entry until Jean asked me to sit. I took a chair by a window that had a clear view of the road.

"You'll hear the bus anywhere you sit." Jean smiled and handed me a cup of mint tea. I took a sip to wet my drying mouth then set it on a side table.

"Have you thought of what to say?" she asked.

"I've learned the direct way is usually the best way."

Jean nodded. She was right. I heard the bus before I saw it. My heart warmed when Rebecca and the Brenner children jumped from the bus step. Happy children. And Rebecca was one of them.

I waited to stand up until the kids burst through the door to appear more relaxed than I felt.

"Sergeant Corky!" Rebecca called.

Tina and Justin were almost as excited. I had discovered they were proud to have a cop for a friend, and my squad car sitting in their driveway earned them points with the school-bus crowd.

Rebecca ran to me and threw her thin arms around me, bumping her elbow on my flashlight holder.

"Ouch. Did that hurt?"

"No, it's okay."

I returned her hug, then ruffled Tina's hair and smiled at Justin.

"Tina and Justin, you head into the kitchen for your snack and wait for Rebecca there," Jean instructed.

They both looked disappointed, but obeyed without protest.

"My grandma?" Rebecca asked, her little face scrunching up with worry. She was very bright and wise beyond her years.

I fought back tears as I nodded. She threw her arms around me again and sobbed. I steered her over to the couch and sat her down next to me. Jean Brenner sat on her other side.

"Does it hurt? To die?"

A question I obviously couldn't answer. I could only guess. "I don't think dying hurts. It might hurt right before. You know, if you have a heart attack, or if you're injured. But your grandma?" Her eyes widened. "She was on medication to stop the pain, so I don't think it hurt her."

Rebecca nodded. "What about her funeral?"

I met Jean's eyes. "She didn't want a big funeral, so we'll have a small, private service. How does that sound?"

Rebecca's mouth quivered when she tried to smile.

"Do you know what cremation is?"

"Uh huh."

"That's what your grandma wanted." More quivering. "So they'll bring her ashes back to us, and we'll have a service for her in a few days. Okay?"

She nodded and leaned her head against my chest.

"Rebecca, I'm so sorry to give you this sad news and leave right away, but I'm on duty."

"I know. It's okay. I'm glad my grandma's not hurting anymore."

I gave her a last squeeze, stood, kissed the top of her head, blinked a goodbye to Jean, and slipped out before I got too swallowed up in sympathy for Rebecca and all she had been through in her short life.

"Six oh eight, Winnebago County."

"Go ahead, Six oh eight."

"I'm ten-eight." Back in service.

"At fifteen thirty-seven. There's a call pending for you. I'll send it to your screen."

"Ten-four." It was a fraud report from the First National Bank in Rockwell.

Smoke phoned me a second later. "I heard you go out at the Brenners' address. Everything okay with Rebecca?"

"I was going to call you. Alvie died."

"How'd Rebecca take it?"

"Pretty well. She's had months of no contact with her, so that's got to help some."

"And you? How are feeling about now?"

"Sad for Rebecca. For myself? Right now, I'm numb. It's surreal."

"It'll come."

"Smoke, do you have time to notify Alvie's mother? I'm on my way to Rockwell and could be tied up for a while."

"I can do that."

"Thanks."

I spent an hour with the bank manager, gathering the information to investigate his claims and collecting the evidence that backed those claims. My report would get turned over to the detective who specialized in financial crimes.

I phoned Sara Speiss on my way back to the office. She was a probation officer for Winnebago County and my best friend after Smoke. She was also one of Alvie Eisner's intended victims. We had come close to dying together. Not the way you want to spend time with your friend.

"Hey, Sara."

"Corky, you heard the news about Eisner? Word is spreading through the courthouse."

"I bet."

"I thought I'd feel happy when she died, but I don't feel much of anything."

"Same here."

"You're off tomorrow, right?"

"Yes and no. I have to meet with someone about an open case, so I'll go into work for a while."

"You got dinner plans?"

"Mom is cooking, and my system is craving a good meal. You are always welcome to join us."

"Tempting, but I'll pass so you can have a little mother-daughter time. How about Friday night?"

"Sure. No date, huh?"

"Casey's working. You cops have awful schedules." Casey was an officer with the Oak Lea Police Department.

"There are advantages to working weekends and having days off during the week."

"Keep telling yourself that."

"You want to go out, or will it be the usual, takeout and a movie?"

"You make us sound so boring."

"Hey, comfortable is not all bad. Saves making a new decision every week."

"All right then, I vote for comfortable. I'll get the food, you get the movie."

"Wow, you are shaking things up. I usually get the food. My place or yours?"

"Yours. We'll have a toast at the scene of the crime. We'll celebrate surviving Alvie's attack."

"Maybe we should invite the ones who saved us. Smoke, Brian Carlson, Todd Mason—"

"Mandy Zubinski, in case you decided to exclude her. You know, I think that's actually a good idea."

"I was half-kidding, but why not? It'll be casual. If they don't have plans and want to stop by, fine. If not, no big deal."

"I'll get the champagne and one of those party trays from Charlie's Grocery Store. You know, with the meats and cheeses. Maybe some shrimp."

"That'd be good. What time should I say?"

"Seven? I'll come over at six and help you with whatever."

"Sounds good."

18

The Coven

The three coven leaders, Cyril, Dieter, and Roman, waited for the fourth to join them at the outdoor temple that evening. Dieter lit two kerosene lamps that hung from poles. They preferred firelight to an artificial alternative, and the lamps provided adequate illumination.

Noris stepped from the darkness into their circle.

"You brought the copies?" Cyril asked.

Noris nodded and handed them to Dieter and Roman.

"The dagger looks like the one we had custom made in my old country for Sparrow," Dieter said.

Roman nodded. "Yes, it does. It's difficult to be certain from this black and white copy, but it does look like it."

"I jotted in the colors of the jewels on my copy from the original color copy in the squad room."

Noris passed the sheet to High Priest Cyril, and they all took turns studying and imagining the color version.

"I'm almost positive it's his dagger. And what about the man, Jeffrey Trippen?" Roman asked.

"He looks like Jeffrey Manthes, all grown up," Dieter observed.

Cyril nodded. "I can only think of two explanations. Either Sparrow lied to us and knew where the family has been all these years, and he's bringing Jeffrey back for a sacrificial ritual. Or, the family stole Sparrow's dagger when they left, and Jeffrey is on his way back to find Sparrow with some silly intention that he can hurt him."

"Jeffrey was a weakling. I can't imagine him going after anyone. Especially Sparrow. He would never have been one of us," Noris said.

"Who was it at the sheriff's department that took the report on Jeffrey?" Cyril asked.

"Sergeant Aleckson. I checked, and she hasn't filed a report on it yet. Either it was an anonymous call, like a friend who feels it's his duty to report it but doesn't want to be involved enough to give his name, or it could be his friend or a family member who gave more detailed information than is listed on the attempt to locate."

"Find out who it is as soon as possible," Cyril ordered.

"Of course. What about Sparrow?"

Cyril looked down his long nose. "It wouldn't be wise to incur Sparrow's wrath by questioning him. Whatever Jeffrey intends to do with that dagger, Sparrow must be aware of it. He has legions working for him.

"We'll do our part to learn everything we can and take the appropriate measures when the time comes. If we learn there is a potential threat for Sparrow, we'll talk to him then, ensure that he knows. Is there any other business?"

When no one answered, he said, "Then we will ask our Holy Master to send his forces of darkness to help us with this matter . . ."

19

Gramps Brandt and I were in his fishing boat bobber fishing for sunfish. My Grandpa and Grandma Aleckson were sitting on lawn chairs on shore, waving at us. My mother was there too, busy doing something. Gramps pulled in a sunnie and smiled. As the fish dangled from his line, dripping water into the boat, my phone rang.

I woke up. No boat. No family. No fish. Just a ringing phone. My work cell.

"Sergeant Aleckson." I forgot to clear my voice, and it was full of frogs.

"Oh sorry, I bet you were sleeping." Gregory Trippen. I glanced at the clock on my bed stand. It was nine ten in the morning.

"It's fine, really. What's up?"

"I got a call from Jeff a while ago."

I threw back the covers and sat up, swinging my legs over the side of the bed until my feet touched the floor. "What'd he say?"

"Same thing he said three days ago. He's on his way to Winnebago County to, you know—" Gregory's voice cracked.

"Anything else, like where he is now? How he's getting here?"

"He rambled for a minute, something about doing a few things he'd wanted to, having a little time before Beltane's Eve, Walpurgisnacht."

I stumbled over to the foot of my bed where I had dropped my uniform on the floor the night before, and pulled my memo pad and pen out of my shirt pocket.

"What is that?"

"You mean Walpurgisnacht?"

I scribbled the word phonetically, as best I could.

"Is that German? *Nacht*? Night? What does it mean, when is it?"

"I'm not sure. I remember hearing the term from my stepfather and at one of the rituals. One where a woman was . . . and then . . ." He stopped a moment. "I never looked the word up. I didn't want to know."

"Greg, let's set a time to meet. We'll figure this out."

"I've tried to put it all out of my mind."

"Very understandable. How about noon, one?"

"I don't want to meet at the sheriff's office with a lot of people around."

"That's fine. I'll see if Detective Dawes is free to join us. How about we plan to meet you in the lobby of your motel at noon? I'll call you back if that doesn't work. All right?"

"Noon, okay."

I left a message for Smoke, then changed into jogging pants and a tee shirt, grabbed the mace from my duty belt, and headed downstairs. I got my small Smith and Wesson out of the gun safe in my office and zipped my cell phone, mace, and gun into my pants pocket. It had been my habit since the past autumn when I was attacked while jogging not far from my home.

I started a pot of coffee and took off for a short run while it brewed. A gentle breeze stirred the brisk, fresh smelling air around me as I ran. As I made my way past my mother's house, then Gramps' house on one side of the road, and thought about my grandparents who lived on the opposite side, I reflected on my good fortune in having a fairly normal family.

What if our widowed mother had married someone who threatened and abused John Carl and me behind her back? Our childhoods would have been stolen, like they were stolen from Gregory and Jeffrey Trippen. Our lives would have gone in far different directions.

I was almost home, pushing pretty hard, when my phone rang. "Smoke," I managed.

"You're running, I hope, and not dying."

I slowed so I could talk more normally. "Just finishing. You got my message?"

"Yup. Noon works for me. Why don't we meet in the department parking lot at eleven fifty? We'll take my car and talk on the way."

"You got something?"

"Working on it."

"See you then."

I clicked my phone shut and went in the side door by the garage to my kitchen. After drinking a tall glass of water, I poured a cup of coffee and took it into the small den office area off the living room. I opened the computer armoire my mother had given me and settled in to do some research.

There were several sites which listed calendars for satanic rituals. Walpurgisnacht, also known as Beltane, was on April thirtieth and one of the most important nights for Satanists. A night for blood rituals and human sacrifice.

Blood rituals and human sacrifice?

According to the calendar, April had a number of dates listed for rituals, especially if Easter was in the month of April. The nineteenth through the twenty-fifth was designated for sacrifice preparation. A time to kidnap, hold captive, and ceremonially prepare a person for human sacrifice.

I printed the calendar, then scanned site after site, gleaning bits and pieces. There were countless stories by people who had been raised in cults and eventually escaped.

I read about Anton LaVey, the man who had started the Church of Satan. He was an atheist who was more interested in serving his own needs than anything else. He thought Satan was a symbol, not a deity. So why did he write the satanic bible and call his hedonistic beliefs the Church of Satan?

I picked up my forgotten cup and took a swallow of cold coffee. Eleven o'clock. Ninety minutes had disappeared. I dashed upstairs, showered in minutes, pulled my hair in a ponytail, did a quick blow dry of the ends, and dressed in a light blue blouse, navy pants, and matching jacket. I attached my badge to a holder and secured it on the left side of my waistband. I pulled the pancake holster from a dresser drawer, clipped it on, retrieved my Glock from the bed stand, checked it, secured it in the holster, and hurried downstairs. I grabbed the calendar I had printed from the den office, and a banana and granola bar from the kitchen. A late breakfast.

Smoke was walking across the courthouse veranda when I pulled into the employee parking lot across the street. I spotted his unmarked gray Crown Victoria and jogged over. We got to it at the same time and climbed in.

"New scent?" he asked.

"What?"

"Perfume? Very clean-smelling."

"My hair is damp. You're smelling my conditioner."

"Nice." Smoke started the engine, and the voices on the sheriff's radio mounted on the dashboard amplified those on the radio attached to his belt. He adjusted the volume. "I finally got a hold of Elaine Van House a little while ago." He shifted into drive and we were on our way.

Alvie Eisner's mother. "Yeah?"

"She cried, didn't have much to say. She did want me to tell whoever was taking care of Rebecca that she hoped they would let her meet her great-granddaughter sometime. I told her I'd relay the message."

"Jean Brenner and I talked about that and agreed that should happen. Sometime."

"You said you were going to have a little service for Eisner. For Rebecca's sake?"

"We are. In a few days, maybe a week. Alvie's mother should probably be there, after all. What do you think?"

"Good question. Van House made a big mistake leaving her children like that, but does that mean she should be punished for the rest of her life, like Eisner wanted? I don't know. Might help give some comfort, to both her and Rebecca."

"It might."

"Back to our current case. I've been checking records on Dr. Royce Sparrow this morning."

"Anything turn up?"

He pulled the memo pad out of his breast pocket, laid it on the console between us, and glanced between it and the road until he found the page he was looking for.

"Nothing negative. Originally from Wyoming, graduated from the University of Minnesota Medical School. Alpha Omega Alpha. Did his residency at the university hospital. Moved to Wellspring twenty-five years ago when he was hired as a general surgeon at Little Mountain Health Clinic and Hospital. Married the widow Jody Manthes twenty-one years ago. They built a home and sold the ones they were living in. No record of a divorce, in Minnesota at least.

"Sparrow left Little Mountain for Saint Cloud General Hospital sixteen years ago. Bought a house there as a single person. No other name on the mortgage. No record of sale for the one in Wellspring. Maybe rents it out, I haven't gotten that far. Moved from general surgery to cosmetic surgery when he went to Saint Cloud. By all reports, he's a gifted surgeon.

"Haven't talked to anyone who knows him yet. That might be delicate. The only record of him being involved in anything suspicious, legally speaking, is the hunting death of Harlan Manthes. No illegal record in Wyoming or Minnesota, aside from two speeding tickets and expired license tabs once. I haven't taken a look at the other two hunters yet."

I followed along as he read his scribbled notes. "Progress, anyway. I did a little research myself this morning. On satanic stuff."

"What'd you find out?"

"Well, when Gregory Trippen called, he said Jeffrey told him he had a little time before Walpurgisnacht—"

"Say what?"

"Walpurgisnacht. I looked it up. It's named after a woman named Walburga. I don't know how it became Walpurg instead of Walburg. Long story, but she was a nun who was canonized—named a saint—on May first back in the eight hundreds AD. So the celebration started out as a Catholic celebration on the eve of May first, but now it's a night for pranks among the pagans and worse among the Satanists. For them it's a night of blood and sacrifice."

"Blood and sacrifice. In Winnebago County?"

I shrugged. "I'm just telling you what I read."

Smoke pulled into a parking spot on the east side of the motel opposite the lobby. We went in and spotted Gregory Trippen pacing by the windows on the south side. He saw us and hurried over. He was clean shaven, and even with his worried expression looked more rested than the last time we'd met.

"Do you know of a good place to meet?" he asked.

"How about here? In your room or by the pool?" Smoke said.

Gregory looked over his shoulder, then back at us. "I'd feel better if no one can hear us."

Smoke nodded, and we trekked out to the parking lot. "You don't mind riding in the back seat of my squad car?"

Gregory glanced in the car window. "Not much room, is there?"

"You're a big guy, but you'll fit."

Smoke unlocked the doors. Gregory wedged himself in and Smoke closed his door, then he and I got in the front.

"Where to?" Smoke turned the ignition key.

"How about Abbey Lake Park? It's deserted this time of year," I suggested and turned to look at Gregory.

"Sounds good to me," Smoke said as he backed out of the space.

"You probably think I'm paranoid," Gregory said.

Smoke looked into the rearview mirror. "What is that expression? 'Just because you're paranoid doesn't mean they're not out to get you.'"

"Smoke," I said beneath my breath.

Gregory surprised me by laughing. "Thanks."

We drove two miles in silence. I thought about the times in my life I had experienced feelings of paranoia, with good reason. When they are out to get you, being paranoid is not a bad thing from a safety and security standpoint.

Smoke turned off County Road 34 and followed the rutted gravel road to the lake. He parked near an open-sided shelter with a few empty picnic tables under its protective roof. Smoke opened the back door, and Gregory slid out. He looked around, apparently assessing the area.

"Private enough, I guess."

"Let's grab a table while there's still one available," Smoke quipped.

"I doubt if we'll still be here in a month when people actually start coming here for summer picnics," I shot back.

As we settled on the wooden benches, Gregory said, "I don't know where to start. Ever since Jeff called, my head has been swimming with images. Things I've tried to forget."

Smoke pulled out a memo pad and pen and laid them on the table, then slid his glasses on his nose. "Greg, it appears we've got three separate, but related, cases going here. Well, four really.

"First, we're looking for your brother. Second is regarding your concern that your father's death was not an accident. The third involves the abuse from your stepfather, which is tied in with the fourth aspect of illicit cult activities, when they actually branded the bottoms of your feet and committed other felony crimes."

Gregory cast his eyes downward. He folded his hands and tapped his index finger against the base of his thumb, rapidly and repeatedly, revealing his discomfort.

I laid my hand on the table next to his. Close, but not touching. "Gregory, all of these cases are related. Why don't you start from what you deem is the beginning. I'd like to know about your mother, your father, your stepfather, your childhood."

He looked up, studied my face then nodded. "My early childhood was great. I didn't know how great until I lost it. My dad was the chief financial officer for Little Mountain Hospital. Smart with numbers. My mom was a nurse there. That's where they met. They got married and bought a house in the country outside of Wellspring. When I was born, my mom quit to stay home to raise me. Jeff came along two years later.

"She was a stay-at-home mom until Dad died. She's very caring and kind of a homebody. She has always liked to knit and crochet. Do crafty things."

"What does she look like?" I asked.

Gregory pulled his wallet out of his back pocket. He withdrew an old photo from its plastic holder and handed it to me. The edges had a few little tears in them.

"The four of us."

"Your mother's very beautiful. You look like your dad, and that's a compliment. Jeff has finer features like your mom."

Gregory's mother had dark wavy hair, large blue eyes, high cheekbones, a small nose, and pouty lips. Gregory was about the same age his father had been in the photo. They could pass for the same person. Jeffrey looked happy, a far cry from the photo we had hanging on the squad room bulletin board.

I handed it to Smoke. "Great photo," he said.

Gregory's lips turned up slightly. "My dad was more social than Mom. He had a poker night once a week. And some good buddies he'd go hunting and fishing with. Not the same ones he hunted with when he was killed."

He shook his head and stared at the photo a moment. "He was a good dad. He and Mom never fought, that I can remember. I take after my dad, and not just in looks. I'm not as outgoing as I was as a little kid, though. I have trouble trusting people now. Jeff is more like Mom. He's always been caring, sensitive. He'd find injured birds and other critters and would try to nurse them back to health. Adults always commented about how sweet he was."

Gregory inhaled and exhaled slowly. "Dr. Sparrow came into our lives when I was seven or so. He was new in town, no family around, and Dad invited him over for dinner. Even as a little kid, I knew there was something about him I didn't trust, or like. He was overly friendly to Jeff and kept staring at my mom. It didn't seem right. He was over a bunch of times after that. And a year later, my dad was dead.

"Of course, Sparrow pretended to be distraught about my dad. Then he started hanging around a lot, comforting my mom and us boys. Taking us places. My mom married him about a year later. He was a good-looking man who could be very charming, and my mom fell for him. Oh, and by then she was working again. Overnights."

"How did Sparrow hide what he was doing to you boys from her?" I asked.

Gregory shrugged. "My mother always looks for the good in everyone. To a fault. She couldn't imagine the man she had married, and trusted to take care of her boys while she was working, was involved in something so evil. Who would? We had some behavior changes. Jeff especially. But she thought they were because our dad had died and we had a new dad to deal with. She told us she expected there would be some problems."

Gregory brushed some oak seeds off the table. "I gave Mom a very watered down version of what really went on. Even though a part of me blamed her for what happened, I couldn't tell her everything I knew. Jeff never said anything about it.

"Then one day when Jeff was about thirteen, maybe fourteen, he started talking in this weird voice. I said, 'Knock it off, you sound like a girl.' He got this funny expression on his face. For a second he looked like a blond version of my mom and said, 'Silly boy, I am a girl. I'm Samantha.'" Gregory's eyes widened, and he blew out a breath of air.

"That would be disconcerting for a teenage boy to hear from his brother. Was that the only incident where he thought he was someone else?" Smoke asked.

"There were a few other times. And after it happened he acted like he didn't remember anything about it. I told Mom, and she finally took him to a shrink, but it didn't help."

I tapped the table. "We met with a psychologist who helps people like your brother. I think you should talk to her while you're here."

Gregory raised his eyebrows and nodded.

Smoke opened to a fresh page in his memo pad. "You said your stepfather would wake you up in the middle of the night and take you to a place by a river. Tell us about that."

Gregory pushed his hands into his thighs, and his huge biceps flexed. "The first night after it happened, I woke up the next morning and thought I had had a terrible nightmare. Then it happened again and again."

"Describe what that was."

"Men in long black robes. Hooded black robes. An altar. A bonfire. Black candles burning. A large piece of wood with a pentagram painted on it. A gong—"

"A gong?" I asked.

He nodded and continued, "A box in the ground where they put people, mostly kids, for a while. It was called ceremonial burying."

My flesh turned to goose bumps. "What do you mean by ceremonial burying?"

"I think it was supposed to be like a coffin. They made people go down there, and they'd close the top. I think some were left there for days, maybe until they really did die. I'm not sure about that. I was in there a couple of times, probably for a few hours."

"Why did they do that?"

"One of the ways to control behavior. And scare the hell out of you. It worked too. You did what they said so they didn't bury you."

I came close to hyperventilating when I thought about being buried alive. Smoke shifted on his seat, notably uncomfortable.

"And there was a large basin they used to drown babies."

Smoke stopped writing. "They drowned babies? You witnessed that?"

Gregory fixed his eyes on Smoke. "Once. Then they passed a chalice filled with the water from the basin. We all had to drink it. I can't tell you what they did to the little bodies. Or about the other people they killed. Or all the sexual orgies. They never made me kill another person, but I had to kill a few animals for sacrifices. Even my own dog. I was nine." Tears filled Gregory's eyes. He brushed at one when it ran down his cheek.

"That must have been unbelievably difficult."

Gregory nodded. "I did what they made me do, hating every minute, but they would have killed Jeff, or Mom, or me if I didn't. They said that over and over.

"Jeff, being such a sensitive guy, really struggled. I think they were harder on him because of it. He would cry and beg them to stop. He spent a lot of time buried. I know there were nights Sparrow took him and not me. Jeff and I agreed never to talk about it."

Gregory looked from Smoke to me. "We were obviously scared shitless. I wanted to tell Mom, but from everything I had witnessed, I knew we would die. And in a very painful way. I think they got off on slow, agonizing deaths. Drowning, burning, or cutting someone so they bled to death. And they'd all be in this circle around the victim, chanting, thinking they were capturing some kind of energy that was being released when the person was dying. I hated being in the circle."

"How long did the abuse go on?" Smoke asked.

"A little over a year. It ended right after my tenth birthday when my mom saw my feet." He resumed studying his hands.

Smoke leaned forward, his chin resting on his hand. "Gregory. Any idea where those things took place?"

"No. We were given drugs. Blindfolded. I don't know if I'd recognize it. It was a ways from Wellspring, but like I told Sergeant Aleckson, it could have been by the Raven River, or a bigger creek. I don't think it was the Mississippi because the Mississippi is big and rushing. Much louder."

The mighty Mississippi.

"How many people were in the cult, taking part in the rituals?" Smoke asked.

"There were quite a few. Between fifteen and twenty. Sometimes more. It varied on different nights."

Smoke's eyebrows rose. "That many? The last time we talked you said there was a doctor, a mortician, a drugstore owner, a deputy, and others from Wellspring. Any you could identify if you saw them again?"

"I'm not sure. The ones I remember are because of the personal connections. One was my doctor, and two were with Sparrow when my father got shot. That's how I figured out it wasn't an accident."

"Their names?"

"Dr. Jenkins. The undertaker was Bishop, the druggist was Munden. He had a foreign accent. All upstanding citizens of the Wellspring community. What a joke. I knew some of the kids, but I think I've blocked out a lot of names."

Bishop, Munden, and Jenkins. The first two were the names Lieutenant Armstrong had given to Smoke.

"I know all this sounds too crazy to believe, but I have proof."

"What kind of proof?"

"Sparrow kept journals. One night, my mother sent me to his office—the one he had in our home—to tell him it was time for dinner. He always made us knock before we opened the door. He didn't hear me, and when I opened the door he was standing by the back wall holding a book. He frowned and said in a low voice, probably so my mom couldn't hear him, 'Why didn't you knock?' I said, 'I did, sir. Mom says dinner is ready.' He was holding a small key in his right hand and a book in his left.

"After that, when he was gone, like when we got home from school and he was still at work, I started looking for that key and the book. I can't explain why I was so driven to find it. I finally succeeded when I found a wall safe behind a painting on the back wall. It took me the longest time to find the key. I figured he kept it with him, but I kept looking anyway. It was taped to the bottom of a desk drawer."

Smoke grinned. "Pretty clever for a young boy. And you found the book?"

Gregory nodded. "I found a lot of books. Journals, like diaries. They were full of detailed information of the coven's activities. Drawings, chants, rituals, awful stuff. I paged through a couple, but couldn't read 'em because it made me sick."

"What'd you do next?"

"I put everything back where I found it, including the key."

"We'd need more than that for a case."

"There is more. When my mom found the crosses on my feet, I wouldn't tell her what happened at first. She asked Jeff and he started crying, saying they were going to kill us. That opened up the whole thing. She really struggled. It was beyond her comprehension. Eventually she admitted there were a few times she wondered if Sparrow had ever hurt us. Jeff and I had changed. I was more quiet, and Jeff was more emotional.

"All of a sudden, she stopped crying. She went into the kitchen and got some plastic garbage bags. She gave Jeff and me each one, and told us to put everything we wanted to take to our new life in them. She grabbed all the photo albums, a file she had with personal records, her jewelry, some clothes, I guess. We didn't waste time. I bet we were packed and on the road within an hour.

"Before we left, she called Sparrow and told him she was taking us boys to do a little shopping and she'd see him later. While she was on the phone, I went to his office, got into the safe, and grabbed a journal out of the stack. He had a lot of them. I didn't think too much about it. I just did it."

"Where is that journal now?" Smoke asked.

"In a safety deposit box at my bank."

Smoke jotted the information down. "So you got on the road?"

"My mom went to the bank and took out a lot of money. We stopped somewhere in Wisconsin and Mom called a few people—her work, our school, our church—to say something had come up with a critically ill aunt and we were going to Texas to help out. She called *my* real aunt, her sister who lives in Georgia, and told her we had escaped from an abusive situation, but we were fine. She said if anyone contacted her she should tell them she had no clue where we were. And in truth, she didn't.

"We drove all night and into the next day. My mother's mother had a good friend who lived in Vermont. Mom figured since no one in Wellspring knew who she was, we'd be safe there. Her name was Emma. She and my grandma wrote back and forth quite a bit back in the old days. Then my grandma died pretty young. All Mom remembered was Emma's name and the name of her city. We found her and literally showed up on her doorstep.

Smoke tapped his pen on his pad. "Your stepfather never found you?"

"If he did, he didn't tell us."

"I would think he'd want his journal back," I said.

Gregory nodded. "I was young, too young to weigh the consequences of taking it. I'm glad I did, but I never thought about the fact that it could have gotten us killed. As much as I hate Sparrow for what he did, I think in the end he probably saved our lives."

"How so?" Smoke asked.

"He couldn't have told the others we had the journal. He must have thought my mother found it, and that's why she took us and left. He was obsessed with her. He didn't give a rat's ass about Jeff and me, but I think in his own sick way he loved my mother. I have a feeling he was protecting her so the others couldn't get their hands on her."

"No one filed a missing persons report when you didn't return?" Smoke asked.

Gregory shrugged.

I leaned forward and raised my hand a few inches. "I can answer that. If they did, the file is missing like all the others. Nothing in the system for a missing Manthes family. Wait, your mother's name was Sparrow?"

Gregory nodded.

"I'll check under that name."

"What others?" Gregory asked.

Smoke hesitated then launched into a lengthy explanation.

"My mother got a copy of the reports when my father was killed, so I have that file."

"Now you're talking. Tell me they're in the safety deposit box with the journal."

"They are."

"Hallelujah! We're building a case."

Gregory and I smiled at Smoke's enthusiasm.

"We should get a copy of the journal and the reports, but leave the originals in the deposit box."

"It's a long drive there and back," Gregory said.

"Could you ask your mother to take care of it?" I asked.

"No. Mom wants to forget the bad things in our past. I've tried to talk to her about Dad's death and my suspicions, but she's convinced herself it was an accident."

"You could fly," Smoke said.

Gregory lifted his shoulders. "I'll go out and get them after we find Jeff."

That reminded me. "Gregory, I looked up Walpurgisnacht. It's the night before May Day and listed as a night for satanic rituals. Since Jeffrey mentioned it specifically, it might be the night he intends to hurt himself."

The color drained from Gregory's face. "The night before May Day? April thirtieth? That's Jeff's birthday. His birthday is on Walpurgisnacht. That's the day he's planning to sacrifice himself."

20

The Coven

Noris was on his way to downtown Oak Lea to run a few errands. He drove past the courthouse where he spotted Sergeant Aleckson, out of uniform, getting into Detective Dawes' unmarked squad car. He was too curious to let it pass. They were up to something. He had his white Lexus SUV, a vehicle he seldom drove. He pulled into the library parking lot across the street from the courthouse and waited for them to leave.

They passed by him and pulled up to the stoplight with the right turn signal blinking. After they turned the corner, Noris stepped on the accelerator, propelling the car forward. He made the right turn before the light turned red, followed them to the motel on Highway 55, and waited in the restaurant parking lot next door.

Dawes and Aleckson got out of his car and went into the motel. Word around the department was that Jeffrey Trippen's brother was the one who had called in the report on him, the attempt to locate. Noris hadn't dug deep enough for the information and needed to do that soon. Cyril was impatient for more details.

A few minutes later, Dawes and Aleckson pushed back through the glass entry doors with a big man between them. Noris kicked himself for not having his Nikon camera with him. He whipped out his cell phone, aimed, and snapped. He was too far away for it to mean much, but he'd enlarge it on his home computer.

When the three drove away, Noris steered into the motel lot looking for out-of-state plates. One from Iowa, one from South Dakota, and one from Vermont. Jeffrey Trippen was from Vermont. He memorized the plate as he sped up to catch Dawes' squad car. He followed it to where it turned into Abbey Lake Park. A meeting place where no one would overhear their conversation.

Noris slowed his vehicle, pulled over on the shoulder, and stopped. He found a pen in the middle console, then searched for a piece of paper but came up dry. Not a receipt or gum wrapper to be found. He opened the glove box, grabbed a map, tore a small piece from the corner, and jotted the license plate number on it.

His instincts told him the stranger at Abbey Lake Park was Jeffrey Trippen's brother, fresh in from Vermont and spilling his guts to the detective and his sidekick sergeant. About what? Where was Aleckson's report on Jeffrey Trippen, anyway? Was she waiting until after meeting with the brother to write it? What was his name?

What was the brother telling them, and why weren't they meeting at the office? Had he figured out Sparrow had killed his father? Sparrow was very powerful, but he'd made a mistake—a stupid, nearly fatal one—all those years ago. The coven was still covering for it. And it would be back to haunt them if the case was reopened.

It was a mess, all right. On second thought, it might be a relief. If they hauled off Cyril and Dieter, Noris would be second in command behind Roman.

What was he thinking? Those two would never confess to being accomplices to a murder. And with no reports? No evidence? The sheriff's department had nothing to charge them with.

Noris turned around and drove back to town to finish his errands. He'd run the Vermont plates when he got to work.

21

Smoke stuck his pad and pen in his pocket. "That gives us a date and a deadline. We need to find your brother between now and the thirtieth."

"Two weeks and a day," I calculated.

"I think Jeff wanted me to know his plans so I'd know what happened to him. But he should have figured I'd do everything I could to stop him."

I leaned closer. "Gregory, the first time we talked, you said you never wanted to come back to Winnebago County. Jeff knew that, right?"

"Sure. I made the statement a lot. That I'd never go back."

"Maybe that's what he was counting on if he's determined to follow this through—that you'd never go back, no matter what."

"I guess." Gregory stood, walked to the edge of the enclosure, and looked out on the lake. "Jeff. What could I have done differently? How could I have stopped him from getting to the point where he believed his own brother wouldn't be there for him? And how could he know names like Walpurgisnacht and when it is? We were little kids."

"Either someone told him—maybe Sparrow did on one of those nights when he took Jeff, but not you. Or he read about it and it stuck in his brain," I said.

Smoke and I got up together. He walked over and stood beside Gregory. I went to his other side.

"He's suffering from mental illness and not thinking rationally," Smoke said.

I touched Gregory's arm. "When we find him, there's a doctor, the psychologist I mentioned earlier, who's had good success helping victims like Jeff. And you."

Gregory's eyes widened. "How?"

"She's got a few techniques she can tell you about. She's dedicated her career to victims of abuse, especially those with dissociative identity disorder, which may be what Jeff has. I think you should meet her."

"Maybe I will. I'll think about it." He turned toward me. "I will talk to her. I've been thinking, back to Jeff. If he's looking at April thirtieth to . . . you know . . . I'm probably going to have to go home to take care of some things. My business. My house. I left on the turn of a dime. I'm not a guy that can sit around and wait very well. I'll drive home tonight, do what I gotta do, and come back in a week or so."

"You'll go to the bank?" Smoke said.

Gregory nodded. "I'll make copies of the journal and the accident report."

"You haven't talked about a wife. Kids. Not married?" I asked.

"Nope, never been married. No kids. Too much baggage. Too many demons."

He meant that literally.

We dropped Gregory off at his motel with promises to contact each other with any new information. If Jeffrey showed up anywhere on our radar, Gregory would return to Winnebago County immediately. We hoped Jeffrey would appear long before April thirtieth.

Sara phoned me on our drive to the sheriff's department.

"Don't be mad."

"About what?"

"Well, I was talking to Ray Collinwood about Alvie Eisner, and how a few of us were getting together, and he said that was a great idea, could the county attorneys join us as a tribute to Arthur Franz, and that the public defenders would probably like to come too, in honor of Marshall Kelton. I said I'd clear it with you since we're having it at your house. What do you think?"

Sara spoke loud enough for Smoke to hear.

"You're having a party?" he asked.

I put my hand over the mouthpiece. "You're invited." I pulled my hand away. "I have to think for a second here. So we might end up with a pretty big party? You know what, why not? They lost good friends, colleagues. Tell them it's fine. They can spread the word in their offices."

"It'll be good for everyone, Corky. I'll say it's potluck and BYOB."

"In addition to the ones we talked about inviting, I suppose I should put an invite on the board in the squad room in case a few more are interested."

"Want me there earlier than six? I can come right after work."

"Nah. Six is fine."

When I hung up, I explained our last-minute plans to Smoke.

"Sort of a celebration slash memorial slash wake?"

"Slash thank you to you Smoke, personally, and to the other deputies who rescued us. That's how it started out. Sara and I are very grateful you all got there in time to save us from probable death. And we're happy Alvie Eisner can never harm anyone again."

"Worth celebrating, all right. So you're saying spread the word?"

"Within reason. Oh, no!"

"What?"

"I suppose I'll have to clean my house."

"Will your mother be there?"

"She doesn't know about it yet, but of course I'll invite her. And the sheriff."

"Then just tell her ahead of time you're cleaning your house. Otherwise she'll show up after work today armed with supplies."

I laughed. "Yes, she will launch into a spring-cleaning frenzy and go at it all night long."

"Probably bring the sheriff along to help."

I laughed again.

My work cell rang. "Sergeant Aleckson."

"Hello, Sergeant? It's Nichole Jaspers. You were at our house a few days ago."

"Of course. How are you doing? I saw your husband made his first court appearance and was released from jail. Everything all right?"

"Yes. Um. Okay."

"What can I do for you?"

"It's not about the other night. I mean, in a way it is, but not in the way you might think."

"What is it?"

"Dr. Fischer talked to me and asked me to talk to you. As a victim of SRA. We both are. Victims. Collin and me."

I was momentarily dumfounded. "Well. Thank you for calling me. This can't be easy for you."

"Um. When Dr. Fischer said it was you who was looking for some information, that made my decision easier. To talk to you. But I really can't right now. I was wondering, maybe we can meet sometime to talk in person."

"Of course. That would be great. When?"

"I work at a factory job. My next day off is Sunday, but we could get together before then if you want."

"Sunday is just fine. What time?"

"Anytime."

"How about four in the afternoon?"

"That works well for me."

"Four o'clock, at the sheriff's department."

"Is it safe?"

A common concern, it seemed.

"We can surely meet just about anywhere. Your house, or—"

"No. That's fine. The sheriff's department."

"Come to the south entrance on the lake side. I'll be waiting for you."

"Okay. I'll let you know if something comes up, if I can't make it."

"I'd appreciate that."

When I hung up, Smoke said, "What was that all about? She had such a quiet voice, I couldn't hear."

I gave him the rundown.

"A whole separate secret world."

"You said it. The occult. Hidden. Secret."

22

The Coven

Noris stopped by the sheriff's department when he thought it would be deserted, and it was. He went to the squad room, sat down at a computer terminal, and navigated to Vermont's vehicle registration records. He typed in the plate number of the green Forester he had seen in the motel parking lot. It came back to Gregory Leon Trippen.

Gregory. The name he couldn't think of. He remembered him from that year Sparrow had brought him and his brother to the gatherings and rituals at the temple. He was a tough kid, right from the start. With time, and the right training, Gregory could have become one of us, Noris thought.

He searched Gregory's driving records, and when his picture appeared on the screen, Noris knew without doubt it was Gregory Manthes. He printed the photo and the records with his statistics and home address.

He disagreed with Cyril on the matter of whether or not to discuss the case with Sparrow. Sparrow was the most connected priest he knew and was bound to discover that their coven had known about Jeffrey Manthes and his dagger for a while. The pictures were on the squad room wall at the

Winnebago County Sheriff's Department, and every deputy was on the lookout for him. It was impossible to deny their knowledge.

Noris snatched the papers from the printer, took one last glance at the dagger photo, and left to go back on patrol.

23

We went into an unexpected holding pattern after many tension-filled days looking for Jeffrey Trippen and his dangerous dagger, and trying to uncover who had stolen the death reports on Harlan Manthes. Was that person still active in the cult and lurking in the sheriff's department?

I phoned the deputies who were on the same work rotation as me and invited them to the party. We were on days off, and they wouldn't see the posting in the squad room or get the department e-mail I had sent.

Expecting a house full of people was the push I needed to attack the nooks and crannies I always avoided as long as possible. Luckily, my mother was the only worker at her shop on Fridays and couldn't help me clean. I greatly appreciated her help, but she had too many commitments the way it was.

My maternal grandparents had given me twenty acres of land from their 1,600 acre farm to build my house. When they'd downsized into a smaller rambler, they'd given my mother their old farmhouse. After Gram died, Gramps had continued to live there, with considerable help from my mother.

All three of us lived on Brandt Avenue, three miles from downtown Oak Lea.

Grandma and Grandpa Aleckson also had a farm Brandt, but spent their winters in Arizona and a month every summer at a lake resort in northern Minnesota. They were in their seventies and tired of maintaining their large farmhouse for the few months a year they spent in Oak Lea. They had been talking about selling it and getting a condo in town and hoped either I, or my brother who lived in Colorado, would want their house if they moved. I loved their home, but it required much more upkeep than my newer home, so it was a tough decision.

I had built my house on the crest of a small hill. In the summer it overlooked acres of cornfields, golden wheat, and soybeans. The back of my land dropped down to Bebee, a small lake. From late fall, when the maple and birch trees shed their leaves until they budded and leafed out again in the spring, I had a full view of the lake.

I opened windows, and the cool fresh air blended with the smells of wood oil soap cleaner and white vinegar as I washed windows and polished woodwork and furniture, hour after hour. I finished with my loft bedroom a few minutes before six.

Gregory Trippen phoned as I was hanging clean towels in the bathroom off my bedroom.

"Hello, Gregory."

"Sergeant Aleckson, call me Greg. I wanted to let you know I got home safe."

"That's good news."

"Any word yet on Jeff? I know you said you'd call, but I had to ask."

"No, no word. And I promise to let you know as soon as there is."

"Okay. I'll take care of all my stuff and be in touch."

"I appreciate that."

"Talk to you later, then."

"Sounds good. 'Bye, Greg."

When I ran down the steps to put away my cleaning supplies, I was pleased that my house not only looked clean, it smelled clean—it *seemed* clean. Mother would notice.

Sara came in the back door and hollered, "Honey, I'm home."

"You're funny," I yelled back from the laundry room.

"What are you doing? You need help?" I heard her setting bags on the kitchen counter.

I walked into the kitchen. "There are paper and plastic products in there—" I pointed to a base cabinet, "—plates, napkins, forks, spoons, cups."

Sara was freshly showered and dressed in a pair of dark blue jeans and a coral-colored belted blouse. Her strawberry blonde hair was pulled back on each side and secured in place by barrettes.

"Cute top. Good color on you."

"Thanks. It's gotten so nice outside, I decided to stop at your mother's shop after work to get something fun for spring."

"She must have just gotten those in. I didn't see them when I stopped in the shop the other day to check out the paint job."

"Which looks very nice, by the way."

"I agree. I was a little skeptical when she showed us the paint samples. I thought it would be more purply-lilac, but it's very subdued."

"Yes, it is. I like the color a lot." Sara glanced around. "Your house looks good. Really clean."

"Thanks. Believe it or not, I found cleaning very therapeutic today. I let my mind wander and processed some things I've been thinking about. A good mental and physical workout."

"Heard from anyone who's planning to come over?" She pulled a bottle of wine from a bag.

"A bunch of people from the sheriff's department. There's Todd and Kayla Mason, Brian Carlson, Vince Weber. Mandy Zubinski can't make it. Darn. Smoke, my mom, and the sheriff. Oh, and Bob Edberg—"

"Deputy Edberg?"

I shrugged.

"I've never seen him at a party before."

"I know."

"Maybe he figures it's time to socialize. He's only like sixty," she said.

"More like fifty."

"Oh, and Casey gets off work at eleven. He said he'd stop by to see if anyone's still here then."

"Any word on the county attorneys or the public defenders?" I said.

"No, I should have told them to RSVP."

"I'm glad you didn't. Saved me answering phone calls. If we get ten people or fifty people, we'll make it work. We can spill into the garage, or outside if we have to."

"You've got a great house for entertaining. Nice and open, so it seems even bigger than it is. Hey, you better get a move on. I'll get things lined up here while you get ready."

Me. The thing I'd forgotten needed cleaning. "Okay."

I showered and shampooed, standing under the warm spray an extra few minutes to loosen my shoulder muscles and relax my body before an evening of hosting. I dressed in a red print V-necked shirt and black jeans. I brushed the snarls out of my straight blonde hair, which hung a couple of inches past my shoulders, then used the blow dryer to remove most of the moisture. The air would finish the job by the time our guests arrived. I pulled on a headband and gave my hair a final brushing.

"Nice transformation," Sara said when I joined her.

"Thanks. You found everything, it looks like."

"And I got the white wine and champagne in the fridge. I hope I got enough champagne."

"It'll be enough. A sip is all anyone needs for a toast anyway. I'm going to back my car out of the garage in case we need the space."

"Won't hurt."

Winnebago County Attorney Ray Collinwood was the first to arrive promptly at seven o'clock, a bottle of wine in one hand and a plate of deviled eggs in the other. My mother and Sheriff Denny Twardy were close behind.

When they came through the door, it struck me how good they looked together. Mother kept trim by continually moving. She highlighted her dark blonde hair to mask the gray and was sometimes mistaken for my sister. Denny Twardy's face was more deeply etched with wrinkles, but he had a youthful appearance when he was relaxed, like when he was with my mother. They assisted Sara and me with the hosting duties, directing the guests where to set food and beverages.

By eight o'clock my house was filled to capacity. People. Beverage coolers. Plates of food. Bowls of chips and salads. Boxes of crackers. Even with the windows open, the house was warm from all the body heat. A few people spilled out onto my deck. The trees had not fully leafed out, so there was a good view of Bebee Lake for the short while before dark. Other guests headed into the garage.

The deputies I had expected came, joined by others I hadn't. I was surprised when Mandy Zubinski showed up.

"Hi, Corky. I hope it's okay to be here. I had a change of plans."

"Of course, join the party."

I was more surprised when my mother opened the door and there stood Eric Stueman, the new assistant county attorney. She pointed him in my direction. The most notable thing about Stueman was his dour expression. Some people were more protective of their smiles than others. Stueman? His were under lock and key somewhere. It was a shame, because he was an attractive man underneath his cover. He nodded at me by way of a greeting.

"Welcome. There are quite a few from your office here," I said.

Stueman looked around, caught sight of Collinwood, and nodded again before walking away. Apparently his words were locked away with his smiles.

Smoke arrived at nine o'clock looking haggard. His sky-blue eyes didn't have their usual sparkle.

"Everything okay?" I asked.

"Yeah. I didn't sleep last night and thought I could catch a nap this afternoon, but no such luck. It'll be an early night for me."

"Help yourself to food and drink."

"You know how to throw a party, little lady. How many are here? Sixty, seventy?"

"Yeah, about seventy. Some are here for their fallen colleagues, others because there was nothing else going on, I guess."

"Mandy Zubinski seems pretty cozy with those guys."

I looked at the group standing near the sliding glass door that opened to the deck. Mandy was laughing and flirting with Deputies Bob Edberg, Brian Carlson, Fred Brooks, and Devin Stauder.

"Edberg. That's a surprise. I need to talk to him. About that deal we got going."

"Too many people here for that," I said.

"No, I didn't mean tonight. Just talking out loud. Speaking of which, I gotta yell to hear my own voice."

"Good thing I live in the country. No close neighbors to call the cops on a noise complaint. It'll help keep you awake, at least."

Ray Collinwood stepped in beside us and clapped Smoke on the back. Ray was Santa Claus, sans the beard. Round and jolly, with a red face and white hair. "Here's the man of the hour. Got the deputies here in time to save our favorite sergeant here."

The long dimples in Smoke's face deepened. "I'm glad it turned out the way it did. Looks like a lot of people from your office are here."

"Arthur was respected by all of our staff. When he died, we found out how much we really lost." He thought a moment. "Corky, should we organize that toast soon?"

"Sure. Anytime."

Collinwood waved at Barbara Jacobs, the secretary and receptionist for the Tenth Judicial District Public Defender's Office. Barbara was past retirement age, but loved her job too much to leave. She ambled over and joined our huddle.

"Hi, Smoke."

"Barbara. You're looking lovely, as always."

She smiled. "You, too. A little tired, but lovely." Barbara turned to Collinwood. "You needed me, Ray?"

"We're going to have that toast, and I wondered if you'd be the first to say a few words about Marshall?"

"I can do that." She patted her fresh-from-the-beauty-shop hair.

"Let's start opening bottles," Smoke suggested.

The inside of my refrigerator looked like a champagne cooler. Sara didn't need to worry whether there would be enough. A number of people had added to the collection.

"Hey, Todd, Brian, you guys want to help pop some corks?" I asked.

Brian cracked a silly grin, and the light configuration of freckles on his face shifted.

"My specialty," Todd said. "What are you talking about?"

"Champagne bottles."

They both laughed and followed me to the kitchen. An assembly line had formed. Sara dug bottles out of the fridge and handed them to Barbara, who set them on the breakfast bar in front of either Collinwood or Smoke. Each was opening a second bottle.

"At your service," Brian said. He and Todd stepped up to the bar and pushed themselves in between stools opposite the other two men. Twelve corks were popped in short order.

Mother, Denny, Sara, and I lined glasses on the counters and poured champagne in each. "Listen up!" Smoke called out to the masses. "We've reached the program part of the party. Corky?"

"We'd like to toast some people tonight. We're pouring bubbly in the kitchen, so everyone come and grab a glass."

I went to the garage, then to the deck, and invited everyone in. About five minutes later we all crowded together, glasses in hand. Sara stood next to me. "You talk," I said.

Sara raised her glass. "Corky and I had the idea to have a get together tonight to thank the people who saved us. And Corky, you know, put up quite a fight against Alvie Eisner, so she's one of the ones I'm personally toasting."

She waved her glass at me and continued, "We were the lucky ones. Arthur Franz and Marshall Kelton were not so lucky. Their colleagues are here to remember them tonight, also." She lifted her glass higher. "So here's to Smoke Dawes, Mandy Zubinski, Todd Mason, and Brian Carlson for rescuing us. We can't thank you enough."

Smoke smiled and winked at me. Zubinski, Mason, and Carlson all shrugged and said they were just doing their jobs. There were shouts of "cheers" and the sound of hard plastic cups clinking together. Sara and I touched each other's glasses first then turned to those around us.

My mother moved next to me, put her arm around my waist and squeezed, then gave Sara a hug. She had tears in her eyes and was as thankful as we were. At least. The sheriff stepped in close to Mom and rested his hand on her arm.

Ray Collinwood spoke next from the other side of the room. "Arthur Franz is truly missed. He ran a tight ship in the county attorney's office, but he never expected more of anyone else than he did of himself. He taught by example. A true professional. He sought justice. He fought for justice in the courtroom. He suffered an untimely death because of it. Here's to Arthur."

"Arthur!" Julie Grimes, an assistant county attorney, called out.

More cheers and clinks.

Barbara raised her glass. "A lot of you probably don't know me because I work for the other side. The public defenders. No booing—"

A few people chuckled, me included. The deputies arrested people, and it was up to the public defenders to mount a good case for their clients, guilty or not.

"—I've been an administrative assistant with the public defenders for about a hundred years. And in all that time, I have to say Marshall Kelton was one of the most brilliant attorneys I have ever known. No offense to the rest of you. And he was fun to work with. He was not the most organized, and far from perfect, but he was a true friend and a great boss, and I miss him every day."

"We love you, Marshall!" I don't know who said that.

I was mingling when I saw the door to my den office open and Bob Edberg step out. As he pulled the door shut, I caught up with him. "Looking for something?"

He appeared taken aback. "Oh, no. Just needed to make a phone call, and it's so noisy out here, I went in there and shut the door. I guess I should have checked first."

"No problem."

Small groups of people, talking and laughing, formed and changed throughout the evening. The unwritten rule was to stay away from work talk at social events, but that was impossible for us. It seemed our best stories stemmed from what happened at work.

I joined Julie Grimes, Vince Weber, and Todd and Kayla Mason. They were sitting in a small circle of chairs on the deck.

Julie was saying, "Collinwood won't say. I don't know what the big secret is."

"Exactly," Todd agreed.

"Secret?" I asked.

"We're talking about the big team-building deal next week."

"Ah."

"You're a sergeant. You know what we're doing?" Julie asked.

I held up my hands. "I know nothing."

"All right. I'll have to work on Ray some more."

"Or wait until the big day."

She wiggled her nose and crossed her eyes. "Way too snoopy for that."

I laughed at her funny expression.

Smoke was leaning against a living room wall watching people. "Nice party. Even the old guys are hanging in there." He indicated Bob Edberg and Dennis Twardy with a small movement of his head. Denny was talking. Bob was listening and nodding.

I told Smoke about Edberg being in my den with the door closed to use the phone. "Why didn't he just step outside if he wanted to make a call instead of going in there and closing the door?"

"That's what I wondered."

"Speaking of which, do you mind if I take a little rest on the couch in your den? I'll get a little shut eye, and it'll discourage anyone from going in there, snooping around, or making out on your couch."

I shook my head and smiled. "I'm sure that's going to happen. Really, Smoke, you're tired. Why don't you go home and get a good night's sleep?"

"Humor me."

I shrugged. When Smoke got something in his head, he did not give it up easily. "Fine with me."

He slipped into the den office, and I went back to the guests. One of the public defenders appeared intoxicated, so I retrieved my PBT—Preliminary Breath Tester—from the briefcase in my den. Smoke was fast asleep and didn't stir.

Some watchdog.

The light on my computer caught my eye, and I realized my computer armoire was open. I had closed it when I cleaned the room earlier that day. Did Edberg lie about making a phone call? Was he on my computer instead? But why? I unlocked my briefcase and grabbed the PBT. I'd pull Edberg aside and ask him about it. When I returned to the living room and inquired about him, Sara said he had told her thank you a few minutes earlier and left.

Sara looked at the case in my hand. "Somebody drunk?"

"One way to find out for sure."

I increased the volume of my voice about fifteen decibels. "Hey everyone, I'm going to PBT you before you leave. Since the party's at my house, I'm responsible, and no one drives if they are under the influence. Okay?"

There were a few protests, but as they left, each one submitted to the breath testing without argument. As it turned out, only one needed a chauffeur: the public defender I had spotted earlier.

By midnight, the few people still on board were Sara, my mother, the sheriff, and a sleeping Smoke. Aside from overflowing trash containers in the kitchen, dining room, and garage, and a recycling bin filled with bottles and cans, my house didn't look bad. People had taken the dishes and crock pots they'd brought back home with them, so cleanup was minimal.

The sheriff pulled a garbage bag out of its container, and my mother started wiping down a kitchen counter. Sara yawned. I took the dishcloth from my mother's hand. When she didn't resist, I knew how tired she was. "Time to say goodnight, everyone. You guys have done enough, helping all evening. I'll finish in the morning."

"It was a really nice party, Corky. Thanks for being such a good sport about how it kind of exploded, number wise," Sara said.

I tossed the dishcloth in the sink. "Hey, we somehow all fit, and it was easy with everyone bringing food. Aside from cleaning, which I had to do anyway—"

"I meant to tell you how nice your house looked," Mother said.

"Thanks. If you want to sit and relax for a while, that's fine, but no more working."

"It's been a long week, so I should get going. Thanks, my dear." Sara gave me a hug.

"Thank you. For all the food and drinks you brought."

Mom and the sheriff followed us to the front door, and we all stepped into the cool night air.

Mother turned to me. "Why is Elton's car in your driveway? I didn't know he was still here."

"Sound asleep in my den office."

"Maybe you should wake him."

"He is perfectly safe, and I am perfectly safe."

"I know that, dear, but—"

"Mother, you are so funny sometimes. If people see his car here in the middle of the night and want to believe we are having mad, passionate sex, that's their problem."

"Corinne Mae Aleckson! What a way to talk."

When I started laughing, Sara broke down too. "Yes, Corinne," she managed to spit out.

Even my mother and the sheriff smiled. I hugged them both, and they walked toward their cars with Sara. I went inside, locked the door, and started thinking about the evening. I wondered why Eric Stueman had showed up. He was hired as an assistant county attorney after Arthur died. He didn't know Arthur and didn't like me. Maybe it was a trial run before our team-building exercise the next weekend. He wanted to find out if he could tolerate being near me for more than an hour.

And Mandy Zubinski had been pretty cozy and comfortable with Deputies Carlson, Stauder, Brooks, and Edberg. She had spent a fair share of the evening with the four of them, acting like it was her personal duty to keep them entertained.

Brian Carlson was one of my best friends and had never mentioned an interest in Mandy. That might have been due to the fact she was *not* one of my best friends. Stauder was married, but that hadn't stopped him from enjoying the attention of an attractive woman all evening. Brooks was very quiet, and I never had figured him out. Edberg was about the same age as Smoke, and almost as nice looking.

It was no secret that Mandy was attracted to Smoke. Maybe she preferred older men over younger men.

None of my business. Any of it.

Edberg. Was he really making a phone call in my den office, or was he looking something up on my computer? And without permission? No one used another's personal computer without asking first.

As I pondered, I cleaned and straightened, despite my earlier decision to wait until morning to finish. By one o'clock all physical traces of the party had been swept from my house. I made my way first through the garage, then the house, turning off lights and locking doors. My car was outside, but there was no hail in the forecast, so I didn't bother pulling it into the garage. I grabbed a flashlight from my kitchen and crept into the den office as quietly as possible.

When I opened the door, the light from the living room lamps fell on Smoke's outstretched body. He was sleeping soundly, his lips letting out quiet puffs of air about every five seconds. Twelve respirations per minute. A normal rate for a resting adult. I smiled at my clinical assessment.

I went to the computer armoire, turned on the flashlight, settled into my swivel chair, and laid the flashlight next to the computer mouse. I wiggled the mouse, and when the screen lit up, I went into My Documents. I didn't have many documents stored, so checking through them went quickly. No one had opened any of them on April sixteenth. I logged onto the Internet and looked at the search history, checking if there were any sites I hadn't been at myself.

Strange. The sites I had searched were there, but they were out of order. The last site I had checked was my personal e-mail. The site before that was my work e-mail. The searches I had done on satanic cults, satanic ritual abuse, and dissociative identity disorder were all done before I checked the e-mail accounts. It was the last thing I did. Someone else had looked at the sites after I had. Had they checked my e-mail, too?

I looked at my mailboxes. There were no new messages opened I hadn't opened myself. But I couldn't tell if the messages I had read had been opened again. I looked in the recycle bin. Nothing there I hadn't personally sent. A wave of anger rushed through me. I had opened my house to friends and work associates, and someone had taken the opportunity to snoop through my files.

Why? Whoever it was had gained knowledge of the research I was doing, privy to information he had no right to have.

Bob Edberg. Was he the dirty cop, the one who had threatened Alden Armstrong all those years?

The discovery guaranteed I would not fall asleep easily. I'd talk to Edberg, but not in the middle of the night. And I needed to verify with Smoke that he hadn't used the computer before he fell asleep. It was remotely possible.

After a day of cleaning and a night of entertaining, I yearned for a long, quiet rest. I turned off the flashlight and stepped over to my bookcase. There was enough lamplight from the living room to read the titles, and I selected a book I had started many, many times. It always put me to sleep. The only reason I kept it was for the rare night I suffered a bout of insomnia.

Smoke wasn't covered and would likely get cold during the night. I went to the den closet and pulled an afghan my Grandma Brandt had crocheted for me off a shelf. When I sat and read in there, I liked to wrap myself in it and remember how I had felt cuddled in her warm embrace. I stuck my face into the yarn fibers, wishing she was still alive.

I set the book on the armoire, freeing my hands to cover Smoke. As I bent over him, his eyes flew open. I caught a surprised yelp before it escaped my lips. His arms locked around me, and he pulled me against his body with enough force to take away my breath. My head was trapped between his neck and the back of the couch, and my arms were locked under his.

"Smoke," I struggled to say.

"What?" He eased his grip, so I pulled my face out of its hold and sucked in a breath of air.

Smoke started breathing heavily. Panting, like he was running.

"Smoke, are you okay?"

"Corky?" He stared into my eyes, inches away from his own. "You're safe?"

"That depends. You've got me in a near-death grip."

Smoke released my arms, but when I started to slide away, he gently eased his hands, one on my back and one on my neck, and pulled me against his chest.

"God, Corky. I didn't even realize I'd fallen asleep. I was in the middle of the worst nightmare. I'm not going to tell you about it, but it was nasty and I'm glad you're safe. More than glad." He massaged my back for another minute.

It felt good resting in his arms. "You can tell me. It's better if you do. It'll help you get over it faster."

"It is not for the faint of heart. I was trying to get there to save you, but my legs were like lead. All I could do was watch."

"Watch what?"

"There were a bunch of men in black-hooded robes standing in a semi-circle around this raised platform. You were lying on it, face up, sleeping, wearing a white flowing gown. Suddenly the guy in the middle of the group lifted up this dagger—like the one Jeffrey Trippen has—and was holding it with his hands over you—"

"That is a bad nightmare. Did he kill me?"

"No. You woke me up in time."

"Even if he had killed me, I heard somewhere that when you dream someone dies, it's a sign of good things to come for that person."

"You think that's true?"

"I have no idea, but in the case of *this* dream, let's believe that it is."

Smoke's breathing slowed, and his heart eased its pounding against his chest wall. And mine. "Okay. Confession time. Truth be told, bad dreams sometimes scare me more than bad things in real life. Glad I seldom have a nightmare."

"Nightmares are scary. I've had a few doozies, that's for sure."

"What time is it, anyway?"

"After one."

"Your house is quiet. Sorry I conked out and missed the rest of the party. I can't believe I slept through the noise."

"Things settled down not long after you came in here, and it's pretty quiet with the door closed."

"It is. I should get home, but I have this gut feeling I should stay here and protect you."

"That's because of your dream. The doors are locked, and I keep my Glock in my bed stand. On the other hand, there's no need for you to leave. Close your eyes and fall back asleep—a nice, dreamless sleep. When you wake up in the morning, the sun will be shining and you'll feel much better."

"At the risk of embarrassing myself, can I make a request?"

"What is it?"

"Will you stay with me until I fall asleep?"

Smoke surprised me now and then.

"Let me shut off the lamps in the living room."

I went into the next room and turned off the lights, then found my way back to the couch in the dark. Smoke turned onto his left side and scooted his body into the back cushion. I picked up the forgotten afghan and threw it over him, then lifted a corner and climbed underneath it, stretching out next to Smoke, and rested my head on his bicep.

My left arm dropped on his chest and his right arm fell across my waist. The one other time we were horizontal on a couch together was very different. We had gotten caught up in a passion that surprised us both. Smoke had stopped us before anything happened physically, but it impacted both of us emotionally and psychologically.

"Ever hear of friends with benefits?"

Smoke shifted. "Now is not a good time to talk about that."

"Thought I'd mention it as an option to consider."

"I'd marry you before I'd do that to you. Or to me."

The M word. Out of Smoke's mouth.

I fell asleep with a smile on my face.

24

The Coven

Noris phoned Cyril, requesting a meeting. Noris lived near the county park where they sometimes met, and they both agreed to be there at nine a.m. Noris jogged the half mile and waited. A few minutes later, Cyril pulled up in his red Cadillac and parked. Noris walked to the driver's window, and Cyril rolled it down. Cyril's dyed, jet black hair was a harsh frame around his face.

"The report?"

Noris handed him the printout on Gregory Trippen.

Cyril nodded. "The other Manthes boy. He looks like Harlan Manthes returned from the dead. He's in town?"

"He was staying at the Oak Lea Motel. I saw him there Thursday, but he was gone yesterday. I drove by the motel a few times and checked some other places, restaurants, stores, et cetera, but he's not around."

"Nowhere? If he came here looking for his brother, I find it hard to believe he would leave without finding him first."

Noris shook his head. "I don't know where he is. We've got his address, so I can have our contact near Burlington, Vermont check on him."

"If he's in Vermont, he's out of our hair. We have bigger fish to fry. But if he's here, we'll need to keep close tabs on him. And Aleckson hasn't filed a report on either of the Trippens?"

"No, and the ATL is still active on Jeffrey, so we know he's still at large."

"We need to find him before they do. You're the deputy. It would be no problem explaining that you had to shoot a man who came after you with a weapon."

Noris was prepared, but if it came to that, he hoped it would happen to another deputy and not him. He didn't want to draw that kind of attention to himself.

"Yes, High Priest. And I was successful in planting the devices. We'll be able to keep better track of Aleckson now. I got things set up on her end before midnight last night. And a little later on my end. I had an errand after the party that took longer than I thought. The equipment is up and running and should be in fine working order."

Noris smiled and nodded. "And I left my mark."

"Good. Keep me apprised."

"Of course, High Priest."

Cyril's smile was more of a sneer.

25

I awoke on my den office couch with sunbeams warming my face. I was alone. It took me some seconds to bring the past night's events to mind. I had fallen asleep in Smoke's arms. He must have woken early and left.

"I thought you'd sleep all day." Smoke appeared in the doorway holding a cup in his hand. The sparkle was back in his eyes.

I pulled off the afghan and sat up. My hair fell across my face, so I tucked the strands behind my ears. "I hope that's coffee."

Smoke walked over and handed me the cup. "It is." He sat down on the other end of the couch. "Did you sleep?"

I took a sip of coffee. It was strong and black, the way I liked it. "Like a rock. You?"

"Surprisingly well. And you were right. I felt much better after the sun came up." He waved at the window.

"I feel a little gross. Something about sleeping in my clothes does that to me."

"Yeah, I'm about ready to head home for a shower and a change."

"You know last night, when I saw Edberg come out of my den office?"

"Sure. The reason I'm still here. I did not intend to go into such a deep sleep, however."

"I think if anyone had come in and seen you asleep, they would have left so they wouldn't wake you."

"I suppose."

"Before you went to sleep the first time, did you use my computer, go online for any reason?"

"I wouldn't use anyone's computer without asking first. Even yours. Why?"

"Someone—probably Edberg—was snooping around on my computer last night."

He frowned. "That dirty bugger. What do you mean by snooping around? How do you know?"

I told him the computer armoire was opened, the computer was left on, and the Internet sites had been viewed in a different order than I had viewed them.

"Not very smart of him. Did he go to other sites, look something up, check his e-mail, or just look at your viewing history?"

"That was it. Unless he deleted what he looked up, but there was nothing oddball in my recycle bin. He didn't go into my documents at all."

"That makes no sense. Anything exciting in the site history? Naked men, naked women—"

"Very funny. No, it was satanic stuff. Trying to understand more about Jeffrey and Gregory Trippen. And Dr. Fischer's work."

"Someone used your computer without your knowledge and was checking your browsing history? Anybody from

Internal Affairs here? Anything you've been involved with I should know about?"

"I spent the night with a Winnebago County detective."

He cleared his throat. "So noted."

"It's possible he didn't know enough about etiquette, not to mention ethics, and wanted to look something up or check his e-mail. Maybe he had a pang of guilt realizing anything on my computer was none of his business. Something could have startled or alerted him, and he forgot to leave it the way he found it. If the computer had been shut down and the armoire closed, I would never have thought about the order of my website history the next time I used the Internet."

"I don't think I would either. Well, let's dust it for prints so we have evidence to back our claims when we go after Edberg. My kit is in my squad car. I'll bring it over this afternoon and take care of it."

"Sounds good."

He rubbed the back of his neck. "What are you doing with your day off?"

"A long run, a long shower, maybe read for a while. I want to spend some time with Gramps, and my Grandma and Grandpa Aleckson invited me over for dinner."

Smoke nodded and stood. "I'll call you later, in the early afternoon when I figure out my schedule."

I got up and followed him to the front entry. "All righty. Later then." When he was out the door, I headed to the kitchen for more coffee.

A few seconds later, I heard Smoke's voice calling from the living room. "Corky, come outside. You're not going to like this."

I jogged out to meet him. "What is it?"

"It's your car. Someone keyed it."

"*No*." I ran outside and stared at the quarter-inch-wide gash that ran most of the length of the driver's side of my classic GTO. My father's car. The car that had sat in a shed for twenty years after he died before my mother gave it to me.

It was old, but almost like new. My father, Carl, had bought it when he was nineteen, a few days before he received his draft notice for the Selective Service of the United States of America. Carl had worked hard to afford the GTO and had driven it fewer than a thousand miles in the short time he had it. I'd added only ten thousand more.

Carl had died in a Vietnam jungle. His car was a physical connection to the man who'd died before I was born. I imagined how proud he must have been, buying a brand new car complete with a V-8 engine, three speed manual transmission, disappearing windshield wipers, bucket seats, and hidden headlights.

My mother had the original sales receipt. He had paid $2,800 for it. Carl would be shocked if he knew the amount of money people had offered me over the years for the old classic. A number of collectors called me on a fairly regular basis, wondering if I was ready to sell.

I ran my fingers over the malicious act of vandalism. The tears in my eyes blurred the damage. "I'm sorry, Dad."

"Ah, Corky, come here." Smoke gathered me into a warm embrace. "I'm so sorry. For your car, of course, but mainly because you never knew Carl. He would have been very proud of you."

There was no way to hold back the tears. I rarely cried, but when I did, it counted for something. Sobs started somewhere deep in my stomach and made me gasp for breath.

"Let's go inside," Smoke directed as he guided me to the door. "There are some guys that do great body work. You won't even be able to tell."

"You think they can match the original paint?"

"I'd like to say yes to make you feel better, but I honestly don't know. It was in storage all those years. And you keep it waxed and in the garage most of the time, so there should be minimal fading from the sun. All the paint codes are on record. They're somewhere in the car, inside the door or the under the hood. We'll look."

I nodded. "I shouldn't feel this bad. It's a thing, not a person."

"It's okay, Corky. I think I understand."

"What bothers me the most is that someone did this on purpose. He—she—must hate my guts."

"Or be jealous of you. Your vehicle is worth big bucks. Call it in, get a deputy out to write the report, take pictures for the insurance company. Give him the names of everyone here last night."

A sob caught in my throat, and Smoke patted my back.

He went on, "Chances are, though, it was random. Someone drove by, saw your car sitting under the garage light, and couldn't resist marring a thing of beauty. Since no one leaving the party noticed it, it could've happened during the middle of the night."

"This side of the car was in the shadows, so I can see how no one would notice when they left my house."

"Yeah, now that I think about it, when I got here last night, I walked next to it on this side, and it was pretty dark."

"Before I call for a deputy, I'm going to take a run, then get in the shower. Another hour won't make any difference, and the deputy might be here for a while."

"Want me to hang around?"

"No, I'll be fine."

"We'll dust it when I come back to do the computer. Anybody from the party could have touched it, but it may give us a lead."

"You never know. I went through the car wash day before yesterday and drove straight home. It was in the garage until I backed it out for the party. Whoever did it might have left their prints."

"Good thinkin'. See you later."

Deputy Holman, a fairly new deputy with the department, pulled up in his squad car ten minutes after I called Communications to report the felony-level criminal damage to property of my vehicle. Smoke heard the deputy announce his arrival at my address on his police radio and arrived a few minutes after that.

"What a bummer way to end your party," Holman said as he inspected the damage.

"For sure."

Holman took the information and snapped pictures. He squatted and stared at the long mar. "Started at the front panel and moved to the back. And the guy was either left handed or was strong and coordinated with his left hand."

Smoke and I both took a closer look.

"You're right, Holman. Would've been too awkward to do this with the right hand. Would have to do it backhanded." Smoke gripped his hand over the pen. "This wouldn't work. He'd have to bend over like this and move backward." He demonstrated pulling the pen, leading with the pinkie finger.

"Not likely." He switched the pen to his left hand and guided it near the GTO, leading with his thumb that time. "Yup."

Smoke touched the scratch with his index finger. "Looks like it was done with a small knife more than with a key. It has a more pointed indentation in the center."

Holman nodded. "Detective, you're about six feet—"

"I am."

"So the guy that did this?" Holman said.

"I don't think you could say with complete accuracy. Depends on height, arm length, and if he squatted a little to give him more force," Smoke said.

I held my hand next to the car at the level I'd be comfortable. "Most likely taller than five five."

"Yeah. I'm six two." Holman ran his hand near the scrape. "I'd guess five ten to six two or three. That'd be with shoes on."

We all knew the chance of finding out who had done it was slim to none.

I assured Holman I would get a list together of everyone who had been at the party, after I enlisted help from Sara, the county attorneys, and public defenders in case I forgot anyone. I didn't have an exact number count of the people at the party, so it would be easy to miss one or two.

"I can think of a lot of 'em, too. Did you do anything to piss anyone off?" Holman smiled when he asked.

"On a regular basis, Holman. Just like every other police officer. It goes with the territory."

He nodded. "I'll write this up and add the supplemental report when you get the list done."

"Thanks."

Smoke and I spent an hour dusting and lifting prints from the GTO. It was tedious work. There were a surprising number on the hood, but only a couple on the side panels.

Smoke chose to use black powder. It showed up well against the red. The hood surface was large, and instead of using the fine dusting brush, he poured a conservative amount of powder onto the hood and blew away the excess. As prints became evident, I lifted them with tape, applied them to glass slides, and marked them using a numbering system.

Smoke pointed at my growing line of slides. "To keep this simple, and so we don't run out of slides, just take the index finger when you've got a hand print that's obviously from the same person."

"Okay."

Twenty minutes later, Smoke said, "Well, that wraps up the hood work." He picked up the dusting brush, with its incredibly fine bristles, and set to work on the driver's side of the car. I assisted, lifting, taping, and marking. It was time consuming, but a task I enjoyed. I loved seeing the prints come into focus when the dust adhered to them, pulling them off the surface, and collecting them as evidence.

"Guess people can't resist touching this old classic, huh?" Smoke said.

"I had no idea."

"The good news is, every county employee has been fingerprinted, so that part of the identification will be easy. The first prints we'll compare them to are the ones from your computer cabinet. If we have a match to any here, it'll be a good starting point."

26

My mother phoned when Smoke and I were in my den office checking the computer and armoire for prints. "Hi, dear. I drove by on my way home and noticed Elton's car was there. Is everything okay? I mean, you were kidding last night when you said that, well, you know, when you made that sex comment."

"Mother. Yes, it was meant as sarcasm. He slept here on the couch in my den—" I left out the part about me being there with him, "—and went home this morning, but came back, as part of an investigation."

"Investigation? What happened?"

She was alarmed when I told her about the GTO.

"Of all things! Who would do something like that?"

Sadly, the sheriff's department got countless complaints of similar incidents on a regular basis.

"I can still see the expression on your father's face when he drove up in that fancy car, fresh off the lot." She was silent a while. "And then you worked so hard to get it back on the road, replacing all those belts and whatever else you did."

"I know, I know. Smoke helped me dust it for prints, and a deputy took the report. Who knows, maybe we'll get lucky and find out who did it. There were lots of people at the party, some I don't really know. And like Smoke pointed out, it could have been somebody driving by that is into vandalism."

"I suppose you've been too busy to think about visiting Gramps. And your grandparents said you were going over there for dinner. They invited me, but I made plans before they asked."

"Hot date?"

"Minnesota Twins opener."

"Seriously? When have you ever been to a Twins game?"

"There's a first time for everything, and Denny's got season tickets. I'll stop by on the way and look at your car."

"If you want. Is Gramps going to Grandma and Grandpa's, too?"

"No. He said he was too tuckered out, that he'd have a sandwich later."

"I can make one for him when I stop by."

"That would be nice, dear. Oh, Corinne? Denny is right here and wants to talk to you."

"Corky."

"Hi, Sheriff."

"I got the gist of what happened listening to your mother's end of the conversation here. Your car was out all night?"

"Yes. From yesterday afternoon about six. We discovered the damage this morning at nine."

"You know the names of everyone who was at your party last night?"

"I'm getting a list together."

"Good. We'll divide up the names and have a few deputies do a quick interview, see if anyone knows anything. It's criminal damage to property. Felony level, with what body work costs nowadays. If it was done by a member of our department, I want to know about it, for godsakes."

I heard my mother say, "Denny," and I knew from her tone she was asking him not to swear.

We hung up after our goodbyes.

Smoke narrowed his eyebrows. "Your mother wondering about possible hanky panky between us?"

I slowly nodded my head. "A mother is a mother is a mother."

"You didn't tell her. Does that mean my secret's safe with you?"

"Your secret?"

"Yeah. That I had a dream that scared me so much I needed you to sleep by me."

I smiled. "Your secret's safe with me."

Smoke worked away with white powder, for that job, and the dusting brush. "I'm surprised. There are only a few prints on the armoire and the computer keys. More on the mouse."

"I cleaned yesterday."

"You did a good job. The armoire has four fingerprints, which must be yours. Small hand. Probably when you pushed the door closed."

I held my hand in front of the prints. The length of my fingers matched the way the prints lined up. "Yeah, that'd be me. No reason to lift those."

"I'm not a fingerprint expert, but looking at the mouse and the few keys that have prints on them, I'd say they're yours, also. Give me your hands once."

I turned my hands palms up, and Smoke examined them. "The thin scar on your right index shows up on the door, mouse, and several keys. The few keys you touched. And that's kind of a cute little whorl next to it. Gives you away. It appears you are the owner of the prints."

"Which means whoever was snooping around here was wearing gloves."

"Do you carry latex gloves around with you, on your person?"

"Only when I'm working."

"Same here. So the snoop came prepared."

Sara stopped by in the early afternoon to see if I needed help cleaning up after the party. I dragged her into the garage to see my damaged car.

She ran over, stopped short, and stared. "Oh no. What happened? Why didn't you call me?"

"I was going to. Smoke just left a few minutes ago, so I haven't had a chance."

I gave Sara all the details, from someone accessing my computer to seeing Edberg leaving my den office to finding the keyed car to dusting for latent prints. Everything except the detail about sleeping next to Smoke on the couch all night. That would come out eventually.

"I am so sorry, Corky. I made you have this party."

"You didn't make me, and stop being silly. I thought about pulling the car into the garage before I went to bed, but I didn't."

"Unless it happened when the party was going on."

"I know. I'm hoping it was a random act, and as much as that irritates the heck out of me, I'd hate to think someone I work with—and actually trust with my life, if it comes to that—would do this. For what? I can't think of a single good reason."

"There is no good reason."

My cell phone rang. It was my brother, John Carl. "Hi Corky. Mother called. Sorry about Carl's GTO."

It would always be our father's car, no matter how many years I owned it. When we were kids, we'd sneak into the shed where Mother stored it. We'd climb in, one of us behind the wheel and the other in the passenger seat, and sit there feeling grown up and a bit smug. When Mother had agreed to let me restore it and put it back on the road, I was thrilled. John Carl had never said so, but I figured he harbored some jealousy that Mother had given it to me.

"Thanks. So where were you in the early morning hours of, say, midnight to nine o'clock today?"

"Does sleeping alone in the guest room of my house count as an adequate alibi?"

That was not what I wanted to hear.

"Yes. Actually, living in Colorado, eight hundred miles from here, is convincing in and of itself, unless you took the red eye, of course."

John Carl rarely gave me private information, so I knew he needed to talk about his marriage. I took a quick breath. "Sounds like things aren't going the way you hoped with Emily."

"No, they aren't. At all. She doesn't want to be married anymore, but she doesn't want to lose the house either. It's not the best arrangement in the world, stuck in this limbo. Trouble is, it takes both of our incomes to maintain this place."

"John Carl, the way she's using you drives me nuts."

Sara's eyes widened, and I lifted my shoulders in a resigned shrug.

"It's not just her. We're using each other, and that's not a totally bad thing. It wouldn't be wise to walk away when we've got so much money tied up in the house. We can't afford to lose it.

"Emily will have to make a decision one of these days. If she wants to go through with a divorce, we'll have to put the house up for sale, and then we'll each have to find a cheaper place to live."

"Are you still thinking of possibly moving back home to Oak Lea?"

"Yes. But it's a tough decision to make."

"That would be the one good thing in all of this, as far as Mother and I are concerned." I hesitated with the next question. "Is Emily seeing another man, or what is the deal?"

"No, that isn't it."

"How can you be so sure?"

"Because she climbs into my bed from time to time."

"Oh."

"Don't be like that, Corky." John Carl was adept at hearing the minutest innuendos in my speech. Even over the phone when he couldn't see the facial expression that went with it.

"I'm not."

"Yes, you are."

"John Carl, your physical relationship is between the two of you. What concerns me is your emotional health."

"Thanks, Mom."

"Now that's hitting below the belt. We both know there is no possible way I could ever worry as much as our mother does."

"You're right. Hey, we got way off subject here. How is everything else?"

"Okay." I wanted to tell John Carl about the Trippen case, but the sheriff had ordered that it be kept quiet during the initial part of the investigation at least.

I heard a woman's voice in the background calling his name. Emily. "I better go, but I'll catch you soon."

"I love you, big brother."

"You, too."

"I could shoot that woman," I said after my phone was off.

Sara dramatically covered her ears with her hands. "I did not hear that." She dropped her hands to her elbows and rested crossed arms on her stomach. "You are talking about Emily, I presume? You and John Carl were having quite the conversation."

"She's using John Carl for money and sex, and that really angers me because he loves her and is so invested in their marriage."

"Let it go, dear. There is nothing you can do about it. He'll get tired of that arrangement before long. Or she will. She may be looking for a new boy toy as we speak."

"Sara, yuck!"

"Yuck is right, but some women are like that."

"Let's talk about something else. The party. People seemed to have a good time. The toasts were a little sad, but it made the colleagues feel better, I think."

I started walking toward the house, and Sara followed.

"I think so, too. I talked to a lot of people I never get a chance to outside of work. Even chatted with the new guy, Eric Stueman."

We went into the kitchen, and I turned to face her. "Did you? I caught him staring at me a few times, but we didn't say more than hi, thank you, goodbye. He's kind of a weird dude."

"Who's pretty cute. He reminds me of a young Harrison Ford, and I had a nice conversation with him."

"Seriously?"

"I mean, I did most of the talking, but he was pleasant enough."

"That confirms it. He does not like me. Why would he even come to my house?"

"He didn't say. Maybe he came with the express intention of keying your car."

"What?"

"I'm kidding."

I gave her a mild shove. "Your date, Casey, didn't show up."

I opened the refrigerator, pulled out two bottles of water, and handed one to Sara.

She took hers and twisted the cap off. "No. He ended up working late. He stopped by, but the lights were out, so he went home."

"And if he had seen someone lurking around my house or vehicle, he would have mentioned it."

"Uh, yeah."

"A couple of years ago there was a rash of vehicle vandalism in Little Mountain," I said.

"That's right. What was it, two or three mornings in a row people got up and discovered their windows, or headlamps, or side mirrors, or whatever had been smashed."

"They wrecked over twenty vehicles before we caught the little darlings."

"I got one of them in my caseload. Jules Worth. At the rate he's going, he'll be one of my probationers until one of us dies, or until I retire."

"He'll end up in prison the next time he offends."

Sara nodded. "That'll be my recommendation."

I spent the rest of Saturday with my grandparents. First Gramps Brandt, then the Alecksons. I debated telling them about the car, but my intuitive grandmother, who knew me better than anyone else on earth, sensed something was troubling me, so I told them. The GTO was parked in their driveway, and we went outside to inspect the damage.

Grandma brought her hand to her chest. "My, that is quite a scratch. I cannot abide vandalism. It has never made sense to me."

It was senseless to every victim.

Grandpa examined the car, shaking his head.

"I guess it doesn't do much good to speculate about who damaged my car until the evidence is processed and the questions are asked."

Grandpa raised his arm and pointed his thumb backward, like he was hitchhiking. "You know that Stan Hemsley over at the garage there on County Thirty-five? He's very talented with body work. I'd look him up."

Stan had a good reputation. I'd heard that from a number of people.

Grandma tucked her finger under my chin. "You still keep that picture next to your bed? The one of your mom and dad on their wedding day, standing by this car?"

I folded my hand over hers. "Still on my bed stand."

"That's a sweet picture." Her eyes misted over.

My grandparents had struggled with the reality of my father's death on and off for thirty years. He was their only son, the one who would have taken over the farm. A man who had left behind a young widow and two babies.

Grandma moved her hand, sliding it between my arm and body in an escort position. "Well, dinner's ready."

We took one last look then went inside.

27

A strong storm moved in Sunday afternoon. Nichole Jaspers and I were scheduled to meet at four o'clock, but I didn't want her to wait in the driving rain for me to open the south entrance door of the sheriff's department, so I advised her to come in the jail lobby entrance. It was open for inmate visiting hours. I said she could either lock her purse in her car or in a small property locker in the lobby. If she brought it in with her, I'd have to search it.

Corrections officer Matt called the squad room a few minutes before four and told me Nichole had arrived. I secured my weapon in a gun locker then pushed the intercom button.

"Can I help you?" Matt asked.

"Sergeant Aleckson to meet one in the lobby."

"Is your weapon secured?"

"It is."

The lock turned, and I pulled the first door open. It took two sets of sally port doors to reach her, the first from the sheriff's department to the inmate side of the jail's visiting-area hallway, and the second from the hallway to the lobby where the visitors gathered.

If she hadn't been announced, if I hadn't been looking for her, I might not have seen Nichole. She was nearly invisible. I had read a fair amount about the victims of satanic ritual abuse, and it made me wonder, was that a protective device? Used consciously? Subconsciously? If people don't see you, they can't hurt you? How many other people were out there, people I passed but didn't notice?

Nichole was slender, with brown hair that hung limply past her shoulders. She had a pale complexion and no prominent facial features. She could have been very pretty, but chose to be plain.

Nichole spotted me when I stepped out of the sally port into the lobby and walked toward me carrying a dripping raincoat. "It's really coming down out there."

I reached for the raincoat. "Yes it is. Thanks for coming. Anything sharp in the pockets?"

"Just my car keys."

I did a quick search and confirmed that. "Okay. Follow me." I grabbed the sally port door handle, and the corrections officer opened it electronically. A number of inmates and visitors watched us with interest, most likely assuming Nichole was turning herself in on a warrant and I was taking her into custody.

When the first door secured behind us, the second door opened in front of us, then closed with a loud click when we were in the hallway. "I have to do a quick pat down before we go into the sheriff's department."

"Oh, okay."

"Just procedure to keep us all safe."

Her face brightened at the word safe. Nichole's tee shirt and jeans were form-fitting on her small body, and there were no unusual lumps. No contraband. As I'd expected. I waved at Matt to open the sheriff's department sally door. Again, when the door closed, the second one opened. I asked Nichole to take a few steps back while I got my Glock out of the locker.

"You sure have to go through a lot, don't you?" she said.

"No weapons allowed in the jail."

"Why is that?"

"So they don't fall in the wrong hands," I said.

"For safety's sake."

"Right. We're big on that around here. Safety and security."

A little of the tension visibly left Nichole's body. Her shoulders dropped from a modified shrug to a more natural position. She opened her fisted hands and wiggled her fingers. She smiled, and it changed her appearance from plain to pretty.

"Detective Dawes gave me permission to use his desk and his cubicle. Or we can go into an interview room. Your choice. Where would you feel more comfortable?"

She considered before she answered. "Dr. Fischer mentioned the detective's name. He was at her office with you." I nodded. "He's not here?"

"No, he's at a family function. The detectives' cubicles are deserted today, if that helps you make up your mind."

"Sure. I think I'd like to go there."

"Nichole, I have another sergeant covering my calls, so take your time. I'll take notes, but I won't record our conversation. This isn't an interview—you'll remain anonymous. You're very gracious to talk to me, to help me understand a subculture I know very little about. Start whenever you're ready."

Nichole shifted in her chair, moved back, then stood. "Okay if I stand?" I nodded. "What happened to me . . . and to Collin, should never happen to anyone."

She stopped, and I waited.

"We are from another state. I can't say where, because they still might be looking for us."

"Why?"

"We escaped. And we took something they wanted with us," she said.

"What was that?"

"My baby. They used my first baby as a sacrifice, and I couldn't let them do it again."

My heart dropped into my lower abdomen. Gregory Trippen had said they drank the water they drowned babies in.

"You had another baby? I didn't notice any signs of one at your home."

"No, after we got to Minnesota, and after my son was born, we gave him up for adoption. So if they found us, they couldn't get him."

"That must have been very difficult."

"Yes, in many ways. I was impregnated during a ritual. I don't know who his father is. There were many men who raped me that night." She silently stared at her hands, and I wasn't sure she'd continue. Finally, she looked at me. "He will never know the circumstances of his conception, and there is no record of his birth."

"What do you mean?"

"We delivered him at home. He was so beautiful. I wanted to keep him, but I loved him too much to take that risk." Her eyes filled with tears, and they spilled down her cheeks. There was a box of tissues on Smoke's desk, and I pushed it closer to Nichole. She pulled out a couple and wiped her face.

"The next day, we took him to a Catholic hospital. I went in alone with him and gave him to a nurse and said I couldn't keep my baby and was taking advantage of the baby safe haven law. I knew they couldn't ask who I was as long as the baby was unharmed. I gave her a note giving the date and time of his birth, what we got for his height and weight numbers, and asking that he be placed with a Christian family."

Nichole had done her homework. In Minnesota, as in most states, a mother, or another person with the approval of the mother, could leave a baby up to three days old with a hospital employee at any licensed hospital in the state.

"Collin and I were in the same cult. Coven. Raised in farm families in a state with miles and miles of privately owned fields and pastures. It's very easy to hide what you're doing from authorities in the middle of all that." Nichole nodded, emphasizing her words.

"My parents said Satan had been enlightening The Family—that's what they called the cult. That he had been enlightening and giving us power for generations. The Family could trace its roots back to the thirteen hundreds, to England."

Nichole sank onto the chair and spoke quietly, almost in a monotone. "I don't know when my torture and abuse began. It was part of my life for as long as I remember. Same with Collin. He was being groomed to one day take over as the high priest, so he was forced to do more things than most of us. If he didn't, they would have killed him."

"Tell me about it."

"It was all part of the rituals. Blood rituals involving animals and people. More than once, when they thought he was resisting, they buried him in a box they had in the ground. For up to three days, without food or water. It was meant to produce great terror in us, and of course it did. Some died in there."

I squirmed in my seat as an imaginary claustrophobic blanket settled around me, like it had when Gregory Trippen had told Smoke and me about the same horror.

"There were many methods they used to make us do their will. Rape, sexual orgies, torture, sacrifice, electrical shock, being hung upside down for long periods, choking, near-drowning, being fed drugs, witnessing what they did to others, being forced to do those horrendous things to others. Most of what happened to us we repressed out of self-preservation, I found out later."

I listened to her voice and watched her expressions and body language when she talked about the horrendous abuse. There was little emotion displayed. Like it was someone else's story. Another survival technique, I imagined.

"As I started to explain earlier, the leaders decided Collin would become the high priest someday. And me? I was a favored one, a bride of Satan. I carried one baby that was given to him in sacrifice. They gave me drugs to make me go into labor, and he was born during a ritual. I saw the knife the high priest held over his little body, but everything is black after that. Collin wouldn't tell me what happened, but I had seen other infant sacrifices, so I could imagine." Tears spilled out of her eyes and landed on the tissues in her folded hands.

I shuddered. "I can't imagine anything so awful. Why would they do that?"

"To offer a gift to the Prince, and to capture the energy when the soul leaves the body."

Gregory had said the same thing. "How is that possible?"

She shook her head. There was no answer. "Then I was impregnated again. But they didn't get him."

"How did you and Collin manage to get out?"

Nichole smiled. "It was a God thing. I was expecting my little baby and terrified about what they would do to him. I even thought for a while about killing myself so they couldn't have him. So they couldn't hurt him."

I reached over and patted Nichole's arm. "I'm glad you didn't."

She nodded. "I wasn't allowed to socialize with anyone outside The Family, except when I went to school, and then I was only allowed to say certain things. We lived two miles outside of a small town. One evening, I snuck out and walked into town. It was a Wednesday night. People were going into this church. Families laughing and smiling. It made me curious. Here were a bunch of people, out in public, going into a church. I had always been taught God was evil. We had to denounce Jesus of Nazareth and pledge our lives and loyalty to Satan."

I thought of the inverted crosses on Gregory Trippen's feet.

"I was drawn into that building with those people. I went in the front door and heard the most glorious sound coming from the choir loft. Voices, men's and women's, singing a joyful song. I was alone in the sanctuary. The others had gone to other rooms.

"I sat down on a pew in the back of the church and listened to the choir practice. My whole body broke out in goose bumps. There were Bibles in the pews, and I picked one up. I had never seen a Holy Bible before and randomly opened to what turned out to be the book of Matthew, chapter eleven, verses twenty-eight to thirty. I memorized them. 'Come to me, all you who labor and are heavy laden, and I will give you rest. Take my yoke upon you and learn from me, for I am gentle and lowly in heart, and you will find rest for your souls. For my yoke is easy and my burden is light.'"

Nichole's eyes filled with tears once more. "Oh, how I wanted rest for my soul and for my burden to be light. Here was this church with Bibles anyone could read. In The Family, only the leaders had access to the Black Book, their book of worship and rituals. I was afraid someone might ask why I was there, and then The Family would find out, so I grabbed the Bible and went back home.

"I hid that Bible and read it whenever I could. I finally told Collin about it and the positive impact it was having on my life and thinking. Collin and I were good friends. We loved each other. We learned from the awful lessons very early in our lives that we had to keep our love secret or it would be used against us."

"How?"

"Threats. Real threats. If Collin didn't comply with an order, they might torture me. And vice versa. How we managed to keep our friendship from the leaders, I don't know. At first I wasn't going to tell Collin I was planning to leave. Then I realized he would think they had killed me.

When I told him my plans, he started crying and said I could never escape. They would hunt me down.

"I said that might be true, but I had to follow a new path, a path of truth. I wasn't afraid for myself anymore, and I would find a good life for the baby. That's when he decided to go with me. Collin was eighteen, I was seventeen. Kids. But kids who had seen as much as seasoned war veterans. Maybe more. Collin's parents had a lot of money hidden away. He figured they wouldn't miss a couple of thousand."

"How did you choose to come to Minnesota?"

"We didn't, exactly. We were hitchhiking and we landed in Minneapolis. We liked it and thought we'd stay awhile. I found out about the baby safe haven program and decided that would be better than adoption. No questions. I turned eighteen a month before the baby was born."

Two teenagers on their own, making adult decisions.

"We got jobs and stayed in Minneapolis for a few years. On Collin's twenty-first birthday, his friends took him out for a drink after work. He hadn't had alcohol since when he was forced to drink it for certain rituals. After a few drinks, he had a very frightening reaction. His friends called me to pick him up. I was supposed to meet him for dinner, anyway. First he was threatening and combative, then he became very childlike, crying and pleading.

"When I said, 'Who are you?' meaning why are you acting like this, he said, 'Micah.' He kept talking in this little boy voice, expressing little boy fears. I was scared enough to begin with, and then when he said he was Micah, I could hardly breathe. Micah was his younger brother. He was buried in the box when he was three. He didn't get out alive."

My throat partially closed. Where were the authorities when all those crimes were taking place? What about all the missing children?

"He went back to being Collin again a while later and had no memory of what he had done or said. We have both always been afraid of doctors and medical people, so we weren't sure where to turn for answers. I started doing some research online. I found out it was common for victims of ritual abuse to fragment into separate, different personalities as a protective device. There are a lot of victim support groups out there, and I started chatting with some people. That's where I heard about Dr. Fischer."

"Ah."

"When we went out to Oak Lea for our appointments, we'd drive around the town, then we started exploring the county. Minneapolis was fine, but we liked the rural setting of Winnebago County. We looked until we found a home we could afford, out in Kadoka."

"It's a very nice place."

A small smile. "Thanks. Dr. Fischer has really helped us. Both of us. I can hardly begin to tell you how much. After Collin had that dramatic episode that brought his condition to light, it made me start questioning things about myself and my memory."

"Like what?"

"Like how I could remember the beginning and end of some rituals, but not what happened in between. You know, like with my baby. We were given drugs sometimes, but not always. And throughout my life I've had gaps where I've lost time. Sometimes a little, sometimes more. I'd get in trouble at school because of it, get chastised for something I said. And I didn't know what it was because I couldn't remember anything about it. I didn't know dissociative identity disorder existed. I thought it was normal to forget things. Collin did, and I did.

"Dr. Fischer is helping us integrate, and Pastor Trondholm is helping us heal spiritually so we can forgive ourselves for any harm we did to people in the name of Satan." Nichole stood. "I better get going. I know I couldn't tell you much, but I hope it helped."

Not much? That was a decided understatement. I wished Smoke had been there to hear Nichole's story. I would never be able to convey it as well.

I rose also. "Nichole, before you go, I have a couple of questions. Did you report any of this to your local authorities?"

She shook her head. "It wouldn't have mattered. The local police chief was the high priest. He knew what to do to hide it from the county and state police, I'm sure."

"But the evidence— "

"There was a crematorium they took the bodies to. I understand bone dust is easy to get rid of."

Bone dust. After a body was burned and reduced to dust, would there be any DNA left in it?

"And all the blood?"

"Yes, for the rituals conducted in an indoor temple, you'd think there'd be some evidence. I know they cleaned very well. Outside? They cleaned up, and the elements and animals took care of the rest over time."

Evidence left outside was compromised, and worse.

"What about the people they used in rituals? After a few people go missing in a given area, even if the police chief was in on it, citizens put a lot of pressure on the authorities to find them. It causes a public panic."

"Most, like the babies and young children, even teenagers, had no birth records. A doctor in The Family had a connection to someone in court records, I'm sure, like if they needed a birth certificate later.

"I don't know how they chose the ones that went to public school. Very few are allowed to. Most aren't. Collin and I decided the reason some were sent was because The Family had to present some semblance of normalcy to the surrounding communities. It would raise questions where there are fifteen or twenty working farms, but no one has any children. Or if any kids were spotted by outsiders but didn't go to school, that might bring the authorities out to check. The Family controlled the information."

"By keeping secret who was in The Family?"

"Right. When I was chosen to go to school, I felt a little safer. I mean, if I died, my teachers would ask where I was. The Family could lie, of course, say I was ill or that my father was transferred and we had to move." Nichole shrugged. "You said if someone disappears from an area, people notice. But people—men, women, teens, children—disappear all the time. I bet for each one that is reported, at least one disappears who isn't reported."

My mother's hovering over-protectiveness seemed like a good problem to have growing up after all. "Do you know of *anyone* who reported the activities of The Family to the authorities?"

"No, and like I said, it wouldn't do any good. They know what they're doing. The Family has been operating for many centuries."

"Nichole, thank you, very, very much." I took her hand in both of mine and squeezed. "You are incredibly brave. Come on, I'll walk you out. And you have my business card?"

"I do."

"I appreciate you being so straightforward with me. Your story would be impossible for most people to tell."

"You're welcome. I wouldn't have been able to a few years ago, but it's gotten easier. I just hope it helps whoever you're working with."

I nodded. Gregory Trippen had revealed few details of what had happened to him personally, with the exception of the box burials and the cross branding. Jeffrey was planning to end his life, most likely because of ritual abuse. The details Nichole had given me provided a better understanding of the abusive practices. I silently vowed to do whatever I could to help however I could.

"Nichole, I'm going to talk to the county attorney, put in a good word for Collin, and request that he not do any more jail time for the domestic."

Her face brightened with another smile. "Thank you."

It had quit raining. I escorted Nichole to the south entrance to avoid going through the sally ports again. We cut through the squad room, where three deputies were working on reports or catching up on department business. I did the customary nods of acknowledgement as we passed through. Edberg, Stauder, and Brooks did the same, eyeing Nichole and no doubt wondering who she was and why she was there.

When we got to the exit doors, Nichole turned to me and whispered, "I have something important to tell you." She looked toward the hallway we had walked down. "Where no one can hear us."

What had suddenly occurred to her? "Should we step outside?"

She nodded, and I followed her out the door. She stopped, glanced at the intercom on the side of the building next to her then walked to the end of the veranda.

"What is it, Nichole?"

Her facial color paled, and a frown replaced the smile from a minute before. "When we went through the room where those officers were just now?"

"Yes?"

"There is an evil force in there."

"What kind of an evil force?" Had she spotted the photos of Jeffrey Trippen and his dagger?

"One of those men is saturated with demonic influence."

28

"Face your demon," my brother always told me whenever I wrestled with a personal or professional struggle. I pondered his words all the way to the squad room. John Carl's words had taken on a whole new meaning given the case I was working on. Ask Nichole Jaspers. Collin Jaspers. Jeffrey Trippen. Gregory Trippen. Greg even said he and Jeff had too many demons.

I looked at the three deputies, men I had known as long as I'd been with the sheriff's department. Because of his connection to the Harlan Manthes shooting investigation, and the fact that I had seen him coming out of my home den office the night of my party, Deputy Bob Edberg was my prime suspect. But saturated with demonic influence? How could I tell?

"A friend of yours?" Stauder asked as I checked my mailbox cubby.

I turned to face him. "A follow-up on a domestic." Not completely truthful. I was not going to reveal Nichole's identity.

Edberg frowned slightly.

Stauder pointed his pen at the bulletin board. "Your ATL guy hasn't shown up yet."

"Not yet."

"What's his story? Why are we looking for a guy from Vermont in Minnesota?"

"He's a transient. Could be anywhere, I guess. He lived here as a kid," I said.

"Thank you for the party the other night," Brooks said, effectively changing the subject.

With the exception of someone accessing my computer and keying my GTO, it was a nice evening. "Sure."

"The county attorneys and public defenders can be kind of fun. I've never partied with them before. We've got Julie Grimes in our group for the team-building exercise, so it was good to get to know her a little better," Stauder said.

"Julie's great. Yeah, we got Eric Stueman in our group. I can't wait." I rolled my eyes.

Brooks cracked a small grin.

"He is one serious dude. I was surprised to see him the other night. He wasn't even around when Eisner was doing her dastardly deeds," I added.

Stauder shrugged. "He hasn't been here long. Maybe he wants to meet some more people."

"Or maybe Collinwood made him go," Edberg said.

That was the more likely scenario. Time to get down to business.

"Bob, I need you for a minute."

Edberg raised his eyebrows, pushed his chair back from the computer, and followed me into the small office set aside for the sergeants to review reports or talk to other sergeants and deputies in private.

The space was limited. The desk wasn't much bigger than a student's classroom desk, and the chairs were molded plastic with metal legs. Someone had told me they had been there since the seventies. I closed the door then sat down in one chair. Edberg sat in the other.

Nichole's words replayed in my mind. If there were evil vibes emanating from Edberg, I didn't sense them. Was I losing my edge, or were my intuitions limited to matters in the physical world, as I suspected? Bob waited while I weighed my words.

"I have a couple of things to run by you, Bob."

"Shoot."

"The other night at the party, when I saw you coming out of my den office, you said you were making a phone call."

"Yes?" He was hesitant.

"Did you use the computer, too?"

"Your home computer? No, why? What's this about?"

"It's okay if you did. I just need to know."

"Are you accusing me of something?" he said.

"No, I'm not. You were in there with the door closed, so you're the first one I'm asking about it."

"I was in there to make a call, like I said. To my mother. I saw I had a missed call from her and needed to check. She doesn't phone me unless she really needs something." He frowned slightly. "Something happen to your computer?"

"No, nothing. It's fine. I'm not trying to blow this out of proportion, but it's a little curious. Sometime in the middle of the party, someone went into my den office and used the computer without asking me first."

"That is downright rude. If you didn't see anyone, how do you know it happened? A guy checking out porn sites and forgot to delete them?"

"No. I had the computer off and the cabinet doors closed before the party. Someone used it and left it on and the doors open."

Edberg scratched his chin, thinking a moment. "Huh. Well, the way I recollect it, the cabinet was open and the computer was flashing when I was there."

"Notice anybody going in or coming out during the evening?"

He shook his head. "Wasn't paying attention one way or the other. I was just looking for a quiet spot to make that call. The bathroom was occupied, so I went into your office. Sorry if I was out of line."

"No need to be. No big deal. I want my guests to feel welcome in my home."

"But not use your computer behind your back."

"Exactly." The next subject was more important. "Bob, do you remember a hunting accident from a number of years ago, during deer season? A man by the name of Harlan Manthes got shot and died."

Edberg's relaxed expression tensed. "Yes?"

"You wrote a report. Remember any details?"

Edberg shook his head and lowered his voice. "We can't talk about it here. They have spies."

First Armstrong, now Edberg. Did they think the place was bugged?

"I'll meet you somewhere," he said.

"Smoke Dawes is interested in what you have to say, too."

A single nod. "I trust Dawes."

"He's tied up this afternoon, but I'll call him later and see what his schedule is like this evening, or tomorrow."

"Winnebago County, Seven oh three," Communications officer Jerry called.

Edberg stood and depressed the call button on his radio. "Seven oh three."

"Report of a speeding motorcycle leaving the roadway and landing in a ditch in Maysville Township. Unknown injuries. My partner is paging an ambulance."

"Ten-four." He gave me a hasty nod and hurried off.

29

I dialed Smoke's phone at five thirty. "Hi. Still at your nephew's ballgame?"

"No, it's over. They won, and *what* a game. The bases were loaded in the bottom of the ninth and Josh hit a home run, so he's pretty pumped. We all are."

I heard an oldies tune playing on his car radio. "You on your way home?"

"Yeah, just coming into Oak Lea. What's up?"

"I had a chat with Edberg about my computer and the missing Manthes reports."

"And?"

"He said he noticed the computer was on when he was in the den office making his phone call. And guess what? When I asked about the file, he acted about the same way Armstrong did when we confronted him. He didn't want to talk at the office."

"Edberg too?"

"I know. It's like a conspiracy theory. What is real? I thought you'd want to be in on the conversation when I talk to him."

"When and where?"

"He's covering the One twenty-six area. We could meet in your driveway. Edberg's not out on anything right now. He cleared from a crash a few minutes ago. Should we say ten to twenty minutes, depending on where he is?"

"That'll work."

When we hung up, I called Edberg. "Bob, what's your twenty?"

"County Thirty-five, passing County Three."

"Are you clear to meet?"

"Sure."

"You know where Smoke Dawes lives?"

"Sure."

"Meet you there in ten?"

"Copy."

Smoke lived a few miles west of me in a log home in the woods, on his own private lake. He was in his yard playing fetch with his dog Rex when I pulled up to the garage and parked. As I got out of the car, I heard a vehicle coming down the driveway. Edberg. He stopped, got out, and the three of us gathered under a tree.

Smoke locked his eyes on Edberg. "Okay, Bob, tell us what you know."

"Why this sudden interest in a closed case?"

"I got a call from someone asking about it," I said.

"It have anything to do with the missing kid? Jeffrey Trippen?"

"Why do you ask?" Smoke said.

"That case has haunted me for twenty years. I see the faces of those little boys nearly every day of my life. Jeffrey

Trippen is Jeffrey Manthes. I recognized him right away when I saw his picture in the squad room. Even with the beard. Brother's name is Gregory. Their mother disappeared with the boys a couple of years after Harlan Manthes was killed."

Edberg was a veteran cop. Very little slid by him.

Smoke shifted. "You said the case haunted you?"

"I didn't think for one minute the shooting was an accident. There were three other hunters with Manthes. If one guy points and says, 'deer,' maybe one other guy will be convinced he sees the same thing. But not two. Just wouldn't happen. I've been on enough hunts to know that much. I was the second one on the scene after Armstrong. The scene was compromised, evidence tampered with. Detective Walden's report, in my opinion, seemed like a cover-up for the hunters. All professionals. Doctor, pharmacist, undertaker. I wasn't exactly quiet about my concerns."

"So what happened?"

"I filed my report, and the next day I got a phone call. The voice was muffled. Deep voice, tried to sound scary. Did sound scary. Told me to shut up about the hunting accident or my mother would be shut up permanently. A death threat. If I dropped it, she would be safe. My mother's crippled with rheumatoid arthritis, has been for thirty years. She has no way to defend herself. She can't even grip a gun.

"That convinced me it wasn't an accident. Over the years, I've been threatened by guys I've arrested—we all have—and I knew half the time they were just mouthing off. I never worried about them. I figured I could take care of myself. But that guy was serious, no doubt in my mind."

He reached up, pulled a leaf off a branch, and gently picked at it with his fingers. "I tried to find out if Harlan Manthes had done something they were seeking revenge for, but I came up dry. He was a social guy, had lots of friends, no drug or alcohol problems. Didn't cheat on his wife. The other three seemed to be upstanding citizens, too. I ran their backgrounds, but since I didn't know who had made the threatening phone call, I didn't delve too deep.

"When Dr. Sparrow married Mrs. Manthes, that gave a motive, but how to prove that? Was she involved with Sparrow when she was married to Manthes, and the one who put him up to killing her husband? But why would the others go along with that? I'd do just about anything for a friend. But kill someone? Never."

He tossed the leaf on the ground. "We did wrong by those kids, and probably his wife, too. She seemed genuinely devastated when we talked to her. After she moved away, I wondered if the same people who had threatened me had done the same to her. Or maybe she found out Sparrow was the asshole I figured him to be, hidden beneath that charming front he puts on. In any case, three hunters who should have been charged with first degree murder are still breathing free air."

"And you have no idea who called you with those threats?" Smoke said.

"Not a clue. And I got a call every year saying about the same thing, just in case I forgot. Whoever it was had a spy in the sheriff's department, I know that much. Said they'd keep an eye on me at work, make sure I kept my end of the deal. It brought up a lot of questions, like was Walden threatened, that's why he did what he did, or was he the spy? And Armstrong, same deal."

"But you didn't ask them?" Smoke asked.

"No. I knew about the three shooters. The creepy caller said someone was keeping an eye on me at work. It made me wonder how big their network was. You know, organized crime. I didn't want anything happening to my mom. She took care of me the first twenty years of my life, and I've taken care of her the last thirty. I don't have much of a social life—by choice—but when I'm at work, she's alone and helpless."

Sweat beaded on Edberg's brow. He reached into a back pocket, pulled out a hankie, and dabbed at his face. "I've kept a close watch on other deputies in the department for years. Looked for signs of who it might be. When Walden retired, the phone calls continued, so I ruled him out."

"And you knew the files were missing?"

Edberg nodded. "Yeah, like I said, I was haunted by the whole deal. I figured someday, whoever was holding my mother's life over my head would go away, and I'd ask to have the case reopened. So I went to the file room and was going to make copies of everything and keep them in my safe at home until the time was right. But lo and behold, they were gone. I felt as sick as I've ever felt in my life. I would've kept a copy of my report if I'd known."

"The last thing you expect is for reports to go missing from our office," Smoke said.

Edberg hitched his shoulders in a mild stretch. "So Trippen and the dagger, that's what brought this up after all these years?"

I nodded. "The sheriff is keeping it under wraps while we do some more investigating, but according to Jeffrey Trippen's brother, Gregory, Jeffrey is planning to use that dagger to sacrifice himself."

Edberg frowned and mouthed a silent, "What?"

"Gregory Trippen said Dr. Sparrow was involved in a satanic cult and brought the boys along to the rituals. Messed Jeffrey up pretty bad, and now he's going to sacrifice himself to Satan."

Edberg's eyes widened and his jaw dropped, leaving his mouth slack. "A bunch of damn cult members are responsible for this? I'm going to redouble my efforts, see if I can figure it out."

"Don't get yourself killed. Or your mother."

Edberg dropped his head and nodded at the ground. "Sergeant." He lifted his head and looked me squarely in the eyes. "Someone was in your home computer. What do you suppose they were looking for?"

"I don't know."

"You keep any info about cases you're working on? Records of your arrests for easier access than paging through your stack of memo books when you want to look something up?"

"No. Why?"

"I've started to do that. I keep copies of all my major crime reports and ones I feel unsettled about in a safe. After the Manthes case, I didn't want any more of my reports to disappear. What I track on the computer is crime, name, date."

I had all my old memo books and as many reports on my zip drive as it would hold, but I had never thought of keeping any professional records on my home computer. They were all public records.

"So no records of your cases?" I shook my head. "How about e-mail communications with Gregory Trippen, or others connected to the case?"

"No. If they looked at either my personal or work e-mail, they wouldn't find anything. There was nothing about him or the case. They did look at the sites I had been on. I had done a bunch of research on satanic cults, rituals, ritual abuse, dissociative identity disorder—"

"Damn. I bet they figured out who Jeffrey Trippen is. I did. And they'd understand better than anyone that he's got that fancy dagger for a reason."

The three of us stared from one to the other.

"The Jeffrey Trippen case is yours. They're looking to find out what you know. A search of your computer gave them the list of sites you'd been on," Edberg said.

From that point on, I resolved to delete all search history, erase my "favorites," change my passwords, uncheck the "remember my username" and "remember my password" boxes, and lock my computer so no one but me could log on in the first place. All things that had seemed unnecessary before. I lived alone. Sara stayed overnight on a rare occasion and used my Internet access from time to time, but she was the only one.

"Sergeant, when I was in your office, I noticed your briefcase lying on the couch when I sat down. Did you check to see if everything was in order there?"

I shook my head. "No, but it was locked. I got my PBT out of it, and I know it was locked."

"And you locked it after you got your PBT?"

"Yeah, I do that out of habit."

Edberg lowered his jaw and drew his eyebrows together. "They may just keep an eye on you and what you're up to or they may warn you to back off."

I wanted to know who *they* were.

Smoke blew out a loud breath. "Corky tell you her car got keyed the night of the party?"

Edberg shook his head, and his frown deepened. "No." He looked from Smoke to me. "I'd say consider yourself warned."

It felt like little crawly things were walking around on my skin. I pulled at my shirt and the protective vest beneath it to ease the sensation.

Edberg nodded a goodbye, climbed in his squad car, and drove away.

Rex nudged my leg with his nose. I reached down, took the ball he was holding from his mouth, and tossed it toward the lake. "Smoke, what do think about all that?"

"Another unsettling conversation with one of our own. Everything Edberg said lines up with Armstrong's story pretty well."

"The way he said 'consider yourself warned' almost sounded like he was the one delivering the warning."

"I think he was just being emphatic because of what he's been through himself. I doubt he'd tell us things like what he keeps on his computer if that was the case. The sheriff is going to have a heart attack before all this is over, I'm afraid."

Rex was back with the ball, panting in front of me. I threw it as far as I could.

"I met with Nichole Jaspers today."

"Yeah, how'd that go?"

I hit all the highlights, or lowlights, of the lives she and Collin had endured and shared. "Then after we walked through the squad room, she told me someone in there was 'saturated with demonic influence.'"

"Someone, or some*thing*, in the room?"

"She said some*one*. Remember when we were talking to Dr. Fischer and she was telling us about that session with one of her clients who asked her if she could hear the angels of darkness screaming?"

Smoke nodded. "Kinda hard to forget."

"Dr. Fischer said the woman was sensitive to the spirit world. She has spiritual discernment."

Smoke kept nodding.

"When Nichole said that, I wondered if she was the client Dr. Fischer was talking about. The one with spiritual discernment. I mean, Nichole was truly upset, very convinced about what she was saying."

"Lots of things we don't understand. So who was in the squad room?"

"Edberg, Stauder, and Brooks."

Smoke bent over and picked up the ball Rex had dropped at his feet. "Brooks has been around over twenty years. Same with Edberg, of course." He tossed the ball. I watched Rex make his mad dash to catch it.

"Brooks is about the quietest deputy in the department. He comes to things and just kind of hangs around in the background. A real wallflower. I saw him with Zubinski at the party for a while, but that's about it. I'm not even sure when he left that night."

Smoke turned to me. "You can learn a lot if you're the one listening, not the one talking. Back to that warning Edberg talked about. If your car got keyed by the same guys who have had Armstrong and Edberg toeing their lines all these years, we need to take that seriously."

"I know, and I am very security-minded, Smoke."

"But that didn't prevent you from being attacked and abducted last fall. Things happen, no matter how careful you are."

The smells, sounds, and terror of waking up in the trunk of a moving vehicle with a splitting headache rushed through my mind.

"I'm much more cautious now. I carry my freeze-plus-three spray and my off-duty Smith and Wesson."

Smoke smiled. "That is a sweet little gun."

"I wear shorts or pants with a pocket for the spray. And a loose-fitting shirt to cover the holster."

"In a couple of weeks you'll have your dog companion. She'll help watch out for you."

I tapped my temple. "I have to remember to tell Rebecca about Queenie. She'll be so excited. Maybe it'll help distract her from thinking about her grandma's death so much."

"You're still planning a little memorial service?"

"Yeah, I have to get back to Jean on that. It'll probably be Sunday—my day off—so I don't have to rush off to work after the service."

"You gonna tell Rebecca about her great-grandma before the service, or sometime down the road instead?"

I shrugged. "Since there are only two sane people in the world who loved Alvie Eisner, it would be nice to have them both there."

"Not counting her brother Henry?"

"I said sane. Jean says Henry's off in his own world most of the time. But there might be some recognition of her name. I don't know."

We played fetch with Rex, alternating who threw the ball, for a few more minutes.

I rubbed my hands together, brushing off some dirt. "Back to the evil Nichole sensed in the squad room. We started talking about Brooks. What do you think?"

"Still waters run deep? Like his name, with an S at the end?" Smoke lifted his shoulders and shook his head. "If you had told me two weeks ago we had some kind of a satanic infiltrator in our sheriff's department, I would have said you're crackers, and here we are. I'll move Brooks to the top of my list to investigate. He was backgrounded a lot of years ago. Could have gone bad somewhere along the way since then."

"Winnebago County, Six oh eight." Communications calling.

"Go ahead."

"There is a Nine-twenty at Location One, Oak Lea."

It was the code for a silent alarm at the State Bank in downtown Oak Lea.

"Copy and en route."

"Hope it's a false trip," Smoke called as I hopped in my squad car. I was on the main road less than a minute later, speeding toward town, lights flashing and sirens blaring.

Robin called for a second deputy. Mandy Zubinski responded that she was a few blocks away. Closer than I was. I turned my sirens off a mile or so from the bank. When I got to the location, I pulled around to the side where there were no windows. Mandy was waiting.

I depressed my radio button. "Six oh eight, Winnebago County?"

"Go ahead, Six oh eight."

"Seven twenty-eight and Six oh eight at location and going in."

"Ten-four."

I signaled Mandy to get down as we crept to the front windows. She stayed on the west side, and I crawled to the east side and stood with my side against the building. Mandy stood and did the same. I leaned my head forward just enough to see inside. A middle-aged Asian man was pushing a vacuum across the carpet.

"Six oh eight, Winnebago County."

"Go ahead."

"Code Four. Accidental trip."

"Copy Code Four, at eighteen twenty-three."

I removed the flashlight from its holder on my belt and used it to rap on the window. After the third tap, the male cleaner stopped vacuuming and looked toward the sound. His eyebrows shot up and his body jerked in surprise. I pointed in the direction of the door. He nodded, shut off the vacuum, and headed to the entrance. Mandy and I met him there.

He pushed open the door. "Hello?"

"It appears you tripped the alarm."

"Oh, man. Sorry, man. I guess I forgot to disarm it when I got here. Sorry to make you come here for that." He walked to the alarm panel and punched in a series of numbers.

"It happens," I assured him.

"Part of the job," Mandy said. "We're glad it wasn't a break-in."

He gave his name, address, and date of birth for my log entry. I jotted the information on my memo pad.

"We'll do a routine walk-through and let you get back to work."

"Thanks."

Mandy and I checked the few offices and walked behind the tellers' counter. The vault door was closed and locked. We called goodbye to the cleaning man, then headed out to our squad cars. "You haven't gone on break yet. Want to grab some supper?" I asked.

She hesitated a second too long. "Um, I was going to meet up with a couple of the guys at Perkins. You want to join us?"

I looked at my watch while I thought of an excuse. "You know, thanks, but I got leftovers from the party I should eat up. I just thought if you didn't have plans—"

Her mouth puckered. "Now I feel bad."

"Don't. Really. I'm just going to grab something quick. I have a few things to catch up on." I reached for my door handle.

"Corky, I wanted to tell you I had a lot of fun at the party the other night. Thanks."

"Sure. I'm glad you enjoyed it."

"We don't see each other much off-duty."

"Don't forget, we have another opportunity at the team-building event on Saturday."

She groaned. "We're all really looking forward to that."

Mandy left and I stayed to type the call information into my squad car's laptop.

I heard Mandy Zubinski, Fred Brooks, and Devin Stauder announce they were going on break at Perkins within minutes of each other. I drove by the restaurant on the way home and glanced at the three squad cars in the parking lot. According to office chit chat, none of the three had any real friends in the department, ones they socialized with outside of work.

Mandy tried too hard to fit in and gossiped too much.

Brooks was quiet, but not unfriendly. He rarely spoke unless he was spoken to.

Stauder was a bit of a braggart. He had the latest and the greatest of whatever was in vogue. His wife had a good job, and it seemed he had plenty of money to spend. A lot of deputies were turned off by his frequent boasting and avoided him.

They struck me as an odd trio to be friends. On the other hand, I hoped they were.

30

The Coven

Roman had a few minutes before his next scheduled patient. He scanned the chart to review the patient's history. His mind wandered, and he glanced at the calendar. April nineteenth. In four days he'd have their victim secured for Saint Mark's Eve. He had convinced himself, time and again over the years that it was for their own good. Dying was better than living as a hopeless, homeless drunk or addict on the streets. It wasn't dignified. And it made the world a better place. That's what they told him. That's what he repeated to himself, over and over until he almost believed it.

It was far better than the baby and children sacrifices. They were the most difficult. Administering drugs that forced young women to go into labor and delivering babies who were used in the ensuing rituals got harder with each passing year.

Roman didn't know what had happened to him. He was suffering doubts, serious doubts. He questioned the practices and rituals he'd been involved with all of his life. He had been coached from early on that he would pursue medicine as a profession. He owed his life, his intelligence, and his success to Satan.

The coven was his family.

He bent down on his knees, intent on calling to Satan for guidance. No words would come. That's when he heard them screaming. They were not pleased. But he would appease the dark spirits when he found a sacrificial offering.

31

I woke up Monday morning less than thrilled with life in general. That often happened when I felt overwhelmed. Gregory Trippen's frantic phone call ten days before had opened four separate investigations for the sheriff's department. A search to find and save his brother, a cold case shooting death, uncovering the mole in the sheriff's department responsible for stealing reports and delivering death threats, and working on charges against Dr. Royce Sparrow, and the others, for abusing the Trippen brothers.

Four separate cases, all related to satanic-cult activities and the cover-up of a murder committed by its members.

The good news: there was no statute of limitations on murder.

The bad news: there was a statute of limitations on abuse.

In Minnesota, victims had only six years to bring their claims of personal injury caused by sexual abuse before the court. If a claimant was victimized as a minor, he or she needed to file a suit before his or her twenty-fifth birthday. In cases of repressed memory, the Minnesota "disability extension" applied. With Dr. Fischer's help, perhaps we could file a suit on Jeffrey Trippen's behalf.

Sheriff Twardy had sent Alden Armstrong and his family away. Would he do the same with Edberg when he learned Edberg had received similar threats? How would we find and flush out the bad cop? Nothing had turned up in the investigations to that point. We had to consider it might not be an officer. What other personnel had been with department for twenty years? I thought of two in the secretarial pool off the top of my head. There might be more.

I was frustrated—more than frustrated. Jeffrey Trippen was out there somewhere, eluding every law enforcement department in the state of Minnesota. I searched for him when I drove the county roads, on-duty or off-duty. I waited for a phone or radio call announcing that he had been spotted. If he was biding his time until April thirtieth in a city like Minneapolis, he would blend in with others like him who wandered the city streets. I assured myself, time and again, that we would find him.

Gregory Trippen had taken the week to manage his trucking business and planned to arrive back in Winnebago County on April twenty-sixth with reports and journal pages in hand. In addition to his internal investigation of Winnebago County deputies, Smoke had sunk his teeth into the Sparrow case, disregarding his growing backlog of criminal cases. He was anxiously awaiting the arrival of Sparrow's journal and the shooting-death reports.

I stared at the ceiling another minute, then climbed out of bed. My work cell rang. Local number, caller unavailable. I'd seen the number before, but couldn't place it.

"Sergeant Aleckson."

"Hi, it's Marcella Fischer. Are you in the middle of something?"

"No, not at all." I plopped back down on my bed.

"I'm touching base with you about Nichole Jaspers. I have to tell you how pleased I am about your meeting with her yesterday. Nichole told me about it and said it would be okay to call you. It is amazing progress, given her general distrust of police officers."

"She has quite the life story, which does not begin to describe it, of course."

"Yes, well, I hope it gave you a better idea of what these victims have been through."

"Oh, man. She's been through similar trauma, some of the same things as the two brothers in the case I'm working on."

"I've treated people from all over, and their stories are eerily similar. You can't make those things up."

"No. In my wildest imagination I'd never think of anything close to that. And what can we do to find these people who are committing these heinous acts? How can we stop them?"

"Whatever we can, but we may have to wait for the final battle."

"The final battle?"

"When Satan is bound for a thousand years, then cast down forever."

"Oh." *That final battle.*

"How are things going in your search for that young man?" she said.

I stood up and pulled my sheets and comforter over the bed. "I didn't think it would take this long to find him, but we think he's planning the event for April thirtieth."

"Walpurgisnacht."

"I guess you'd know that." I wandered to where my clothes were heaped in a pile and started picking them up.

"Major night for rituals."

"And it happens to be Jeffrey's birthday."

"Ah. I can see why he'd choose that. I understand one's birthday is the most important date for rituals. It must be a bonus if it falls on one of the more important satanic holidays of the year. Jeffrey's most likely convinced himself he will be freed of his suffering by pleasing Satan in that manner."

"That is so warped." I tossed my clothes on the bed.

"Yes it is. Have you given any consideration to talking to Pastor Daniel Trondholm? He's had vast experience with victims of cults and covens. Spiritual warfare."

"I was thinking of giving him a call. I've done some research online, but I would like to hear it firsthand from someone else who has experience and expertise in that area."

"I'd recommend it."

"Thanks, Dr. Fischer."

"You're welcome. And don't forget to call me when you find Jeffrey. I'd be more than happy to help in any way I can."

"Will do. Thanks again."

Sheriff Twardy phoned an hour later. I was sitting in the living room staring out the window. "How are you coming with that list of party guests?"

"I got it done. It's in my briefcase, and I gave a copy to Holman for his supplemental, but I forgot to leave a copy in your box last night."

"Just drop it by when you report for work today. I'm turning that part of the investigation over to the chief deputy, so he'll make the contacts and do the questioning. It'll be a while yet before we have results on the fingerprints."

"I wish we knew if it's related to the cases we're working on. If it is, it's important. If not, we could put it on hold."

"That's true. Dawes said the two of you talked to Edberg. What he had to say was another shock. I'm going to meet with him this afternoon and decide what to do. I'd like to know what in the Sam Hill happened. I've been in charge of this department all these years, and not once did Armstrong or Edberg come to me. Doesn't the sheriff deserve to know when there's corruption in his own department?" His voice grew louder with each sentence.

"Yes, but—"

"Is this the tip of the iceberg?"

"What do you mean?"

"We know about Armstrong and Edberg because of their connection to the Manthes case. Are there other cases? Other threats? Other cover-ups?"

It was possible, but we had to stay focused. "With all the aspects of the Manthes case we're uncovering, I think I'd concentrate on that before worrying if there are others. Now that we're looking for the dirty cop in our department, we're bound to find him. Hopefully soon."

"You're wise for being so young, you know that?"

I felt much older than I had one short week before.

"Sheriff, Armstrong left on vacation. What about Edberg? Same deal?"

"Should be, but Edberg's kind of a stubborn old coot. He may not fly away as easily as Armstrong did."

I went on a long run, but it didn't chase away my racing thoughts. There were many levels and facets to the cult investigation, and the implications were frightening. There was a dark dimension in our midst, invading our county's primary law enforcement department, and we needed to identify it. Stop it. The sheriff had good reasons for his grave concerns. We all did.

Sheriff Twardy had brought up valid considerations. Were there other cult-related cases? Other personnel in the sheriff's department who had bowed to personal threats and enabled more cover-ups?

I mentally reviewed the discussions I'd had with the victims, professionals, and officers, including Gregory Trippen, Dr. Marcella Fischer, Nichole Jaspers, Alden Armstrong, Bob Edberg, Smoke, and Sheriff Twardy.

Bob Edberg had indicated my damaged car was meant as a warning. If so, whoever had done it had given me more credit for connecting the dots than I deserved. Acts of vandalism were committed by a wide range of people, with any number of motives. It could be an act of revenge, or it could be an emotional display.

I thought of one man I had arrested. He was mad at his girlfriend for breaking up with him and had cut the arms off two of her coats. One was a sable fur. Very expensive. It was possible someone I had arrested had keyed my car out of revenge. Or was it done as a warning?

I dropped by the sheriff's office before the start of my shift, and he waved me in. "Close the door."

I did, then handed him the list of party guests and sat down in a chair. "More questions about my mother's birthday gift?" I kidded.

The sheriff snickered softly. "Thanks. I needed a little comic relief. You talk to Dawes today?"

"No."

"I called Edberg to come in shortly after I talked to you this morning. He was relieved I knew about the whole ordeal and offered to do everything he could to help clean house here. Expose those you-know-whats for every bad deed we can uncover. Edberg had no interest in taking his mother away, but he'll probably move her to a friend's house until we get to the bottom of this."

"That'll give him some peace of mind."

"The other thing you should know. I unofficially assigned Edberg to investigations. Dawes is very efficient, but he needs help."

"That's a good idea, Sheriff. Edberg seems motivated to find whoever was behind all those years of threats."

"He's a damn good detective. I've tried to talk him into taking a position in investigations for years, but he would never go for it. He likes being a patrol deputy."

"I'm willing to put in more hours, help with whatever," I said.

Twardy nodded. "It takes so much time when you want answers yesterday. Dawes is concentrating on the three hunters, mostly Sparrow, for now. Their personal friends. Professional contacts. Bank records. Holdings. You name it. Basic background, which takes a hell of a long time.

"There are men and women in this department I know with certainty are not the Benedict Arnold. Kenner is one, Captain Randolph is another. Edberg is going to work with them, figure out a game plan to catch that bastard."

"Good."

"I still can't understand how two—not one but two—of our sworn officers told no one, not one person in the department, what was happening."

"I know. I've thought about that a lot. We put ourselves in personal danger. It's part of the job. But if someone threatens the life of your loved one and you're convinced they will do what they've threatened if you don't follow their instructions, that's a different story. Both Armstrong and Edberg said they thought they'd figure out who it was, but they never did."

"Yeah, I guess we can't say for sure what we'd do unless we were in the same boat. Officers have a strong need to protect others. That's part of the deal. I'd have maybe done the same, if I think of it that way. I want to say I wouldn't, but I don't know."

I nodded.

I stopped by Smoke's desk to check on his progress.

"I may have to take a trip to Germany, darn it," he said.

"Meaning?"

"Dieter Munden, the pharmacist. Born and raised in Germany. Came to the U.S. for college and stayed. Got his citizenship fifteen years ago. Attended the University of Wisconsin in Madison. Went to work in the drugstore in Wellspring after graduation then bought it three years later. I talked to the former owner. He said Dieter paid cash, which tells me his family has money or he has friends in high places. Or Sparrow paid him big bucks for the hunting episode."

"Gregory Trippen and Nichole Jaspers both said they were given drugs. A pharmacist would come in handy."

"Very. No complaints against Munden are registered with the Board of Pharmacy. But in the past, drug traceability ended at the manufacturing process. Now regulations require a certified chain-of-custody to improve security and prevent counterfeiting, which had been a huge problem. But if you're unlawful and smart, there are creative ways around regulations."

"Really?" I quipped.

"I've done some very informal interviews, so people I've talked to don't know who I am or that I'm conducting an investigation, or that I'm doing anything other than making general conversation. I found out Munden belongs to the Lions and the Presbyterian Church."

Smoke thought for a second. "This is interesting. He had a wife who died in childbirth, apparently on the way to the hospital. She was home alone and called an ambulance. Don't know where Munden was. No other kids and he didn't remarry." He referred to his notes as he talked.

"Wow. That's a little suspicious."

"Lives in a nice house, not extravagant. I'm close to accessing bank records, but that's a little trickier." He flipped another page in his notebook. "And I paid a visit directly to Cyril Bishop of the Wellspring Mortuary and Cremation Services."

That surprised me. "You did?"

"I may not have used my real name, or the official purpose of my visit."

I smiled. "You were not there as a Winnebago County detective. And you're sure he didn't recognize you? You've never had any calls there as a deputy, or as a detective?"

He nodded. "I responded to a call there a number of years ago when family members actually came to blows over their mother's funeral arrangements. But no, he didn't recognize me. I may have looked different this time, changed my appearance some." Smoke raised his eyebrows up and down several times, and I smiled again.

"I went in for some pre-planning of my funeral and was able to weasel a little info out of him. He inherited the business from his uncle. Uncle had no sons or daughters to leave it to. It's been in the family for three generations. He's married, has a son who will be joining him in the business when he finishes college. Belongs to the non-denominational church out there."

"How did you get him to talk about his family?"

"It's amazing what a guy will tell a lonely older man when he wants to make a sale. Then I went to the local café and chatted with some folks. Word is no one knows much about Bishop personally. He's friendly out in public, but it appears his family members are his only real friends, as far as they could tell. Has one assistant who is on call to pick up bodies when Bishop is away. I'd like to talk to him, but he has another job, and we haven't connected yet."

"So how did Bishop strike you?"

"Like he isn't the same underneath as he is on the surface. Superficial, but in a much darker way. And I don't think it's from all the embalming fluid he's inhaled over the years."

"The crematorium is connected to the mortuary?" I said.

"Yep. Both Armstrong and Edberg did some version of checking them out twenty years ago, and probably since, but came up with nothing. The sheriff mentioned hiring a private eye, if need be, and it may come to that. I'd like to put twenty-four-hour surveillance on these yahoos."

"Anything on Sparrow yet?"

"Not much. I talked to some people at the Little Mountain Hospital. There again, just casual conversation so as not to arouse suspicion. I'll head up to Saint Cloud tomorrow, see what I come up with."

"Gregory Trippen will be back next week. His paperwork should help."

"I am praying for names and dates and specific criminal acts, so we can nail them good."

"Me too. You're making fine progress. You've gotten a lot in a few days."

32

The Coven

Roman pulled his car over to the curb beside a parking meter in the last available spot, two blocks from the Harbor Shelter in downtown Minneapolis. He hurried out of his car to the curb and dropped some coins in the meter. Roman was dressed in jeans and a navy sweatshirt. Nothing to call attention to his appearance. He walked at a near-jogging pace to the shelter, signed in, and went back outside to wait for the van. It was six minutes before eight p.m. He had a two-hour shift, from eight to ten p.m.

Seven minutes later, a blue van with bold white letters spelling out HARBOR SHELTER stopped a few feet from where he stood. A tall, chubby black man climbed out of the driver's seat and waved at him. "Hey, Doc, good to see you. Can you give me a hand?"

"Hi, Pete. Busy night?"

"Oh yeah, nicer weather gets 'em out of their winter hiding places. Talked two into coming with me to sleep it off in a nice bed."

Roman walked over and opened the side door. Strong, mingled odors of different alcoholic beverages escaped the van then drifted into the evening air. He offered his arm to an older white man with gray hair and whiskers. The man's head bounced slightly as he grabbed Roman's arm for support and tried to find his balance.

"There you go, sir. Nice and steady." When the man was on the ground, Roman walked with him into the shelter. A couple of volunteers stepped forward and took over. When he turned around, he saw Pete was holding onto an American Indian.

Within minutes the drunks were safely delivered inside, and Roman began his tour of duty. At nine o'clock, he added more coins to the meter his car was parked by to avoid a ticket. He stopped at various places, finding an occasional intoxicated man or woman who was willing to go with him. By nine thirty he'd made three trips back to the shelter with people.

At nine forty he found him: a thin, bearded man in his thirties who strongly resembled Jeffrey Trippen from the printout Noris had given him. He was wearing blue jeans and a black tee shirt stamped with a logo that was no longer readable. No jacket to keep him warm on the chilly evening.

The young man was completely wasted.

"Hey, dude, what are you on tonight?" Roman moved in for a closer look. Constricted pupils, watery eyes, droopy eyelids. Roman touched the man's arm, and his skin felt clammy.

The man focused on Roman as best he could, wondering if he knew him. "Found me some smack."

Heroin. Perfect. Putty in his hands.

Roman needed assurance the man wasn't carrying a weapon and gently patted his back, then around his waist and pocket area. The man didn't seem to notice. No weapon and no wallet.

"So where's your backpack? Your ID?"

His words were slurred. "Sold my ID awhile back. Traded my backpack and stuff for the smack."

"Nothing of value, I hope."

"Yeah, but I can't tell you. Secret." It came out she-cret.

"Where do you live? Can I give you a ride back to your family?"

He grunted. "My family gave up on me a long time ago. I live everywhere, and nowhere."

"It's okay, we'll see what I can do to help you. I got some smack of my own, enough to share if you want."

"No shit. Whadda I gotta do?"

"Not a thing. I'm rich and I like to share my wealth."

"Serious, man?"

"Yeah, we'll drive this van to my car, and you can wait for me there."

"Iz a deal."

Roman helped him into the van and drove to an alley half a block from his car. There was no one hanging out there, so Roman parked, got himself and the other man out, then assisted him to the sidewalk at the edge of the building.

"Okay, you wait for me in my car. Can you do that?"

"Yeah."

He pointed. "Walk to the blue car there. I'll open the lock and you climb into the back seat. You lie down there and rest for a few minutes."

"Okay." He seemed to understand and managed to get to Roman's vehicle without falling. Roman hit the keyless-entry button. The man struggled with the handle and finally got it open. He climbed in the back seat, closed the door, and disappeared.

Roman smiled. He was easier than most. He usually had to repeat instructions several times to an impaired person. He was still standing in back of the van when a couple, a man and a woman both badly in need of showers, walked down the sidewalk toward him. He willed himself to be calm, smiled, and said, "Good evening."

They glanced his direction, but didn't respond. When they passed, Roman hopped in the van and drove back to the shelter. He signed out and handed the keys to Mac and Cindy, a husband and wife team who often volunteered.

Roman jogged to his car and climbed in. Calming relief washed over him when he looked over his shoulder at the young man passed out on the back seat. He pushed the trunk release button, got out, and retrieved his medical bag from the trunk. He slid back behind the wheel and laid the bag on the front passenger seat. A syringe loaded with a sedative was in the bag, if needed.

The young man slept through the entire forty-five mile drive to Wellspring. The closer they got, the more uneasy Roman felt. Usually it was the other way around. Were all the years of securing sacrificial offerings catching up with him? Something was wrong.

The young man stirred when they pulled into Dieter Munden's driveway and stopped. "Huh?" he said, making an effort to sit up.

"Let's go inside the house where it's warm." Roman climbed out and opened the back car door. The young man latched onto Roman's arm and got out. Roman assisted him to the door, where Dieter greeted them.

"Come in."

They went in and walked directly to the door leading to the lower level. The two older men held on, preventing the younger one from falling down the steps. Dieter had the basement room prepared.

"Heroin?" Dieter asked.

Roman nodded.

"His name?"

"I didn't ask, and he said he sold his ID card."

The young man lifted his heavy eyelids as best he could. "Talkin' about me?"

"Yes, son," Roman said.

"Lost my home, lost my family, lost my name. They call me Blue."

"Okay, Blue. Let's get you cleaned up."

"Where's the smack?"

"First you take a shower and change into clean clothes," Roman said.

Blue was nearly sober when they finished scrubbing him with soap and a shower brush. Roman toweled him dry then Dieter slid a white gown over his head.

"What's this?" Blue asked.

"Something comfortable," Roman said as Dieter stuck a short needle in the side of Blue's neck and pushed the syringe plunger with his thumb, emptying the contents in seconds.

They grabbed onto Blue as he collapsed and laid him on the specially-equipped table. They secured restraints around his waist, hands, and ankles. There was no reason to tape his mouth shut. No one would hear him. In twenty-four hours, he would be freed from his life on the streets forever.

33

The small Winnebago County Courthouse conference room was filled to near capacity with deputies, corrections and communications officers, office personnel from the sheriff's department, county attorneys, and probation officers. The other sheriff's employees, attorneys, and probation officers had either gone through the adventure in the two days prior or were scheduled for the afternoon session. Those who had gone through the course were sworn to secrecy about it.

I noticed Smoke and Chief Deputy Mike Kenner standing in the front of the room when I walked in. Smoke blinked his eyes twice to acknowledge me. I scanned the sea of people and spotted Mandy Zubinski, one of my team members, sitting in a middle row. I took the empty chair to her left.

"Hey," she offered.

"Hey," I returned. "Good-sized crowd, lots of teams."

"Yeah."

Most of the people were in jeans and hooded sweatshirts. A few wore sweatpants. A number had on hiking boots, and the rest were in athletic shoes. Two things distinguished the deputies from the civilians: a sidearm and a badge, either attached to a belt or hanging from a neck chain. A day off from Kevlar vests, at least.

The chief deputy drew his hands together in a loud clap. "All right! If I can have everyone's attention, we'll get started." It took a minute for the din to die. "You all know your team assignments. Is there anyone missing?"

I looked around and located Vince Weber in the back row to my left. He nodded at me. Donny Nickles was sitting in the second row, and assistant county attorney Stueman was standing against the back wall to my right. My friend Sara Speiss was next to him.

Sara caught my glance, smiled, and lifted her eyebrows in a way that said, "I wonder what this exercise will be like?"

I smiled back and caught Stueman staring at me in a near scowl. *I'm so glad he's on my team.*

"Okay, team up and we'll hand out your instructions. But do *not* open them until we say so."

Mild pandemonium swept through the room as people rose from their seats, waved, and gathered their teams into one area or the next. The space around Weber cleared, so he stood and motioned the rest of us to join him in his corner.

Smoke and Kenner passed out sealed packets to each team as they assembled. When Smoke handed one to me he said, "No peeking." I rolled my eyes then looked at the thick, sealed envelope. I held it up so the others could get a glimpse.

The chief deputy clapped his hands together again. "Listen up. We have ten teams, the largest group scheduled. Two of the teams had to switch to this time slot due to unforeseen conflicts, so we did a little last minute scrambling to add a couple of courses. If there are any glitches, I apologize ahead of time. If you run into any real snags, call me on my cell phone. But with your training, that shouldn't be necessary. You've had to figure your way out of things a time or two."

I felt Mandy's eyes on me and chose not to return the look.

"All right, then. I'll turn this over to Nathan Gillette from our human resources department to fill you in on the details of the exercise."

"Thank you, Chief Deputy Kenner." Gillette's mustache covered his entire top lip and curled around at the sides, touching his bottom lip. "We researched a number of team-building activities and found one we hope you'll think is worthwhile and fun at the same time. You have high-stress jobs dealing with crimes, criminals, victims, and legal proceedings. Your various departments interact on a regular basis, so we determined that it's important to open the lines of communication, build bonds, increase trust. Our hope is this will lead to higher performance and an increase in morale."

I heard a few quiet groans. Many, if not most of the deputies, were not touchy-feely types.

Gillette went on, "It can be easy to point fingers at others when things don't go the way we think they should, either during an arrest, or in court proceedings, or with probation. We want to move away from that. Hopefully, by getting to know each other better and working together on this exercise, you'll feel comfortable talking to a person in another department if you have an issue with something they have done professionally."

More hushed groans.

"Every team has their assignment in the packets. I'll give a rundown of what we're doing. You will ride together in a squad car to an appointed spot. Then, using the set of directions and a compass, you'll navigate on foot to your destination. Once there, you will each write a haiku."

I have no idea how I contained my laughter when others couldn't.

"A high what?" someone asked.

"A haiku." Gillette was matter-of-fact, like it was something we all did on a regular basis.

"What is *that*?" another asked. Apparently he had missed high school English class that day.

"It's a short poem about everyday things. The details are in your packets."

"You have got to be kidding me!" Weber's voice was low and emphatic.

"There is no way," I heard Carlson complain from a nearby group.

I shot Smoke an "I don't want to do this" look, and he shot me a "who does?" one back.

"Any questions?" I guessed everyone was too shocked for words, because no one spoke. "Okay then. Each driver has been contacted ahead of time. Follow him or her to the cars. Open your packets when you are all in your vehicle."

I looked at Weber and Zubinski.

"Yeah, it's me," Weber said. "Come on, team."

We trampled off to the parking lot. "Sergeant, where do you want everyone to sit?" Weber asked.

Donny's legs were the longest. "Weber, for this exercise we're a team and each of us has equal status, but I'd say Donny should take the front passenger seat so he doesn't have to sit completely sideways." I handed Donny the instruction packet.

"The back seats of squad cars are not exactly roomy," Zubinski said to Nickles and Stueman.

Weber unlocked the doors, and we piled in. I ended up sandwiched between Zubinski and Stueman. Weber pushed shut the driver's side back door, and Donny closed the passenger side door, then the two of them jumped in the front.

"You sure have a lot of bells and whistles in your squad cars," Donny admired.

"We all know each other, right?" I asked, and everyone nodded or said "yeah."

"Your weapon's poking into my ribs," Stueman said.

"Sorry." I wedged my knees up and shifted them to my right, turning my body toward Stueman to move my Glock and holster away. "Is that better?"

His hazel eyes met and held mine. He cleared his throat and nodded. "I've heard officers describe taking prisoners into custody as 'cuffed and stuffed.' Now I know what they mean. Literally stuffed. Between the small space, no door handles, and the cage between the front seat and the back seat, a person might feel a little claustrophobic."

I was amazed by what I interpreted as his attempt at humor and cracked a half-smile.

"Breathe in slowly through your nose and out through your mouth," Weber said.

Stueman opened his mouth to answer, but didn't.

"Forget about seat belts," Zubinski complained.

"You know we can't do that. We gotta use them," I said.

"Yeah, our luck, we get involved in a crash and it's all over the news my passengers weren't wearing seat belts."

"Because that would be more important than what happens to us." Zubinski's tone was sarcastic.

"Zubinski," Weber shot back. "Come to think of it, it might be easier to explain that to the news media than how the taxpayers are footing the bill for all of us to get together to write a dumb poem."

"Probably less painful for us, too," Mandy said. She snapped her buckles together.

"Donny, why don't you read our assignment while we buckle up." I reached down to locate my belt, but couldn't find it. "Mine is stuck between the seats, I think."

"Slide forward a little. I'll dig for it," Stueman suggested, and I moved a little closer to him. He was pulling his right shoulder strap down. As I settled back to locate my belt, I felt Stueman's left hand on my bottom.

"S-sorry," he stammered. "I didn't mean—"

"Forget it."

"H-here's your belt." Stueman wrenched it free and handed it over.

"Thanks." *Let me wake up from this bad dream, and soon,* I silently pleaded as I buckled in.

Donny ripped open the packet. "Okay, here are the instructions. 'Drive to Lynden Township to the farm access road located between fire numbers ninety-two forty three and ninety-two forty-five Pequot Avenue Northwest—"

"That's a ways out there," Weber interrupted.

"On the way, each of you is to share something about yourselves with the others. When you get to your first destination, park the car and hike to the second appointed destination, closely following the directions. When you get to said location, you are each to write a haiku about your experience."

"Do they say, exactly, what a high, a high—"

"Koo!" Mandy's impatience was evident.

"Gesundheit!" Donny said.

We all laughed, all except Stueman.

"That was really bad, Donny," I said.

"I know. Couldn't help it. All right. It says a haiku is a seventeen-syllable poem in three lines. Five syllables in the first, seven in the second, and five in the third."

"You have got to be kidding me," Weber said for the second time that morning about the exercise.

"There is no way," Mandy said. They agreed on one thing.

"People actually get paid to come up with this stuff?" Weber again.

"And they get smart people to believe this is good team-building," Donny added.

I cut in before any more negatives flew around. "Redirect, everyone. Our first order of business is saying something about ourselves. Then we have a long hike. Then we worry about the poem. Weber, you want to start?"

"Sure. Hello, everyone. My name is Vincent Weber, and I am *not* an alcoholic."

"Hello, Vincent," Donny and Mandy mocked together.

"Weber." My tone was like my mother's when she was warning me to shape up.

He bounced his head, first to the right then to the left. "Okay. I grew up in Ely, a little town up north. Got my associates' from Saint Cloud State, did my skills at Alexandria, been with Winnebago County for eight years. I married my high school sweetheart. We went to Saint Cloud together. She died in a car crash a year later." He paused a second, then quietly added, "A big part of me went with her."

Zubinski and I exchanged shocked expressions. I had worked with Weber for years and didn't know that significant piece of his past. Apparently, Mandy didn't either. She reached her hand up and splayed her fingers against the cage behind Weber's back.

Our uttered sympathies mixed with Donny's. "Sorry to hear that, Vince."

"Yeah. Next." Weber's voice cracked.

It took a moment.

Then Nickles went. "My legal name is Donny, not Donald. People have a hard time believing that. I do not carry my birth certificate around to prove it, however. I thought about being a cop through my teen years, but when I got to college I changed to probation. I like doing the presentence investigations, going to court, giving my recommendations to the judge, following the lives of my clients. I feel good when my guys and gals decide to follow the straight and narrow, and bad when they don't. I'm from Wisconsin—yeah, don't say it—married, two daughters. Been here three years."

Mandy shifted and took the next turn. "I'm from Saint Paul originally. I went to college at Metro, did my skills there too. Started my career with Ottertail County and was there a few years. I wanted to get closer to the Twin Cities and family, so I was happy when Winnebago hired me, going on three years ago. Not married. I have an older sister I hang out with when I can, but she is busy with her three kids. All of whom I adore, by the way."

Mandy listed her sister as her friend. Her only real friend?

I went next, sensing Stueman didn't want to go at all. "I was born here in Oak Lea. I have one brother, ten months older than me. My father died before I was born, so my mother was very protective of John Carl and me, to say the least. I was always interested in law enforcement and thankfully have a grandmother—my father's mother—who supported that and helped convince my mother to let me pursue my dream. I've been with Winnebago for seven years and made sergeant last year. Oh, and not married, or anything close."

I had left out a few key things. First, my job had cost me a developing relationship with Nicholas Bradshaw, the Oak Lea Hospital Administrator who had made me choose between him and my career. He had asked me to leave the thing that mingled with the blood flowing through my veins. But I wondered how it might have been, as Nick's wife and his daughter Faith's mother.

Second, my job had brought me to death's door a few times. Twice in the past year. That's what Nick couldn't handle. He was shocked I loved a job that involved personal peril, and I had no logical way of explaining and defending it.

Third, my brother's marriage was crumbling. He lived too far away for my mother's eagle eye to keep a close watch. We had to be content with the brief snippets of information he gave us from time to time.

Fourth, my mother, who had not dated in thirty years, was seeing Winnebago County Sheriff Dennis Twardy, a fact that continually astounded me.

Fifth, I had hoped for years that my mother would get together with Detective Smoke Dawes. Instead, I found myself suddenly, strangely, and strongly attracted to him. He had nipped the near romance in the bud for several reasons he believed were valid, and maybe they were.

All those thoughts raced through my brain in the seconds before Stueman began. "I started here January second. City kid. Edina—"

Rich city kid.

"Edina," Mandy muttered.

"My father is a corporate attorney. Putnam, Stueman, and Rose—"

One of the top law firms in Minneapolis. I hadn't made the name connection. What was he doing as an assistant county attorney in Winnebago County?

"Whoa," Donny admired and turned to glance at Stueman with new eyes.

"The decision for me to become an attorney was made when I was still in the womb. My mother's father is Gerald Putnam, the founder of the firm. To condense a long story: I worked for the firm for two years and was miserable. My interest is in criminal law. My grandfather was the first to cave and gave me his blessings to leave. My father and mother are both in denial that I did. But my older sister is doing her best to fill any void I may have created. Very high achiever. Always has been."

"Sounds like you took a huge pay cut," Vince said.

Stueman shrugged.

"Married, engaged?" Mandy asked.

"Not anymore. The engaged part. I was, to another attorney in the firm. It's over."

Stueman sent out a silent message that it was all he had to say on the matter. Any unasked questions remained that way.

"We're here," Weber said with fake cheerfulness. He pulled off the gravel road onto a raised, flat embankment, designed to give farm equipment access to the fields, and parked.

Stueman unsnapped his buckle and mine, and reached for the door handle that wasn't there.

"Forgot," he admitted.

Weber and Nickles opened the car doors, allowing us to flee our cramped quarters. I slid out Mandy's side, the lesser of two evils.

"We are out in the middle of nowhere," Donny said, looking at acres of pastures and fields. There wasn't a house or building visible from where we stood.

"So where do we go from here?" I asked.

Donny fumbled with the packet then withdrew the instructions. He read, "Hike west to the first gravel road, then south for three quarters of a mile to the sign on the tree. Turn west and hike another half mile to the next sign. Go south a quarter mile to your destination. There will be a sign on the building. Go inside and write your haiku on the provided tablets. When you are all finished, read your poem to the others. And be supportive of one another."

I stifled a giggle. Weber and Zubinski guffawed out loud. Nickles rolled his eyes, and Stueman frowned. What a team.

Attitude adjustment, Corky.

"It's a beautiful day. Sunny, cool. Onward and upward, guys. Who wants to carry the compass?" I said.

Stueman stepped forward. "I will, Sergeant." Donny handed it to him.

"Call me Corky, today at least."

"I can't."

I raised my eyebrows.

"I had a dog named Corky. A Welsh Corgi."

Vince Weber belly laughed, and the other two smiled and waited for my rebuttal. I didn't know what to say except, "A Welsh Corgi named Corky."

Weber roared even louder. Zubinski and Nickles were close. I was ready to wring all three of their necks.

Stueman acted like he didn't hear them. "I'll call you Corinne." His stare turned into a mild frown. "How did Corinne turn into Corky anyway?"

A direct, personal question from Stueman to me. I shrugged and said, "My brother, you know, the one who is ten months older than me," as an explanation. I had never thought much about my nickname, nor had to defend it to anyone before. I felt slightly insulted.

"Maybe you can turn that into a haiku," Weber suggested. He held up one hand, fingers spread. With each word he spoke, he put a finger down. "My Cor-gi's name was Cor-ky. Oops, seven syllables. That would have to be the second line."

Zubinski gave Weber a backhanded swat on his bicep. "Why don't you just shut up, Weber?"

I cut him off before he could answer. "The sooner we get to our destination, the sooner we're done."

"Yay," Mandy said enthusiastically. Not.

We walked west to the gravel road a short distance away, headed south on the gravel road, and turned right at the first checkpoint. The next leg of the trek was rougher on the uneven ground of pastures and fields. After what seemed like more than a half mile, we came to a rutted field road.

I stopped and assessed the area. "This has got to be wrong. We're not far from the Raven River, and we're supposed to be close to a building about now. I don't know of any farms close to here."

"This is a private road. It's not even on the county map," Weber said.

Mandy pointed. "There's something over there."

We walked another twenty yards to a picnic area, surrounded on three sides by a small woods. The grass was mowed, and a long wooden table, six or seven feet long and about four feet wide, sat in the middle. It was unusual looking, with supports that curved from under the thick surface to the base on all four sides. The base was almost as long and as wide as the top. There were three wooden chairs on either side of the table. Six kerosene lamps hung from shepherd's hooks around the outside edge of the clearing, and a bonfire pit was near the western edge.

"That is one weird-looking table," Donny said

Mandy stepped closer. "Donny, you wouldn't have enough leg room, for sure."

Nickles pulled out a chair and sat down. His knees hit the base, and his body was still a couple of feet from the table. "Well, I got long enough arms to reach, but not to be comfortable," he said, then stood up again.

"The river is on the other side of the trees there. Not too far. Read the directions again, Donny," I said.

"Hike south for one mile to the sign on the tree. Turn west and hike another half mile to the next sign. Go south a quarter mile to your destination. There will be a sign on the building."

"We are clearly not in the right spot. If we go any further west, we'll end up in the Raven. I'm sure we've gone further than a half mile, and we haven't come to the other sign," I said.

"Chief Deputy Kenner said they put a couple of these together at the last minute. We must have drawn the short straw. Should we call him?" Donny asked.

Weber, Zubinski, and I all said "No" together.

Donny held his hands up. "Whoa, you guys scared of Kenner?"

Stueman raised his eyebrows. Weber laughed.

I rested my hands on my hips. "The chief deputy said we should be able to figure it out. They might have even done this on purpose, so we work together to find a solution. So team, what are your wishes?"

Zubinski went first. "I say we head back to the last sign and go east instead of west."

"I agree with Mandy here. For once," Weber said.

I sent a silent plea for him to be nice.

"Donny, Eric?" I asked.

Nickles shrugged. "I'll go along with the rest of you."

"I'm open," Stueman added.

"Okay, let's head east."

34

The Coven

Cyril heard voices and moved closer to the clearing. He stayed out of sight behind a thick grove of trees and tried to figure out what that group of people was doing on his private property. It took a minute to realize three of them were armed and wearing badges. His heart picked up its speed. Why were they here?

He noiselessly set the cloth bag he was carrying on the ground, pulled out his cell phone, snapped a few pictures, then turned it off before it rang and alerted them. One of the officers looked familiar. He recognized her as the deputy who had responded to a burglary complaint at his mortuary business a couple of years before.

Aleckson. That was her name. The one they were keeping an eye on.

He listened to their prattle about the table. They didn't appear to be looking for anything in particular, and they weren't in uniform. Undercover? What were the other two doing with them? If they were out there for an official reason, they would all be armed, and they wouldn't be wandering around like a bunch of lost lunatics. He had a few good shots of their faces to show Noris. He should have an explanation of what was going on.

Cyril quietly backed away, deeper into the woods. He had every right to be on his own land, but he did not want to talk to them or answer any questions. The group stayed a few minutes, then took off. Cyril waited a long while. When he was confident they wouldn't return, he went to the temple area. He brought something they needed for the evening's rituals. Dieter, the executor, normally handled that task, but Cyril enjoyed it. It enhanced his mental preparation.

Dieter, Cyril's greatest convert. It was as though he had been born into the coven. He was a natural, gifted Satanist. At his initiation ritual he had recited with certainty, "I swear to give my full allegiance to our Lord Satan and worship him; to strive to undermine the faith of those who practice false religions; and bring them to the true faith, when desirable. I swear to give my mind, body, and soul to further the work of our Lord Satan."

Yes, Dieter was a true success.

Cyril went to the storage unit that was buried in the ground, close to the river. He brushed away the leaves and lifted the trapdoor. No one had disturbed the contents: the gong, woven pentagram, chalice, black candles, matches, and a basin. He looked in the bag at the newly sharpened dagger then set it in the box. He pulled down the lid and covered it with leaves. Everything was there. Everything they needed for the human offering to their Master.

35

Weber locked his hands together in a loud clap. "Miracle of miracles, we actually found it. A barn, no less."

Most of the red paint had peeled off the outer siding. We piled into the old, weathered structure. It was fairly clean. We found hay bales and all sat down for our final project of the exercise—composing seventeen-syllable poems.

The packet was crumpled and worse for the wear after traveling miles clutched in our hot little hands. We had taken turns carrying the precious cargo so Donny wouldn't have the lone responsibility. Zubinski dug into the envelope and extracted five memo pads and five pencils. She handed a set to each of us.

"Anyone here ever written a haiku before?" she asked.

"I have," Stueman admitted in a barely audible voice.

"Why?" Weber looked puzzled.

"I got my BA in English. If it had not been preordained that I pursue law, I would have been an English professor."

Weber tapped his pen on the notepad. "Oh. Huh. So you think you can give us a few pointers here?"

Stueman's eyes moved from point to point in the barn, then fixed on Vince. "Keep it simple. It can be about something in nature, maybe something you noticed on our hike."

"Why don't you write one to give us an idea," Weber said.

"I'm not much of a creative writer."

"Vince, you're putting Mr. Stueman on the spot," I said. As if we were in school and Mr. Stueman was our teacher.

"Eric," he corrected me. "Okay, give me a minute. All of you should give it a try."

Weber drummed his hands on his thighs. "I can't believe we're being held hostage in a barn until we write a dumb poem."

"That's a good point. The sooner we write, the sooner we're free." Donny's face brightened.

We kept silent for five minutes, diligently writing, counting syllables, scratching out some words and writing down others.

"I'm done." Stueman stood and brushed some hay off his behind. "Here goes.

"Sun cutting a path
across fields green once again
Show us the way back."

Mandy lifted her chin. "Not bad at all. Way better than mine, Eric."

"Read it," he encouraged.

She held up her paper. "Don't laugh. Since we're in a barn, it's about a pig. Okay, you can laugh.

"I dig the big pig
The pig grunts and snorts and eats
I dig the big pig."

We all chuckled. "Nothing wrong with that," Donny said.

Weber coughed to get our attention. "I'll go next. I used the barn theme, too.

"Hay, straw, makes me sneeze
Old barns make me almost wheeze
Let me go now, please."

"Yes, let me go with you," Mandy groaned.

"You done, Corky?" Donny asked.

"You go ahead." I picked a piece of straw out of the bale.

Donny sat up straighter. "All right.

"Flow on river flow
from rise of sun to moon's glow
To where does it flow?"

Stueman nodded his approval, and Donny smiled.

"Your turn, Sergeant. Corinne," Stueman said.

I sucked in a breath and twirled the straw between my fingers as I read.

"The thoughtful flower
reflects the sun on its face
Lift your flower face."

I raised my eyebrows and shrugged.

"Isn't that sweet?" Weber said, jutting his lips forward when he talked.

"Very good. Everyone. Original. All of them," Stueman said and stood.

Each of us tucked our notepads and pencils into our pockets, and Donny picked up the packet.

Weber sprinted to the door. "And we're out of here!"

"Yes!" Mandy jumped off her bale and took off after Vince.

The rest of us jogged to catch up with them.

36

The Coven

Cyril left a cryptic message for Noris. It was Noris's day off from work and he had plans, but when the high priest beckoned, he had no choice. He drove to the outdoor temple, following the dirt path next to a newly planted field. In two months, the corn would be as tall as he was. The road ran south for a half mile then veered to the right toward the river.

Noris had seen that look of wrath on Cyril's face many times in his life and reminded himself, once again, that one of his jobs was to calm Cyril or they would all pay.

"Can you tell me what the sheriff's deputies would be doing out here?" Cyril demanded and handed Noris his phone so he could have a look at the photos.

Noris covered the feeling of surprise that immediately gripped him. He knew each one of them, of course. "Those morons. They were on a team-building exercise and obviously didn't know where they were going. Chief Deputy Kenner wouldn't send them on private property without permission."

Their stupidity was their salvation. Well, not everyone's, Noris thought.

Cyril stepped close to him and exhaled an unpleasant combination of onion and garlic near Noris's face. "Is there a reason to move our outdoor temple to a new site?"

"Did any of them act like they were suspicious of anything?"

"As you said, they are morons. One sat down for a minute, and they left soon after that. I moved further away, so I couldn't hear much."

"Then I say no. There is no reason to relocate. This is the best site we've had to date. It looks exactly as we intended. In the very rare event that anyone should happen on it, no one would think it is anything other than a picnic area, plain and simple."

Cyril looked around and smiled. "It does look like a picnic area, doesn't it?"

"Anything else we need for tonight?"

"Things are in order here, and Roman and Dieter are preparing the sacrifice."

"Good. I will be here early to adorn the temple."

37

We hashed over the team-building exercise experience all the way back to the station and agreed on two things. We had worked well as a team, and none of us would ever write another haiku in our lives, unless we were threatened with death or dismemberment if we didn't. Donny added the death and dismemberment clause, just in case.

We pulled into the sheriff's parking lot a little after one thirty. My stomach growled loudly enough for everyone to hear. "I'm going to grab something at The Sandwich Shoppe, if anyone's interested." I didn't care how disheveled I looked.

Donny opened his car door, climbed out, and opened the back door. "Thanks, but the family's waiting for me. We're taking a little trip to the in-laws' house."

Weber jumped out and opened the back driver's side door, leaving his own open. "I got a lot of stuff to take care of."

"Me too, but thanks," Mandy said as she slid out.

"I'll go," Stueman said.

My team spirit disappeared, and I willed it to return. "Um, good." I would eat as fast as possible.

We exchanged hasty goodbyes.

Eric and I took off on foot as the other three took off in their vehicles. Neither of us spoke on the walk to the deli. When we arrived, I reached for the door pull, but Eric stepped around me, opened the door, and held it for me.

"Thanks," I said.

We walked in and read the day's menu. A glance at the selections told me all I needed. The soup choices were chili or corn chowder. Check by the corn chowder. The chicken salad on whole grain bread with lettuce, tomatoes, cucumbers, and Swiss cheese was my favorite. Another check. I pulled a bottle of water out of the beverage cooler and set it on the counter.

I gave my order to the ponytailed teen behind the counter, paid, and stepped aside while Eric did the same.

"The back table okay?" I asked, heading that direction before he answered.

"Sure."

We sat on opposite sides of the table, and Eric resumed his habit of silently staring at me.

I swallowed a bite of sandwich. "Eric, I can't stand it anymore. Have I done something to offend or upset you?"

The puzzled look on his face seemed genuine. "What?"

"We spent the morning crammed into the back seat of a squad car, hiking over fields and pastures, and writing dumb poems. You even accepted a lunch invitation from me, knowing it would be just the two of us."

He dipped his spoon into his soup bowl. "I don't know what you're getting at."

"You don't talk to me, and you stare at me like you're mad at me."

"I didn't realize that. I'm not mad at you, Corinne," he said.

"You can tell me if you don't like me. It's okay."

"But I do like you."

"What is it then?"

"I went to school with *him*. College."

"Him, who?" I said.

"Langley Parker, the one who—"

"I know what he did." The name sent a wave of nausea through me.

Eric searched my face and his eyes squinted. "Sorry. Are you okay to talk about this?"

"I'll let you know. Go ahead. You have me curious."

"He's one reason I'm here, in Winnebago County. You're the other reason."

I opened my mouth to speak, but could not force out one single word. A sound similar to "eh" finally spilled from my throat.

"You dropped your sandwich."

I looked down. My plate was blurry, and I couldn't focus well enough to see it.

"You're wondering why." He sounded like he was talking to me from the next room.

I think I nodded.

Eric picked up my glass and put it to my lips. "Here, take a drink." I managed a sip, and he set the glass down.

"Last summer, when you—Winnebago County—had that case with the dismembered woman they found up by Lake Pearl State Park, I followed it closely in the news. Then when they caught and identified the serial killer, after he attacked you, imagine how shocked I was he was someone I knew. Granted, I didn't know him well, but we had a few classes together."

Langley Parker had sat in classrooms, walked the streets, and raped and tortured and killed and dismembered.

"I'd go over the case in my mind and think of the arguing statements that would put Parker away for life. The victims' faces are etched in my mind. They were gone, like too many victims, and I wanted to be the attorney that mounted solid cases against people who did unthinkable things to others. I had trouble sleeping for a while until I made the decision: I needed to be a prosecutor."

How did I fit into his decision? "You said I'm one reason you're here."

He nodded. "You survived the attack, and then you went back to work. I didn't know you, of course, but I admired you for not letting something so awful stop you from doing the work you loved."

"And you *didn't* talk to me because?"

"You awed me."

That was a first. "I *awed* you?" I took a quick sip of water.

He leaned a little closer. "Don't take this wrong, but I think you are quite beautiful."

There is nothing more embarrassing than blushing when you're trying to look unaffected by someone's words. I took another swig of water, hoping it would cool my burning face and body.

"The first time I saw you was in court during my orientation. I was there observing, and you came in to testify. When they called you to the stand, I was surprised how petite you were. It made me admire you all the more. I wanted to tell you that, but I was always a bumbling idiot around you." Eric smacked the tabletop with the palms of his hands. "All right, I said it. I hope I didn't offend you, Corinne."

"No, um, not at all. Thanks."

Sara would not believe it.

I stopped by Sara's house after lunch, and I was right. She did not believe it.

"Corky, Stueman is not like some stalker dude, I hope." She opened a bag of Oreos and passed it to me.

"Sara, I can always count on you to cheer me up." I took a cookie and handed her the bag.

"That came out wrong."

"Don't try to take it back. I know what you mean. But after I confronted him, he seemed normal for the first time."

"That's encouraging. So how did your team do?" She bit into a cookie and it crunched between her teeth.

"I would rather run seven miles through the woods of Lake Pearl State Park than hike to a barn and write a haiku."

Sara laughed. "I think I would, too. And I don't run. My team was okay, but still, it was a strange, strange day. I'm going to be honest on my evaluation form, but I'm having trouble thinking of a diplomatic way to say, 'It sucked.'"

I reached over for another cookie. "That would be blunt. First our team got lost. Our directions sent us the wrong way, which we figured out when we ended up at a little park by the Raven River and couldn't go any further. So we all trooped back and went the other way. That error took up a good half hour. But the funny part is, we all got along pretty well as the morning went on."

We exchanged details on our adventures, laughing until our sides hurt. I stretched my arms. "Okay, I can't take any more. I am going to take this sweaty body home and soak in a nice lavender-salts bath."

"Hot date?"

"Yeah, trying to decide on Cornwell or Reich."

"Why do you read cop and forensic stuff, anyway?" she said.

"For fun." I took a third and final cookie.

"You should come over here tonight. Casey wants to watch a movie, and you are welcome to join us."

"Sara, I am not going to join you on your date."

"We could invite Eric Stueman to even things out."

"I am *so* out of here."

Smoke phoned after I'd finished bathing. "What did you think of the exercise this morning?" he asked.

I groaned as an answer.

"Yeah, it was painful, all right. And the worst part is the time it took when we got hundreds of hours of work on our open cases. That's the reason I called, to tell you I did a little unplanned surveillance last night."

"Oh?"

"On our mortician and our pharmacist."

"How'd that happen?"

"I was heading home when I heard a coroner call out by Wellspring. I was in the area, so I swung by the funeral home and parked down the block where I still had a view. Bishop himself came for the transport vehicle, headed out, and returned a half hour later. I waited until he left again and followed. He went straight home. So I decided to swing by Munden's house, and something there struck me as odd."

"What?"

"I was maybe two blocks away when the house came into view. There was a car in the driveway and two guys at

Munden's door. Munden opened it, and they went in. It was late, about eleven. I didn't get a good look at either one of the visitors, but I ran the license plate, and the older guy seemed to match the description of the owner. It was Roman Jenkins."

"The doctor Gregory Trippen talked about."

"That's the one. There was something about the other guy that got my attention. He was scruffy looking, long hair, a young hippie. The older guy had his hand on his arm. And when Munden opened the door, he acted like he was expecting them."

Jeffrey Trippen's photo flashed through my mind.

"The younger guy could have been Jenkins' son, I suppose. I waited an hour and nobody left. Since it was after midnight, I headed home. From what I read, midnight is a prime time for satanic rituals. I figured they would have gone to wherever they go before then."

"That's kind of late to be stopping by someone's house. Nichole talked about indoor temples and rituals. Maybe the three of them were having an indoor worship thing."

"Which is not a crime. Friday night, who knows? They could have been at a party and headed to Munden's for a little after party. Munden could have gotten there a minute before they did. Could be for any number of reasons. I know I don't trust Munden as far as I can throw him. He was Sparrow's fellow shooter. He and Bishop. And Jenkins? I saw him going into Munden's house, so now we have proof they're connected."

"And Gregory Trippen saw them at the rituals. They were all members of the coven—at least they were twenty years ago."

"Everything seems like it's out of control. We need to find our dirty cop. We're not even close to being as effective as we should be with only a handful of people in the department knowing the whole story. If there's a satanic cult operating in the county, every deputy should be aware of that. And we don't know if they're still active or not. Like you just said, Gregory Trippen was speaking about experiences from twenty years ago."

"What about the threats Armstrong and Edberg continue to get?" I said.

"May have nothing to do with a cult. The three of them committed murder, and they keep a mole in the department to make sure the case is never reopened so they are never tried."

"You have a point. Neither Armstrong or Edberg thought they were being threatened by Satanists, per se. Gregory knew the men who shot his dad were in the cult, so we all thought the two were connected. Maybe they aren't after all."

"It makes my head spin. My gut tells me they are. We just need the evidence to prove it," he said.

"We'll keep working. Do you want me to keep an eye on either Bishop or Munden tonight?"

"It's your day off. You already had to endure hours of hiking over hill and dale with your best friends, then sitting around writing poetry."

"You have a way of making sitting alone in a vehicle on surveillance sound very appealing," I said.

"I do, at that. But no, we'll see what we can do to pull in some more forces. There are only so many hours in the day, and we need to spend some of them sleeping."

"Very true. After the stressful week, I'm just going to relax tonight. Tomorrow's the service for Alvie Eisner."

"I got it on my calendar, to give Rebecca some support."

"I'm glad. That's one thing I need to do tonight—talk to Jean Brenner and Rebecca, see how the meeting with her great-grandma yesterday went."

"I've been wondering about that myself."

"See you tomorrow." I didn't get into the discussion I had had with Eric Stueman about Langley Parker. Or the other things he'd said.

"Right."

Jean handed the phone to Rebecca.

"Sergeant Corky. I have another grandma."

I could picture the smile on her face. "I heard about that. And you met her?"

"She came over yesterday, and she's really old and really nice."

I laughed silently as I sat on my den office couch and pulled my grandma's afghan over me.

"She's really sad about my grandma dying, and she cried. So I sat close to her and put my head on her chest and cried with her."

Rebecca. She took me from laughter to tears with one touching sentence.

"Sergeant Corky, are you still there?"

"Yes I am, dear." It was my mother's voice, soft, soothing.

"It made me feel better, and I think it made her feel better, too."

"I'm sure it did. When I feel bad, it always helps to share what's bothering me with someone who cares."

"Not everyone goes to Heaven," she said.

"That's true."

"I prayed that my grandma did."

"And we know God hears every prayer."

And answers each one, but not always the way we hope.

"I love you, Sergeant Corky." Another first.

"I love you too, Rebecca. I always have, and I always will."

I went to bed with a new resolution to think of at least one thing I liked about everyone I knew, especially those I wasn't very fond of. I decided to start with the day's team.

Mandy Zubinski. A very good officer and I trusted her.

Vince Weber. Amazingly strong, and I liked his deep, raspy voice.

Donny Nickles. Friendly and dedicated to his family.

Eric Stueman. Eric Stueman. Easy to look at and full of surprises.

The next thing I knew it was Sunday morning.

38

The Coven

As the midnight hour approached, the assembly was ready. The sacrificial offering was lying on the altar, aware, but unable to move. The paralytic-like drugs in his system were powerful, invisible restraints. For the first time in years, his mind had clarity. What drugs did that, he fleetingly wondered. Evil was around him, and it was impossible to use his body for battle. His spirit was all he had left, and all he would be leaving this world with.

What were his bedtime prayers as a kid? "If I should die—"

A gong sounded off to his right. He counted nine strikes. Men in hooded, black robes closed in around him. One held a large knife with jewels that sparkled in the firelight. They looked down at him, and he closed his eyes against the shining malevolence in theirs.

"Are you ready, High Priest?" one said.

"Yes, Deacons, let us begin." He extended his hands, palms downward, over the offering on the altar.

"O mighty Lord of Darkness, we implore you to accept this sacrifice which we offer on behalf of your assembled coven. You have given us your mark, and we ask you to help us prosper, and give us long lives for your service. Keep us under your protection for the fulfillment of our desires, and the destruction of our enemies.

"In the unity of unholy fellowship we honor thee, Lucifer the Morning Star, and Beelzebub the Lord of Regeneration, and all of your angels, the mighty hosts of hell, and by whose assistance we may be strengthened in mind, body, and will."

Noris lifted the dagger and drove it into the man's heart.

The rituals, celebrations, and orgies continued long into night. When the last "Hail Satan" was said, Cyril signaled for two teenage boys to assist with the removal of what was left of the body of the young man they knew only as Blue. They zipped his body into the leak-proof bag and loaded it into Cyril's van. By the time the sun rose, he would be reduced to dust. Dust to be mingled with the earth or thrown into the river. There would be no earthly trace of him left.

39

The Brenners had asked their minister, Pastor Boyd, to say a few words over the ashes of Alvie Eisner.

Our small group gathered under a maple tree in the Oak Lea cemetery. Rebecca held her great-grandmother Elaine's hand on one side and her great-uncle Henry's on the other. Elaine was only a few inches taller than Rebecca, and Henry towered over everyone present. Jean, Dale, Tina, and Justin Brenner, Smoke, Alvie's attorney, Gib Conner, and I completed the circle.

Pastor Boyd didn't address the issue of where Eisner would be spending eternity, but he spoke words of comfort, then asked anyone who wished to say a few words. Elaine talked about Alvie as a small child. How she loved to play with kittens and her brother, Henry.

Henry said, "Alvie."

Rebecca spoke with love and affection of the woman who had raised her and cared for her. Pastor Boyd closed in prayer.

The attorney, Gib Conner, asked if he could have a short conversation with me. We walked some feet away from the others. "As you know, Alvie Eisner's estate is very large, but will be fairly easy to settle. She has set up a monthly stipend for you, as Rebecca's guardian—"

"I can't take it. Why should I get money for being a guardian? The final adoption is about to go through."

Conner rested his crossed arms on his ample belly. "It's the way Eisner set it up. If you don't want the money, donate it to a charity. The Brenners will also receive a generous amount monthly until Rebecca turns eighteen. Henry, of course, is set for life. And there is a large trust fund for Rebecca. She will receive four large chunks during her college years, then the bulk when she turns thirty-five."

"That sounds smart. Thank you, Mr. Conner."

We hung around, chatting for a while. When it was time to say goodbye, I hugged Rebecca, Tina, Jean, and Dale. Justin looked worried he was next, so I gave him a high five instead.

Smoke and I walked to our cars together. "Thanks for coming, Smoke."

"I'm glad they had a service, something positive for Rebecca to remember in the years to come." Smoke pointed at my car. "You ever going to fix this thing?"

"Maybe—" My cell phone rang. It was an 802 area code. Vermont. But not Gregory Trippen's number. Smoke lifted his arm to wave goodbye, but I shook my head and held up my hand for him to stay.

"Sergeant Aleckson."

"It's me."

A reason not to identify himself? "Hi."

"Got a couple of problems. Two guys are watching me, and they tampered with my car."

My heart picked up its beat. "What do you mean?"

"I went in the bank yesterday morning to do some business. You know. When I left, they came up to me and one of them said, 'The sparrow can fly anywhere in the world.' I acted like I didn't care and pushed past them, walked to the parking lot behind the bank. I was pretty shaken and didn't notice my oil light came on when I started my car. Bastards drained my oil, and the engine seized up a little ways down the road. Ruined my engine."

"I'm so sorry."

"I had it towed to a shop, but they can't get a new engine for a few days. My friend picked me up at the shop. I was watching for those guys, and I don't think they followed us to his place. Oh, so you know, I'll be sending a package to you tomorrow."

"Okay. Good. But the main thing is to take care of yourself. And call right away if you see those guys again. All right?"

"I will. Goodbye."

"Now what?" Smoke asked when I hung up. I filled him in on the latest update from Gregory Trippen.

"The sparrow, huh? I'd like to shoot that nasty bird right out of his tree."

"Someone must have seen Greg when he was here and recognized who he was. They told Sparrow, who traced him to his home in Vermont. Our not-so-esteemed colleague in the sheriff's department?"

"Or Sparrow's known all along where they've been and keeps an eye on their activities."

40

I knew it was important to find a balance between work and play, but the Trippen case was consuming me, and time was running out. I had two more scheduled days off, but I needed to work. I wanted to keep going until we found Jeffrey and learned the identity of the person in the department responsible for all the years of corruption and threats.

Since Gregory Trippen's initial phone call, the dimensions of the cult activities and their capital crimes had expanded on a daily basis. I was impatient with the time it took to investigate and build solid cases. Conducting interviews, maintaining surveillance, record-searching, and evidence-gathering all involved scores of hours. Limited human and financial resources were legitimate deterrents to streamlined efficiency.

We had only a few days to find Jeffrey Trippen, if April thirtieth was his intended death date. Learning the dirty cop's identity was a priority, but finding Jeffrey was the top priority. We needed to save his life. Then he could get help from someone like Dr. Fischer, who had had marked success with people who'd suffered similar trauma.

In addition, Jeffrey and Gregory were eyewitnesses to the crimes committed by the cult.

Why hadn't we thought of it before? I called the sheriff.

"Sheriff, remember when Smoke and I talked to Gregory Trippen last week, and he mentioned that a deputy had been at one of the rituals?"

"Of course."

"He might be able to help us find him."

"But he couldn't see his face."

"No, but he remembers his voice. I know Trippen was young, but he says he can still hear the voice in his memory. The voice was low and like a smoker's, and belonged to a man in his late thirties or early forties. We have, what, twelve men in the department who were here twenty years ago?"

"Sounds about right," he said.

"If you figure out a way to let Trippen listen to their voices, it might narrow the pool of suspects."

"You may be on to something. I'll run it by the officers working on it."

"Good."

"Thanks, Sergeant."

"Sure. 'Bye for now."

I picked up my memo pad and paged through notes I'd taken. Dr. Marcella Fischer's card was taped to a page. I flipped it over and stared at Pastor Daniel Trondholm's name and number. Dr. Fischer had said he worked with the spiritual aspects of healing and might be another good resource for the Trippen brothers.

A woman answered the phone. "First Congregational Church. May I help you?"

"Hi. I'm Corinne Aleckson, a sergeant with the Winnebago County Sheriff's Department, and I'd like to make an appointment with Pastor Trondholm, please."

"Of course, Sergeant Aleckson. I'll transfer you to his phone."

A click and a beep and he was on the line. "Pastor Trondholm." His voice was gravelly and very deep.

"Pastor, it's Sergeant Aleckson—"

"Ah, yes, Sergeant, Marcella Fischer said you might call."

"I'm glad she mentioned it."

"So what can I do for you?"

"I wondered if we could meet."

"Of course. When would be good for you?" he said.

"Do you have any openings today?"

"I do this afternoon. Two o'clock?"

"Perfect. At your church?"

"Yes. I'll be expecting you."

Pastor Trondholm was standing at a bookshelf in his office, replacing a book.

I paused at the door jamb. "Excuse me, your assistant said to come right in."

"Yes, yes, please do." Trondholm closed the space between us, his steps heavy, feet planted firmly like he was carrying a heavy load. He was in his sixties with large features—thick lips, prominent jowls, a bulbous nose, and drooping eyes. His fading brown hair was graying at the temples. Trondholm wasn't a giant, but he likely bought his clothes at a big man's store.

He took my hand in his and shook it firmly. His brown eyes searched mine, and I felt he was looking into my very soul. He nodded as he stared. I wondered what he saw.

Trondholm would be an effective investigator. I was prepared to tell him anything he wanted to know.

"You've been brought into the battle."

"I guess that's one way to put it."

He extended his arm toward a group of chairs arranged next to the bookshelves. "Let's sit." And we did. "Dr. Fischer said you were working on a case involving a young man who was in a satanic cult as a child. She didn't feel it was her place to give any other information, but wanted to give a little background in case you called."

"Yes. It's one of the more traumatic cases I've worked on, for a lot of different reasons, and we've got this guy out there who is nowhere to be found, it seems."

I told the pastor nearly everything Gregory Trippen had told me. How he suspected his stepfather had killed his father, the rituals at the outdoor temple, Jeffrey's mental and emotional decline and his plans to kill himself.

"We're waiting for Gregory to get back with some reports, some evidence we can use in a case we're building against his stepfather and others. But he was delayed because his car was tampered with. I feel like our efforts are being thwarted every step of the way," I said.

"Sergeant, you are seeking the truth. Justice. They will do whatever it takes to hide the truth. They are working for the Great Deceiver." He lowered his chin and looked at me over the top of his glasses.

I nodded. "Dr. Fischer said you also work with people suffering from dissociative identity disorder."

"Dr. Fischer refers people to me, and I to her. Years ago, as a young minister, when people came to me for help with particular symptoms, I thought they were plagued with demonic possession. As I counseled these people and studied extensively, I discovered their problems were the result of demons, all right, but not in the way I thought.

"You see, demons seek to destroy people. On the other hand, alternate personalities help people cope with realities they cannot face. It took me a long time—and a lot of that was on my knees in prayer—to understand the difference. The alternates hold painful memories and need love, compassion, understanding, and acceptance to be healed. It's a very long process."

"You and Dr. Fischer impress me with your commitment to being there for the long haul. I wish I had that kind of patience."

Pastor Trondholm smiled. "I was not always the most patient of God's creatures, but after He called me into this work, He gave me the tools I needed. It started with a young woman who came to me at the end of her rope. She had consulted psychologists, ones her parents chose. She had been hospitalized for depression. She was on any number of medications.

"She said they had been following and tormenting her for two years, and she could no longer cope. She was going to end her own life. She came to me asking me to bless her before she did that, because she did not want to go to hell and spend eternity with the people who had made her life on earth a living hell."

"What did you do?" I said.

"I told her I would not let her kill herself. That's when one of her alternates came out and told me the evil that had been done to her at the hands of her parents. They were leaders in a satanic cult. At first I thought the poor woman was completely insane, suddenly taking on a different look and talking in a more confident voice. I had never seen anything like it. Surely, I thought, she is possessed by a demon. But the more she talked, the more God opened my mind and my heart to the concept that a demon would not be saying the things she was saying.

"Thankfully, her story had a happy ending, eventually. And then other people with DID seemed to come out of the woodwork. My main responsibility is this congregation, but I spend a great deal of time working with abuse survivors." He raised his hand and shook his finger. "And not without consequence. There have been a number of threats over the years."

"What kind of threats?"

"I must stop, or else."

I smiled. "But you didn't." Like Dr. Fischer didn't.

"No. My ministry is to bring people to the knowledge of salvation through Jesus Christ. But my theme, if you will, is from Ephesians, chapter six: 'Put on the full armor of God so that you can take your stand against the devil's schemes. For our struggle is not against flesh and blood, but against the rulers, against the authorities, against the powers of this dark world, and against the spiritual forces of evil in the heavenly realms. Therefore put on the full armor of God, so that when the day of evil comes, you may be able to stand your ground . . .

"'In addition to all this, take up the shield of faith, with which you can extinguish all the flaming arrows of the evil one. Take the helmet of salvation, and the sword of the Spirit, which is the word of God. And pray in the Spirit on all occasions with all kinds of prayers and requests. With this in mind, be alert and always keep on praying for all the saints.'

"So I put on the full armor of God and keep praying."

I drove away contemplating the work Pastor Trondholm, Dr. Fischer, and all the others like them were doing. The kind of work I had had little knowledge of mere weeks before.

Sheriff Twardy phoned me as I pulled into a parking spot by my mother's dress and accessory shop. "Hi, Sheriff."

"Corky, we came up with a plan. It's been a few years since our longtime deputies have had their photos updated on their ID badges. The chief deputy sent out a memo asking every deputy with photos older than two years to stop by his office in the next three days—that'll cover everyone on days off—to have their picture taken for new badges. We're installing a camera in the ceiling sprinkler, and we'll have everyone on tape. Including me."

"That's pretty clever. As long as no one notices." I looked at my mother's colorful window display.

"Do you study the sprinklers in our offices?" he said.

"Well no—"

"I doubt if anyone else does either. And it'd be very difficult to see. Oh, before I forget, we've talked to most of the people who were at your party. So far, no one saw anything, or knows who may have keyed your car."

"I can't say I'm surprised."

"No. Expected as much. And we're still waiting to hear about the latent prints we sent to the Bureau of Criminal Apprehension last week. We'll see if that turns anything up."

"Thanks, Sheriff. I just stopped by my mom's shop. Want me to ask her what she wants for her birthday?"

"As long as my name is not mentioned."

I laughed. "I'll just say 'hi' from you."

"Okay."

When I got out of my GTO and shut the door, my eyes were again drawn to the damage. I pushed the shop door open, and the little "ding" announced my arrival. Mother was straightening shirts on a rack.

Her face lit up in surprise. "Corinne. What are you doing here?"

"Day off. Sara got a cute top here, so I thought I'd visit you and shop at the same time."

Mother hugged me. "There are some bright, fun colors for spring. Look around." She pulled away and looked at me. "How is everything?"

"Okay." I filled her in on the details of Alvie Eisner's service, and we talked about that, and Rebecca, as I looked at nearly every clothing item in the store. I selected two tops, a pair of shorts, and some earrings.

"Aren't you going to try them on?" she asked when I laid them on the counter and handed over my bank card. "Put that away."

"They'll fit fine." I put my card in her hand. "Take this. You need to at least cover your costs." She rang up the purchases with an overly generous discount.

"I'm going to head out to the body shop on Thirty-five to get an estimate on my car," I said.

"I'm glad. You've seemed a little down since it happened."

I didn't correct her perception of why I had been under par. It wasn't the car. It was all the things at work I wanted answers for, the crimes I wanted solved.

"And what are your plans for the rest of your day?" She put my things in a bag and set it on the counter.

"I'll stop by to see Gramps. Maybe I'll pick up something at the deli for his supper, if that's okay."

"That would be nice, dear. I was having trouble thinking of what to fix."

"I'll get enough for all of us."

She smiled. "Thanks. It'd be a relief for me to have the evening off."

Mom didn't complain, but keeping tabs on Gramps and managing all the other things in her life was wearing on her.

"And I'll tuck him safely in bed."

She stepped around the counter and hugged me again. "Thank you, dear. The whole night off. I may have to rent a movie, or read a book."

"Do you think you can sit still long enough to do either one?" I teased.

"I'm slowing down. I'll be fifty this year, you know."

"You'll be fifty, but you are not slowing down."

Stan Hemsley at Stan's Body Works gave me a written estimate to turn into my insurance company. They had asked that I get at least two estimates, but Stan was the best and the cheapest. If the company insisted I get another, I would. Stan had a few jobs ahead of mine, and we set an appointment for the following week.

It was late afternoon when I finished my other errands and stopped by Charlie's Grocery Store for whatever looked good in their deli. I'd decided on a broasted chicken, potato wedges, and coleslaw when a voice behind me said, "Do they have good chicken here?"

I whipped around. It was Eric Stueman, looking downright dapper in his suit and tie. "Oh, hi. Um, Eric. They have very good chicken. It's one of my regular staples. I'm not much of a cook, and I'm bringing supper to my Gramps."

"Well good." He waited while the deli attendant asked if I wanted anything else, and handed me the food when I said I didn't.

I turned back to Eric. "All recovered from Saturday's excursion?"

"That was the oddest team-building exercise I've ever been a part of. But I'm glad we were together and finally had a chance to talk."

I smiled. "Well, I better get going before the food gets cold."

His hand on my arm stopped me. "Corinne, is it okay if I call you sometime, outside of work? You mentioned not being in a relationship during our little personal-facts session."

I managed to hold a poker face. "Um, sure." There was a growing line of customers behind us. "See you."

"'Bye, Corinne."

Spending the evening with Gramps was exactly what I needed. He and Grandpa Aleckson were my surrogate fathers. Gramps had been my faithful fishing buddy for years, and I wondered if we would make the walleye fishing opener in a few weeks. I doubted I could get him in and out of the boat by myself.

"Hi, sweetheart," he said as he fumbled with the television remote. He hit the off button, and the room noise went from blaring loud to calming quiet in a split second.

I bent over and gave him a kiss. "Hi, Gramps. You ready to eat?"

"It smells good. I reckon I could eat something." He leaned forward and reached for the TV tray by the side of his chair, then slid it into place while I went into the kitchen to dish up our plates.

I returned and set his plate in front of him and mine on another TV tray. I turned my chair to face Gramps, settled in, and pulled the tray in close.

"How was your day, Gramps?"

"Fine, fine. Your grandma and grandpa came by, and we played cards for quite a while. I read some and watched a little TV. And then my favorite granddaughter came with supper."

I reached over and gave his arm a gentle squeeze. "Your only granddaughter. Sounds like you had a good day. You know what? It is so nice out, Gramps, after we finish eating let's take a little walk. It'll strengthen our legs and make it easier to get in and out of the boat this summer."

"Corky, I see you running down our road most every morning. You don't fool me. You're hoping to get these old legs of mine working again. All right then." He took a last bite and set his tray aside. He rocked forward a few times and propelled himself to a standing position on the third try.

I took his hand in mine, and we made it out the door eventually. It was a slow process, strolling down his driveway. I willed myself to relax, to clear all the clutter from my mind and enjoy the time with Gramps. Each step we took was good for his bones, muscles, and tendons.

As we neared Brandt Avenue, I noticed a car slow to a crawl as it passed my house. A black BMW. It was too far away to read the license plate or identify the driver, but I could see it was a male who sat tall in his seat. It was probably my imagination, but it seemed when the driver spotted us, he decided to turn around rather than drive past us. He stopped the Beemer, backed into my driveway, and went back the direction he had come from at a fairly fast clip.

There was little traffic on our rural road, and it struck me as strange. My nearest neighbor was a half mile away. I knew of no one in the area who owned a BMW. If the driver was lost, why wouldn't he continue to the main county road instead of returning to the back roads? Then again, he might have been at a friend's house, realized he had forgotten something, and went back to retrieve it.

"Everything okay?" Gramps asked.

"Yes. Sorry, I was thinking about something for a minute and didn't realize I'd stopped walking."

Why would a car turning around in my driveway put me on heightened alert? It happened sometimes, that sixth sense when I knew something was off, but didn't know why. It took nearly ten minutes to get back inside Gramps' house. I watched for the BMW, but it didn't return.

I stayed with Gramps until he went to bed, hours before my own bedtime, then headed home. The telephone was ringing when I walked in the door, and I rushed to the kitchen counter to answer it before the machine came on.

"Hello?"

"Corky, you didn't answer either of your cell phones all evening." It was Smoke.

"I was at Gramps' and left my work cell at home, but—" I pulled my personal cell out of my pocket. "Oops, my other one is off. Forgot I turned it off when we were eating. You know how Gramps hates phone calls during meals. What's up?"

"I spent part of the day talking to people about Dr. Sparrow at his former clinic in Little Mountain and his current clinic in Saint Cloud. He's built a sizable practice.

Apparently he's a very talented cosmetic surgeon. Nice house. Big. Owns three vehicles, a Toyota Tundra pickup, a Lexus SUV, and a BMW, all late models—"

"What color BMW?"

I heard papers shuffling. "Color? Ah, black."

"A black BMW turned around in my driveway a while ago."

"License?"

"Too far away. Gramps and I were outside at his place when I saw it coming our direction, very slowly. It seemed like the driver spotted us, then turned around instead of driving by and getting too close. At first I thought it was my imagination, but I don't think it was."

"Those cult people seem to have connections everywhere, even in the sheriff's department. If Edberg figured out who Jeffrey Trippen is, our dirty cop probably did too. You're working the case, and someone accessed your computer and keyed your car. Maybe Edberg's right—maybe that was done as a warning." Smoke sneezed loudly. "Sorry."

"Bless you."

"I started sneezing about an hour ago. I'm hoping it's spring allergies. My brother had a bad cold at the game Saturday, and I am going to be less than happy if he gave it to me."

"That'd be a bummer. Those guys found Gregory Trippen in Vermont and gave him that warning. Maybe someone saw him in Oak Lea and recognized him. He looks just like his father did in that old picture he showed us. Would they be after the boys, all these years later?"

"Truth be told, I am downright confused. I want evidence. I want witnesses. I want those responsible for the crimes we are investigating to be put away. For life. With no chance of parole."

The BMW kept niggling at me. "I doubt if Dr. Sparrow himself would have any reason to drive by my house. It just seemed weird, that's all."

"He'd be after me if he got wind I was snooping around. You're only a few miles away. If your car damage was done by one of his evil cohorts, he might have driven by hoping to see the job they did. Or, our imaginations are just running wild." Another sneeze.

"Bless you, again. We are speculating, but that's what makes us eager to find answers."

Smoke sneezed again, three times in succession. "I wonder if I have any aspirin?"

"Maybe you should drink some tea with honey and go to bed early."

"A hot brandy toddy sounds better."

41

A brown UPS delivery vehicle pulled up to my house a little after nine o'clock Tuesday morning. I watched the driver jump out with a package and opened the front door to meet him.

He handed me a shallow, letter-size box, scanned the code, then set the signature pad on top of it. I signed, we both said "thank you," and he was off to the next stop. I looked at the return address. No name. A UPS box number in Vermont. Gregory Trippen's, I surmised. I had not expected the documents to be shipped to my house.

I closed and locked the door, then stood in the entry and stared at the package. The vital information we had been waiting for. I pulled out my cell phone and dialed Smoke's number. No answer. I didn't leave a message.

I stared at the package some more. Evidence. It was addressed to me, but I wanted someone there when I opened it. A witness. Another set of hands, another set of eyes verifying the number of pages and what was on them.

I carried the package to the gun safe in my den office closet, punched in the code, pulled open the door, and laid it on the top shelf. My Smith and Wesson and extra ammo were asleep on the bottom shelf. I locked the safe, paced around the room for a while, then sank onto the couch, sliding down until my head rested on the seat cushion and my feet were stretched out straight in front of me.

That's when I noticed it.

My computer armoire was open. The interior contained a top shelf filled with reference books and statute manuals. The main shelf housed the computer and screen. There was a pull-out shelf for the keyboard, a drop-down shelf for the mouse, and another pull-out shelf on the bottom for the printer. Above that was a small shelf where I stored printer paper.

That's where it was.

I slid to the floor and crawled on my hands and knees to the armoire. I bent my head and stuck my face under the shelf for a closer look. A black box, approximately two inches wide by three inches long by one half inch thick, clung there. A bugging device. Damn.

A bugging device.

My emotions flew back and forth between fury and fear, fear and fury. Someone was spying on me? I could barely contain myself. I stopped myself from yelling at the top of my lungs only because I didn't want them to know I knew.

Were there other devices in my house, my phone, my car? A hidden camera somewhere? My cell phone was usually on my person, except when I was in the shower or in bed. Even then it was within reach. I concentrated for a minute, searching my memory, trying to recall if I had let anyone use my cell phone for any reason. I could not think of a single incident A.J.T. After Jeffrey Trippen.

I began a search of every room of my house, starting with the same corner each time and moving to the right. I looked behind every wall hanging, in and under each piece of furniture. I didn't find another intrusive device, but that didn't mean there wasn't one. It could be in a pen or a calculator or any number of places.

Throughout the exploration, I tried to recall everything that had been said in my den office. If they were monitoring the device the night of the party, they knew Smoke had slept over. Had they heard him describe his nightmare? Our banter? Our conversation the next morning?

We had talked about someone looking at the computer files, about suspecting Edberg as the culprit. We'd mentioned Gregory and Jeffrey Trippen. And Dr. Fischer. The next day, Smoke and I had dusted the armoire for fingerprints and talked some more.

When I had finished checking my entire house, I ran back upstairs to my bedroom, grabbed my duty flashlight—a maxi-beam magnum—and headed for the garage. The GTO was parked in the middle of the two-car space. Smoke and I had checked under the hood to get the code for the paint color, but I popped it open anyway and had a look. Nothing evident. I got down on all fours, ducked my head, and craned my neck, searching under the car. I started at the front and moved around to the passenger side, down the length of the car, wishing I had a mechanic's dolly so I could lie on my back and roll around instead.

It was in front of the right rear tire well. A global-positioning-system device keeping someone apprised of each journey I took. If it was attached the night of the party, it had been on eleven days, according to my quick calculations. I left it in place and ran back into the house to the kitchen. Why would a person key my car and plant a tracking device, knowing I'd be taking it to a body shop for repairs, where it might be found? Or was it not the same person? Had the device been installed before my car was vandalized?

I grabbed a notepad and pen from a drawer and sat at the counter, contemplating. Where had I driven? Saturday I had gone to my grandparents' houses. Sunday morning Deputy Schorn had dropped the squad car we shared off at my house. I had driven it for the six-day work stretch and hadn't taken my personal vehicle anywhere significant that I could recall. My first day off, Saturday again, was the team-building exercise. I had driven to the courthouse, then home. Sunday was Alvie Eisner's service. Monday I had gone to see Pastor Trondholm.

If a cult member was tracking me—and I believed he was—he would most likely know of Pastor Daniel Trondholm. I should inform Trondholm.

My thoughts were processing at an adrenaline-enhanced speed. What should I do first? I went to my gun safe and withdrew the loaded Smith and Wesson. I ran up and got the pancake holster, clipped it on my jeans, and flew down the stairs for a last look at the safe. Should I take the package of documents or leave them? They were secure where they were. I locked the door behind me and gently jogged to the end of my driveway, keeping a lookout for unfamiliar vehicles. When I hit Brandt Avenue, I flat-out ran to Gramps' house and up his front steps, landing on the porch huffing and puffing.

I sighed in relief that his door was locked. I knocked on the door then rang the bell. He didn't hear well, and depending on where he was or what he was doing, sometimes he heard the bell, sometimes the knocking. Why hadn't I brought my keys?

"Gramps," I yelled, then darted to the front window, stuck my face against the glass, and put a hand on each temple, blocking the sun from my eyes.

Gramps was making his way toward the door. "Coming. Slow, but sure." He opened the door and his bushy white eyebrows rose, deepening the creases on his forehead. "Your face is all red. You all right, girl?"

I stepped in the house. "Yeah, just ran faster than normal." I moved close to Gramps and put my hands on his elbows. "Gramps, I have a question. In the last couple of weeks, has anyone, like a repairman, or any kind of salesman, or anyone you didn't know, stopped by your house, come in for any reason?"

Gramps frowned in thought. "Not that I recall." He shook his head. "No. The only ones who have been here are your mother, your grandparents, and you. No one else."

I hugged him. "Good. Now I have a couple of favors to ask. Can I use your phone then borrow your car for a while?"

"You know you can. My, I wonder if the car'll run? I haven't driven it in a long time." He didn't ask why I needed it.

"Mom used it last month when hers was in the shop for repairs," I reminded him.

"Oh, that's right. Well, you make your call, and I'll go find those keys."

Gramps headed to the kitchen, and I sat down in the chair next to his recliner in the living room and dialed the sheriff's number.

"Sheriff, it's Corky."

"Something happen?"

"A lot. I found a bug in my computer cabinet and a tracking device on the GTO."

"For godsakes! What's next? Did you disable them?"

"No, I left them as is. I didn't want to alert whoever is listening that I'd found them until we figured out what to do."

"Good. Good."

"I went through my house and only found the one, but it'd be a good idea to double check with our detection equipment."

"Right. I'll check with Kenner. Either he or Edberg will take care of it," he said.

"There's also something I want to talk to you and Smoke about, but not over the phone."

"Dawes called in sick. Chief Deputy said he sounded awful."

"Shoot. He thought he was coming down with a cold. I don't want to bother him, but I really need to talk to him."

"He told Kenner he'd be making some calls, checking on a few things from home."

"Okay. I'm at Gramps' house. I'm a little freaked about using my cell phone until I know, positively, that it's clean."

"I'll call you when I have a time arranged with Kenner. What's the number there?"

After I gave it to him, we hung up, and I called Smoke's home phone.

His voice was raspy, with a nasally twang. "Oh, it's you, Corky. I saw it was your grandpa's number and was wondering why he'd be calling."

"You don't sound so good. I heard you actually called in sick."

"Sicker than an old dog."

"The brandy toddy didn't help?"

"Oh, it helped. Until I woke up this morning. Got something?"

I told him about the devices in my home and car.

"Damn, that really irritates the hell out of me. We have got to find and *stop* them. How did we miss that bug in the armoire when we dusted it?"

"Trust me, you'd had to be looking for it. The sheriff is sending someone over to check for others I might have missed."

"That really irritates the hell out of me," he repeated.

"The other thing you need to know. I received that delivery today."

He was silent a second. "Ah. It came to your house?"

"Surprise. So I was hoping to bring it over as soon as possible."

"I don't want you exposed to this crap."

"I am way too angry to get sick. I'll see you after we take care of the bugs."

Chief Deputy Mike Kenner pulled into my driveway in a car he must have borrowed from the impound lot and parked next to Gramps' older model, white Oldsmobile. I unlocked my front door when I saw who it was and went out to meet him. His trunk popped open then he climbed out of the car, walked to the back, and lifted the small instrument from the trunk floor. He waved me over.

"Nice car," I said.

He squinted against the sun. "Isn't it, though? The sheriff and I decided I should be as low profile as possible. We also discussed some tactical options and made a decision we hope you can live with."

"What's that?"

"We don't want the people who installed the bugs to know you found them. Gives us the ability to feed them information, mislead them about what we know as we uncover more and more. 'Course it does infringe on your privacy."

"Let's see if we find any other devices. Then I'll let you know."

"We don't want to alert them that I'm here so we won't talk out loud until we're done and back outside. The plan is, we'll do a check of the outside perimeter first, then head inside. We'll start with the upstairs and move down to the main level, then to the basement, and finish with the garage and your vehicle."

"And Gramps' car? It was locked in his garage, but who knows?"

"Sure. Okay. Ready?"

I nodded.

Kenner pointed at my house. "Let's do it."

I followed the chief deputy around the outside of my house, then through each nook and cranny inside the house and garage as he operated the machine, moving as quietly as possible. When we were in the den office, I hummed a tune and made noises like I was straightening papers. He checked my landline phones and my cell phones, and he took special care examining electrical connections. He checked both vehicles. There were no more hidden privacy-invading devices to be found, a relief for both of us.

"Jump into my car a minute," Kenner said as he climbed into the old beater. I joined him on the passenger side. "No sense us standing out there for anyone to see." He turned toward me. "Either they didn't get the chance to plant any other bugs, or they think your office is the best spot to collect the information they're interested in."

"I keep everything locked—my doors and windows—when I'm gone, and there's been no sign that anyone broke in, so they had to have planted it the night of the party. It would have been hard, but not impossible to place a bug somewhere in the living room or kitchen or even my bedroom. Thank God they didn't. I feel violated enough."

"I suppose you've gone over everything in your mind, everything that might have been said in the office."

"Over and over." I told him how Smoke had fallen asleep on the couch that night and awoken from a bad dream, which he had shared with me. I summarized the conversation Smoke and I had had relating to Edberg, the Trippen brothers, and Dr. Fischer the next morning. He already knew the other details: that I had been looking up information on satanic cults and ritual abuse, that someone had been on the computer, and that we had checked the cabinet for latent prints.

He didn't probe why Smoke had spent the night. "If they heard you talk about Edberg, they'll think he's your prime suspect. That plays nicely for our investigation. So what's your decision? Pull the bugs or leave them?"

"Let's leave them. Now for the big thing that happened before I discovered the bug this morning. Gregory Trippen sent me copies of his stepfather's journal and the reports of his father's death investigation, via UPS."

A loud, quick "ha" escaped his lips. "Does Twardy know that?"

I shook my head. "Not yet. I told Smoke, though. I'm going over to his house and was hoping Twardy, or maybe you, could join us. Then we can examine the documents together."

"Where are they?" he said.

"Locked in my gun safe."

He nodded. "The sheriff has a number of meetings today, but I can work it in. I'll call him."

Kenner talked to Sheriff Twardy. He told him about the search and the delivery from Gregory Trippen. When he hung up he said, "Sheriff says we should take a look at the papers right away, see what we got."

I nodded and opened the car door. "Will you call Smoke? I'll get the package."

We drove in separate vehicles to Smoke's house. He opened the door with a dust mask over his mouth and nose. I suppressed a giggle and smart-aleck remark when his bloodshot, watery eyes met mine and I sensed how miserable he felt.

"Looking a little rough. Sure you're up to this?" Kenner asked.

"I look worse than I feel, believe it or not. No fever, at least. I wiped down the doorknobs and kitchen table and chairs with alcohol. Are you sure you want to enter the germ factory?"

"I'm not worried. I prefer any of your bugs over the one in my house," I said.

The crow's feet by Smoke's eyes, visible above his mask, deepened. He wasn't too sick to appreciate a little humor.

Kenner smiled too. "My kids expose me to stuff all the time."

I held up the package. "Kitchen table, you said?"

Smoke led the way. Kenner and I stood on one side of the table, and Smoke stood on the other.

"Got a letter opener or knife?" I asked.

Smoke pointed at a drawer behind me. I pulled it open, selected a small paring knife, returned to the table, picked up the box, and sliced through the taped top edge.

"Like Christmas," Kenner said as I lifted out two large brown mailing envelopes and laid them on the table.

"Keep slicing," Smoke said, so I did. First the thinner envelope, which I handed to Kenner, then the thicker one, which I offered it to Smoke, but he shook his head. Kenner and I pulled pages out simultaneously.

Kenner flipped through the stack. "Yup, reports written by Edberg, Armstrong, and Detective Walden." He sat down on a chair and started reading.

My pile was very different. The original journal pages were smaller than the eight-and-a-half-by-eleven-inch copies, perhaps six by nine inches. "The first page has a prayer, or chant maybe, written in a foreign language."

Kenner leaned toward me and looked at the writing. I turned it around for Smoke to see. "Looks like Latin," he said.

I tucked it on the bottom of the pile and looked at the next sheet. "The second page is dated February seventh, twenty-four years ago. That's before Harlan Manthes was killed, before Sparrow married Gregory and Jeffrey Trippen's mother. Listen to this:

'To Satan, giver of youth and happiness.

Come mighty and eternal devil.

We are with you, armed and ready

to offer this transient's life to you.

We are here as your

Masters among this failing species.

'M.W. delivered offering, Keith James Nutting, age thirty-seven, a transient he found on patrol to C.B. Held for three days. Sacrificial ritual performed at indoor temple on February tenth. C.B. took remains.'"

"Oh. My. God!" we all said, nearly in unison.

Kenner stepped in close to my side and read over my shoulder. He reached for the page, and his hand trembled when he touched it. "A handwritten confession of murder. M.W. on patrol—"

"Miles Walden?" Smoke sneezed into his mask, and his reading glasses fogged up. He pulled off his glasses, lifted the mask, turned away from us and blew his nose, then went to his kitchen sink, washed his hands, and pulled the mask back in place.

When he got back to the table, he held out his hand and Kenner gave him the page. He put on his glasses and stared at the writing, moving his head back and forth. "Sparrow is going down if it is the last thing on earth I do."

A shiver ran down my spine. Sparrow was going down, all right. And I hoped it was not the last thing on earth Smoke did.

Kenner rapped the table. "If Walden was still alive, if he was M.W., nothing would give me greater pleasure than taking him down right along with Sparrow."

Smoke nodded.

The pages weren't numbered, so we took care to keep them in order. I got the first look then passed a page to Kenner, who read it and passed it to Smoke. When he finished reading a page, he turned it upside down and added it to the growing pile. Each of us made a sound here and there, indicating our disgust and disbelief at the depraved and despicable acts committed by the monsters of the coven.

"This is worse than any horror film I've ever seen. All the horror films I've seen put together," Kenner said when he finished the last page.

Smoke sniffled, left for a minute, and returned with a notepad and pen. He sat down and pushed the pile closer to me. "We'll go through and make a list of the actual crimes. Most of the rituals are not against the law. Religious freedom and all that. Let's start with the first one on February seventh."

"Abduction and false imprisonment of Keith James Nutting, age thirty-seven. February tenth, torture and murder of Keith James Nutting." I set the page aside. Kenner picked it up and reread it. I paged through prayers and rituals that asked Satan for a variety of things, from special powers to riches.

"Next?" Smoke asked.

"February eighteenth. Initiation of neophyte Crystal Planer, age sixteen, to coven. High Priest Sparrow represented Satan in the coupling ritual."

"Neophyte?" I said.

"It means novice, I believe," Kenner said.

"First degree criminal sexual conduct against C.P., a minor, age sixteen, committed by Dr. Royce Sparrow, aka asshole to the nth degree," Smoke said as he wrote.

Kenner hit the table with his fist. "Bastard. My daughter's sixteen."

"I wonder where she is now? Crystal Planer?" I said.

"We'll investigate," Kenner said.

I searched through the pages. "How do they do this stuff? Drink a mixture of urine, blood, sperm and/or vaginal fluid from a chalice? Recite these chants? Sacrifice animals? And *people*? I don't get it."

Smoke and Kenner shook their heads.

I continued searching. "There's a black mass which ended with a sex orgy, but no names listed. The last date is February twenty-seventh. A month's worth of entries. If he's got one for every month, maybe he wouldn't notice one is missing. How many is that, over twenty-five years?"

"About three hundred," Kenner said.

Smoke multiplied the numbers on his paper. "Yeah, three hundred." He picked up the copies of the shooting reports. "Let's confer for a minute here."

"Yes, we need a game plan," Kenner said.

"This journal has documentation of criminal activities. We need to locate Keith Nutting's family and Crystal Planer."

Kenner nodded. "I'll work on getting a search warrant for Sparrow's house. Now that he lives in Stearns County, it complicates things. He must still have ties with the cult, if it's still active here. I'll talk to the chief deputy in Stearns. I know him pretty well. I'll write up a search warrant and get the judge there to sign it," Kenner said.

"I'd sit on Sparrow, watch his every move until we can execute the warrant," Smoke said.

"Done. We'll do eight-hour shifts. Sergeant, I'm going to pull you off the road for special detail, but the only people who will know that fact are the ones working on this case. Officially, you're home sick for a couple of days."

I nodded, but thought, *Oh great, Smoke's sick, I'm sick. Maybe there is something between us. Those who were eavesdropping in my home office would think so.*

Kenner pulled out his cell phone and punched in a two-digit code. "Clayton?" Captain Randolph, the next in command after Kenner. "Say, I forgot to take care of something before I left for a meeting. Sergeant Aleckson called in. If you could get a replacement. . . . Great, thanks." He closed his phone and nodded at me. "We'll get you a fully-equipped car from the drug task force. Think you can handle eight hours of surveillance?"

To help nail Sparrow for the evil things he had done over the years? "No problem."

"We'll watch him, Dawes. I'll see what I can find out about Nutting and Planer, and write up that warrant when I get back to the office. May not get it all done today, but I'll try."

Smoke nodded. "Understood. Now for the reports."

Kenner spread the sheets on the table and pointed to one. "Armstrong tells it like it is: evidence compromised, hunters reported Manthes had been wearing an orange hat, but that was never found. Reports the facts, calls for a deeper investigation."

"Which Walden supposedly did," Smoke said.

Kenner raised one eyebrow then looked down at the papers. "Edberg, same deal."

Smoke's finger moved down the page as he read. "And Walden's supplemental doesn't say much. How did he slide this through? He lists brief statements from each witness/shooter. No mention of how they compromised the scene, moved evidence. There was no autopsy. And there's the matter of the missing cap. They were hunting together, so Manthes' orange cap should have been nearby. One of them must have taken it."

Kenner shook his head. "That was stupid. Why didn't they just toss it somewhere in the woods, not far from the body? They should have been interrogated and charged. Compare Walden's four-paragrapher to your detailed reports, Dawes.

"Trouble is, with no autopsy, we have no estimate of how far away they were when they all shot. We got no physical evidence. Unless we get a confession from one of them, at this point we're screwed. Walden had to have been in on it. One of them. Dirty. The M.W. who picked up a transient, *on patrol no less.* I want every one of Sparrow's other journals."

Smoke nodded. "Yeah, he probably documented what really happened on that deer hunt. His house over in Wellspring? There's no record of him selling it, but we should see if he's rented it out. If he hasn't, I'd get a search warrant for that place too. Gregory Trippen saw the stack of his journals in the safe there."

"Will do. When is Trippen coming back to Oak Lea? The thirtieth is only a few days away."

"He'll be here Thursday. Since his car is taking so long to fix, I talked him into flying and renting a car at the airport. With plates from anywhere but Vermont. He's very worried, of course. Jeffrey hasn't contacted him for a long time. I can't imagine how Jeffrey can hide when the whole state's looking for him," I said.

Kenner nodded then shrugged. "A couple things to consider. For one, other agencies aren't looking for him as diligently as we are. And he could have changed his appearance dramatically, making it harder to spot him." He clasped his hands. "Well, we've got a lot of ground to cover. Sergeant, dress down for your detail. You got a wig?"

"No." Except for a silly orange clown wig I had worn to a costume party once.

"Then put your hair up and wear a baseball cap. Give me a call before you come to pick up the vehicle and I'll tell you which one is available. Your squad car key will work in the ignition."

Smoke cleared some phlegm from his throat. "I can take a surveillance shift."

"No, you rest. You'll get better faster." Kenner gathered the documents and put them in the envelopes.

"Smoke, you got the list of Sparrow's vehicles, license plates?" I asked.

"Yeah, in my briefcase. I'll get 'em."

He went into another room and returned with the vehicle registration printouts. I jotted the data in my memo pad.

Kenner checked his watch and looked at me. "It's twelve thirty now. Think you can get to Saint Cloud by two thirty or three?"

"Sure, maybe before that. I'll go home, get ready, eat something then I'll be ready to roll," I said.

42

The Coven

They were assembled in the county park by Noris's home, waiting, when he pulled in. Cyril, Dieter, and Roman had agreed to meet him there from time to time so Noris could swing into the park when he was on duty. He steered his squad car to the right and stopped a few feet from them. Noris got out, and they all stepped into a small circle.

"Give us your report, Deputy Deacon," Cyril said.

"I'll start with Aleckson. She hasn't filed any reports on Jeffrey or Gregory Manthes, aka Trippen. I went through the call log from the day the ATL was posted and there are no summaries either. When calls are handled and don't require a full report, the officer makes a two or three-line entry with the report number, and ends it with NRN, which means no report needed."

Dieter frowned. "Tell us what you have learned from the recordings you're taking at her house."

"I got the equipment set up on my end about three o'clock that morning. When it detects someone is in the room, the bug activates and turns on. It's very sensitive. Aside from noises people make when they're sleeping, it was quiet until nine. Detective Dawes was there with Aleckson. I think he was the one who slept in her office.

"They talked about someone being on her computer and planned to dust it for prints. They suspected it was Deputy Edberg because Aleckson saw him leaving the office during the party. The next day, we were in the squad room and she pulled Edberg into another room.

"I teased him about it later, asked him what he was in trouble for, and he said she had some questions, but he didn't have any answers. As far as I know, she quit bothering to find out. She and Dawes probably still think it's Edberg, but they can't prove it. No fingerprints.

"Nothing much to report since that first morning after the party. She goes in the office to use the computer, makes a few phone calls. But none to, from, or about Gregory Trippen."

"Keep checking the recordings. And her car trips?" Cyril asked.

"Not many, nowhere special. A cemetery, a church, that's about as exciting as it gets." Noris smiled. "That was one awesome warning I left on her car."

No one else smiled.

He went on. "A deputy named Holman took the call on her car and wrote a report. The chief deputy was the one who talked to me about the damage. He said they were talking to everyone who had been at the party. He asked me if I had done it, or knew who did. I said no, of course. They have no clue it was me."

"Did you reach your contact in Vermont?" Dieter asked.

"I did, and the message was delivered to Gregory Manthes Trippen in downtown Burlington. From the way it was phrased, he'd think it was from Sparrow. And they disabled his vehicle."

Cyril nodded. "Good. I find it strange Sparrow has been so reclusive. I've phoned him several times. He doesn't answer and hasn't returned my calls. I finally called his office, and his scheduler said he was on vacation this week and will be back on Monday."

"He always keeps us apprised when he leaves town in case we need his help or advice. Where would he go during such an important time?" Dieter asked.

"It's not like him at all, but there's nothing we can do until he gets back in touch with us," Cyril said.

They silently considered options for a while.

Cyril turned to Noris. "And the abduction is set?"

"Yes. Dieter will assist me in securing our sacrificial offering. She is a worthy gift for our Master. Full of energy. We'll celebrate Walpurgisnacht well into the morning."

Dieter nodded. "I will meet you at eleven forty-five, and she will be in the preparation room by twelve fifteen."

"We miss your Uncle Miles, but you have been a very worthy replacement, Deacon. You improve every year," Cyril said.

"Thank you, High Priest. I am honored to serve our Master."

"Hail, Satan," Cyril said.

"Hail, Satan," they chanted.

43

The older model silver Chevrolet Venture minivan was the perfect surveillance vehicle. Who really paid attention to minivans? They were all over. My mother had driven one when we were growing up, so when I saw one, I thought, "Mom's vehicle." Had I ever stopped one for speeding? Probably a few times, but not often.

I cruised through the parking lots of both the clinic where Sparrow practiced and the hospital where he did surgeries. None of his vehicles were in the doctors' reserved spots, or anywhere else in the lots. If Sparrow was at work, he hadn't driven there.

I consulted the map, figured out where he lived, and found it ten minutes later. The street was a few blocks from the state university in a quiet neighborhood. The house was a stately, two-story brick Cape Cod complete with shutters on the windows. Unless one personally knew Sparrow and the clandestine life he led, there would be no obvious reason to suspect a monster lived there. I drove to a street a block away and parked. I had a front view of Sparrow's house, between two others.

Three o'clock. There were few cars and little activity. Sparrow's house was closed up tight. Curtains and blinds covered all the windows, including the one on the front door. He had a two-car garage and owned three vehicles. If two were in the garage, where was the third?

I called information for the clinic's phone number then dialed it. "Hello. I'm from out of town, and my friend recommended Dr. Sparrow as a great surgeon. I was wondering if he had any openings today or tomorrow?"

The receptionist on the other end was abrupt when she said, "I'm sorry, Dr. Sparrow is out of the office all week."

"Will he be back next week?"

"Yes, but he is completely booked. I can put you on a waiting list, in case there are any cancellations."

"No thanks, I'll be leaving before then. 'Bye." I hung up before she could say more.

Had Sparrow left town, or was he taking his vacation at home?

Neither Smoke nor the chief deputy was happy with the news. When I told him, Kenner said, "Stick to your detail. We'll continue watching, in case he's still around. Edberg will relieve you at twenty-three hundred."

"Sounds good."

I drove to different locations about every two hours. First down the block on Sparrow's street, then to a cross street, then to another. The outside temperature was in the seventies. Comfortable in the shade, hot sitting in the sun. To stay cool as the sun's light moved to the west, I moved with it.

An older gentleman approached my vehicle shortly before five o'clock. I opened my cell phone, hit the camera button, snapped his picture then pretended to dial.

I smiled at him and held a finger up as if to say, "I'll be with you in a minute." I talked into the phone to no one, making imaginary plans to meet. When I clapped the phone shut I said, "Hi."

"Hello. I'm checking to see if everything is okay. You've been waiting out here a very long time."

"I know. I am such a dimwit sometimes. I just talked to my friend, who's wondering where I am. I got the address mixed up. But it's nice of you to check. Well, I better not keep her any longer." I started the engine.

"Then I'll get out of your way. Drive safely, young lady."

"I will, and thanks." When he was back on the sidewalk, I drove to a new spot.

I vowed that the next time I was on a long stakeout, I'd bring something to read. I ran the license plate of every vehicle that passed on the car's laptop. I examined the few items in the glove box. I sent text messages to Sara and John Carl about nothing special and one to Smoke with an update on the absent Sparrow. I studied the Saint Cloud map and memorized side street escapes to two state highways and the interstate that looped by the city. I didn't eat or drink anything, except a few sips of water, for fear I would have to leave my post to find a restroom.

Hour after hour passed with no sign of Dr. Royce Sparrow. The sun finally set at eight fourteen. I watched the darkness settle in for another twenty minutes then climbed out of the car. Slowly. After all those hours of sitting, I was very stiff. I could relate to how Gramps felt. The more he sat, the harder it was for him to move. I resolved to take him on more frequent walks.

I stretched. I walked around the car. I did a few jumping jacks and half push-ups from the car hood. Still no Sparrow.

Edberg phoned me shortly before eleven to get my location. "Hasn't shown up yet, huh?"

"No."

"If he's off all week, he probably is out of town. But Kenner says we stay put until Sparrow returns. Kenner'll be up here tomorrow, at the courthouse, taking care of that search warrant."

"I hope you brought something to read."

"Are you kidding? That'd put me to sleep in about two minutes. Happens every time I try to read at night. I'll stay in the shadows and get out of the car when I need to, play solitaire and tic tac toe on my phone. And I brought some crossword puzzle books."

"That was smart."

Edberg drove by me and nodded. "Take off."

"I'm gone."

44

Chief Deputy Kenner pulled six deputies off the road to keep Sparrow's house under watch twenty-four hours a day. They were all fairly new hires and still on probation. Kenner assigned them four-hour shifts and swore them to secrecy, assuring them their probation would end abruptly if word leaked out to anyone what they were doing. They didn't know any specifics. But if anyone entered the home, they were to call the chief deputy immediately. I knew all of them well enough to know they would follow Kenner's directive. They valued their jobs.

I was anxious for Gregory Trippen to return and even more anxious for Jeffrey Trippen to turn up, walking down a county road or eating in a county restaurant.

Smoke phoned Wednesday morning sounding more like himself. He didn't sneeze or cough during the entire conversation. I walked outside with my cell phone. I was not one hundred percent convinced there was only the one bug in my house.

"Kenner's on his way to Saint Cloud now. He's hoping to get the warrant signed within a couple of hours. His buddy up there will be with him when he brings it to the judge. Kenner, Edberg, you, and I are the selected search team. Edberg'll be at my house in an hour. We can swing by to pick you up."

"Nah, I'll drive over."

"Don't forget your vest."

Deputy Holman was near Sparrow's house in a different stakeout vehicle than I had had the day before. The task force had a number of them. He was crouched down in the driver's seat looking at a magazine. Chief Deputy Kenner had sent him a message saying we were going in on a search warrant and to keep watch for any unusual activity, and to call his cell phone if there was. We purposely ignored him when we pulled up, and he seemed to do the same.

Edberg, Smoke, and I were in Smoke's personal vehicle, a silver Ford Expedition. Edberg rode shotgun, and I was in the back seat behind Smoke. Kenner was behind us in his unmarked squad car, a gray Crown Victoria. Smoke stopped a block away from Sparrow's house and parked. Kenner did the same. Edberg got out, walked to Sparrow's house, and rang the doorbell. He waited a minute, rang it again, and banged on the door. Edberg turned our direction and jerked his head to one side in a quick movement.

Smoke, Kenner, and I piled out of our respective vehicles. I glanced back at Kenner, checking to see if he had remembered the ramming bar. He held it in his right hand. We quickly and cautiously made our way to the back door. We knew no one had entered or left the house for twenty-four hours, and there were no signs of life inside. But there was a slim possibility someone was there. Edberg held his position in front.

Smoke pounded on the back door and shouted, "Open up, it's the sheriff's department and we have a warrant to search the premises." There was no response.

Smoke nodded at Kenner who lifted the bar, both hands on the metal grip, and forced it into the door. The lock released on the third push. Kenner set the bar on the ground, and the three of us drew our weapons and entered the house into the kitchen. We checked the kitchen, then the dining room on our way to the front entry, off the living room. Smoke opened the door for Edberg, and he stepped in.

"Sheriff's department. Anybody home?" Kenner called. There was no answer. "Okay, we'll finish sweeping through the house, make sure no one is here, dead or alive, then dig deeper. Edberg and Aleckson, take the basement and garage. Dawes, you and I will finish this level, then head upstairs."

It took about five minutes to discover no one else was in the house. Dead or alive. We regrouped in the living room.

"It doesn't seem like anyone really lives here," I said.

"No, it doesn't," Edberg agreed.

"It's like one of the models for the Parade of Homes," Kenner said.

Smoke scanned the room with his eyes. "Yeah, just enough perfectly placed furniture in each room, tasteful art on the walls, decorative pieces set just so. Twenty classics on the bookshelves. There's not even much in the closets. Clothes in the master bedroom closet, some hygiene stuff in the bathroom."

"Basement's virtually empty. There're two vehicles in the garage, but that's about it. Not even a rake. Must hire a lawn service," Edberg added.

"It won't take hours to look through everything, that's for sure," Kenner said. He gave us our assignments, and we divided up again.

My first room was the master bedroom. I pulled on latex gloves and got to work. The shelf above the clothes rod in the closet was empty, but there were a number of suits, shirts, and pants hanging from the rod. I looked in the pockets of his clothes for slips of paper with incriminating information. No slips of paper, or anything else. There were four pair of dress shoes and one pair of athletic shoes sitting on the floor. Nothing else was in the closet.

I checked each item of clothing in his drawers. I opened the small drawer in his bedside stand and discovered it was empty. I pulled back the bedcovers and lifted the mattress. Nothing. It appeared the man slept and dressed and showered there. Maybe.

After an hour, we wrapped up the search. Every inch of Sparrow's house had been checked. No hidden safes. No trapdoors in the floors. Nothing unusual in either vehicle. Kenner pulled a copy of the warrant out of his back pocket and threw it on the dining room table.

"It's like he knew we were coming and removed anything and everything incriminating," Kenner said.

"I have weird vibes in here. And touching his clothes, his bed, felt creepy, even with my gloves on," I said.

"You three talk to some neighbors, find out about his habits. I'm going to head back to Oak Lea. I have to pick up my son from ball practice. Let's meet in my office tomorrow at oh nine hundred. Does that work for you?"

We all agreed it did, and Kenner left. Smoke determined which house each of us should visit. Thirty minutes and seven neighbors later, we met back at his Expedition and settled in. Deputy Holman had moved, and I stole a glance at him when we drove by. The only part of him that moved was his eyebrows when he raised them a quarter of an inch.

"Holman must be dying of curiosity," I said.

"Think how good he'll feel when we get Sparrow locked up and everything is out in the open, knowing he did his part," Smoke said.

Edberg ran his hand through his hair. "I expected to find a helluva lot more inside that house."

"Like Kenner said, it's like one of those Parade of Homes models that nobody lives in," I said.

"Think he's stupid enough to store anything at his office?" Edberg asked.

"I don't think he's stupid at all, but he may be bold enough to think nobody can touch him. And then do something that stupid because he thinks that way. We should try for a warrant for his office, but I wonder if a judge would sign one. My guess is he's got a storage unit somewhere. But where? No paperwork, no bills, no files whatsoever at his house. He might keep a locked file cabinet with personal papers at his office," Smoke said.

"Or in the trunk of his car. Remember that eccentric attorney that kept a bunch of his clients' files in his trunk? Found 'em after he died when they went to sell the car," Edberg said.

"Yeah, not too bright. Sparrow driving around with records in his BMW?" Smoke shrugged. "I'm taking a different route home so we can drive past his Wellspring place, see if there's any activity."

Smoke reached for something tucked in between his seat and the middle console. He tugged, came back with a ball cap, and put it on his head. He pulled the bill down to his eyebrows. He reached down again, found another cap, and tossed it over his shoulder to me. "Put it on."

"None for me?" Edberg asked.

"No, but you're on the other side of the car, not as easy to identify. Not that I expect Sparrow to be there looking out the windows anyway."

Smoke slowed down slightly. "It's the tan one on the left. Number six thirteen."

"Grass is mowed," Edberg said.

I studied the house and property. "Almost looks boarded up, doesn't it?"

"It's been kept up over the years since he moved, but no signs of life around—kids' toys, lawn furniture, wheelbarrow," Smoke said.

Edberg leaned forward to get a better look around Smoke. "Kinda like his other place."

"Shades or blinds on the windows, even on the garage windows, so we can't sneak a peek to see if there's a car in there," I said.

"He seems to be pretty good at keeping things well hidden."

45

The Coven

It would be over at the stroke of midnight Friday. Walpurgisnacht. The final sacrifice. Where was Jeffrey? Sparrow's instructions were clear, and Jeffrey had agreed.

"Come home to the altar."

"Yes, Father."

Sparrow picked up the framed photo and studied it a long time. Jody. He hadn't known it was possible to love a human being the way he loved Jody. That had astounded him for years.

When Sparrow started his practice at Little Mountain, Harlan Manthes had invited him to his house for a home-cooked dinner. He walked into what looked like the set of a 1950s television program. Comfy house, nicely decorated. Two happy, healthy boys playing a board game on the living room coffee table. Harlan handed Sparrow a bourbon on the rocks and told him to sit, to make himself comfortable.

They were making small talk and watching the boys when the most stunning woman he had ever seen came in from the kitchen. Her dark hair was pulled back into a bun, but curling tendrils had pulled loose and framed her flushed face. One look and he knew she was his reward for being sent to Wellspring to assume a position of leadership in the local coven.

The only thing that stood in his way was Harlan. Jody loved her husband and had not picked up on any romantic hints Sparrow had thrown her way. Harlan had to die, and the hunting accident was easy to stage.

Sparrow had counted on Miles Walden being the first officer on the scene. That was the arrangement. Walden was waiting in a nearby park, listening for the call on the radio so he could tell Communications he was close and would respond to the scene.

The problem: Walden had a flat tire. Armstrong and Edberg had shown up before Walden did. It had been a thorn in Sparrow's side ever since. Sparrow wanted Armstrong and Edberg eliminated, but Walden said that would make it worse. If two cops on a case disappeared, or got killed, everyone in the department would get involved, and Walden would lose control. He said he'd handle the cover-up.

Sparrow had gotten Jody, but only for a year. The memories of their time together still kept him going. The thoughts were a pleasant distraction while he was dealing with coven responsibilities, or performing surgery after surgery.

That was all coming to an end.

Where was Jeffrey?

Jeffrey and Gregory were part of the package. Jody worked overnights, and Sparrow got the boys. He'd instructed them and taken them to the temple, enlightening them about the real truth. The boys had to learn to endure and appreciate the rituals so they would prosper and be awarded power someday. Like they all did.

Sparrow was shocked when Jody took the boys and left him. He was beside himself when she didn't return that night. The next day he went to get the key for his safe. It was in the front part of the drawer bottom. He'd always put it at least halfway back. When he opened the safe, it was obvious someone had been in there. A few of his journals were pulled out, not lined up with the rest of the pile. He checked and discovered one was missing: the month of February, from his first year in Wellspring.

He didn't know how Jody had found his key, or why she had taken that particular journal. The weeks, months, and years of rituals ran together, and he didn't remember what was in that one journal. Sparrow had deliberated for a long time and decided the only way to keep her safe from the others was to let her go.

There wasn't a word for almost twenty years. Then last month, when he had answered the phone, he thought it was Jody calling. It was a woman who sounded exactly like Jody had. She said her name was Samantha, and she was calling for Jeffrey Trippen. He was having problems and needed Sparrow's help. Satan's angels were surrounding him and telling him the time to sacrifice himself was near.

"I'm afraid I don't recognize that name," Sparrow had said.

"You knew him as Jeffrey Manthes."

After all those years. "Where is Jeffrey now?"

There was a pause then a male said, "I'm here." His voice had the same quality as Samantha's, only deeper. His sister? Did Jody have a daughter after she left him?

"Jeffrey, who's Samantha?"

"Greg's talked about her, but I don't know her."

"Is there a woman with you now?"

"No, I'm alone. Who's this?"

"Royce Sparrow, your stepfather."

"Oh."

"I understand you need help. Satan is calling you home," Sparrow said.

"The angels told me that, but I don't know how to get there."

"Yes you do. A fine dagger works well."

"I don't have one," Jeffrey said.

"I will send you mine. I haven't used it for years."

"Okay."

"Where do you live, Jeffrey?"

"Nowhere special. I'm in New York City now."

"What's your address?"

"I only have a box number."

"All right, give it to me and I'll get the package in the mail. Call me as soon as you receive it."

Sparrow had carefully laid the custom-handcrafted dagger in its case, then into another box, addressed it, took it to the post office, and mailed it.

The next day, the results of the medical tests Sparrow had taken at the Mayo Clinic in Rochester came back. He was more than surprised by the news. The cancer in his body had metastasized to his brain, lungs, and liver. He had not anticipated that. He thought Satan would want him on earth for many more years.

The decision was easy. He wouldn't wait for the disease to take him. He would go willingly, as a sacrificial offering. It was time to see his Master, to discover what position of leadership in hell awaited him.

Sparrow chided himself for sending his dagger to Jeffrey. What a fool. Had he known the day before, he would have sent him another. Sparrow hadn't known he'd need it for himself. He'd waited two days without a word from Jeffrey, or Samantha. He'd tried the number Jeffrey had called from, but there was no such number. Probably one of those disposable cell phones that was used up.

Sparrow had paced around his Saint Cloud house, deliberating what his next step should be. He'd scratched out a note telling Jeffrey he needed to return to his home in Winnebago County and to call him immediately. Sparrow had left his home, driven to the post office, mailed the letter, then kept driving until he was home in Wellspring.

He always came and went in the dark. He had disabled the light by his garage door opener so no one would see him drive in. His yard was full of trees and bushes, and the other side of the street had never been developed, so it was very private. He was certain his neighbors hadn't seen him in years.

Jeffrey had called three days later, crying. He said he he'd gotten the package, but didn't know what to do next. Sparrow told him to come home. Jeffrey said he didn't have any money to get home. Sparrow wired enough for a bus ticket and plenty more for food.

"We will perform the ritual on Walpurgisnacht. You need to be home before then. Come home. You will sacrifice yourself on Satan's altar, then I will take the dagger and do the same."

"Okay."

"Will you be all right, traveling all the way here?"

"We'll be fine," a woman's voice answered.

"I can come and get you," Sparrow had offered.

"No, we'll be fine," Jeffrey said again.

Jeffrey had turned out to be worthy, after all.

Walpurgisnacht was the next day. And where was Jeffrey and the dagger he carried? Sparrow wanted more than a single day to prepare the two of them for the journey. It was their final triumph, their step into eternity. It should be done well, and done right.

46

The sheriff called a meeting for eight a.m. Friday morning to brief the officers working on the cult case, which trumped the one the chief deputy had planned for nine.

"It's time to get everyone together for a progress report. We've been looking for Jeffrey Trippen, so far without success. It's April thirtieth, and there's been no sign of him.

"His brother Gregory got into town later than expected last night. He'll be here in an hour and will watch the videos we took of the officers when they were getting their pictures taken for their ID badges. He'll have a close listen, see if he recognizes anyone's voice. And we're sending out a department-wide e-mail informing everyone that Jeffrey Trippen was involved in a satanic cult and his brother thinks he is planning to kill himself tonight, as a sacrifice on his birthday. Every deputy should be on high alert."

"I think that's a good idea. So be it if our dirty cop reports that to the cult," I said.

The others nodded.

Twardy looked at Kenner. "Chief Deputy?"

"I'm working on warrants for Dieter Munden and Cyril Bishop. Search warrants for their homes and businesses and arrest warrants for them, as well as for Royce Sparrow. So they'll be ready to be signed and executed as soon as Sparrow rolls into town, sometime between now and Monday morning when he's due back at work.

"We had chats with Sparrow's old neighbors in Wellspring. One of the kids, a few houses away, takes care of the yard and removes the snow from the driveway in the winter so it looks like someone lives there."

"Someone should tell Sparrow it's not working. Place looks deserted," Smoke said.

Edberg and I nodded.

Chief Deputy Kenner continued, "He mails the kid a check every month, drawn from an account at a Saint Cloud bank. Nobody in the Wellspring neighborhood has seen him in years. When he moved out, he told the guy next door that he wasn't ready to sell quite yet. We'll see what turns up when we bring Sparrow in, then we'll decide about a search. I hate to waste man hours going through an empty house. That's all I got for now."

"Dawes, Edberg?"

Edberg shook his head.

"Nothing new since we saw each other last night. I haven't uncovered anything incriminating on any of our deputies. I'll be interested to see if Greg Trippen remembers anything when he watches the videos," Smoke said.

"If that's it, then the meeting's over," Twardy said.

Kenner stood. "I'll call you when Gregory's done."

Kenner phoned later that morning to report that Gregory Trippen had gone over the video tapes several times and could not match a voice from any on the tapes to the deputy that was at the rituals.

When we finished our conversation, I called Gregory and asked if he could meet me for lunch. "That'd be good," he said. We agreed on a Chinese restaurant. He was waiting in the parking lot and got out of his car when he saw me walking toward the door. "Sergeant Aleckson."

I turned around and waited for him to catch up. I wanted to hug him, offer some comfort for all he was going through, but settled on a handshake instead. We went inside and found a table in the back corner next to a window overlooking Bison Lake. We didn't say much until we'd finished eating.

"Is there anything else I can do?" he asked and threw his napkin on the table.

"I've been asking myself the same thing for two weeks."

He nodded. "Something might have happened to Jeff on the way here. If he was hitchhiking and got into a car with the wrong person . . . or if he started acting like he does sometimes, you know, when I said he talks like a girl."

"Yeah, if someone thought he needed help and called authorities, and then they found that dagger, who knows? He might be in a hospital somewhere."

"Why hasn't he called?"

"I wish I could answer that. But we're not giving up. The whole department is on alert."

"I don't know how I'll tell my mom if he dies. She blames herself for marrying Sparrow, not knowing who he really was."

"That happens to a lot of people. I mean, maybe not marry a guy as evil as Sparrow is. But each of us has had some experience where you think a person is one way and they turn out to be another."

Gregory nodded.

I laid my napkin on the table. "I better get home and get ready for work. Oh, I meant to give you Dr. Marcella Fischer's contact information." I handed him her card. "She's an excellent resource and may know doctors in Vermont who specialize in helping SRA victims." I reached over and put my hand on his. "I wish I could promise a good ending for all this, but I am praying for one."

"Me too."

47

Deputy Holman tracked me down in the squad room Friday afternoon. "Zubinski hasn't shown up for her shift. She call in sick?" Holman had covered the 135 area for the day shift, and Mandy Zubinski was his replacement for the evening one.

"Not that I know of. Let's go ask the chief deputy." Kenner had so many things going on a shift coverage might have slipped his mind.

Kenner hung up his phone when we knocked on his door frame. "What's up?"

"Did Mandy Zubinski call in?" I asked.

"No." He looked at Holman. "Didn't report in yet?"

Holman shook his head. "The latest she's ever been is ten to, and it's ten after."

Kenner glanced at his watch. "Can you stay until we get you covered?"

"Sure," Holman said then left.

"That's not like Mandy. Where would she be that she wouldn't at least call us?" I asked.

Kenner lifted his desk calendar and pulled out a sheet with names and phone numbers from underneath it. He picked up his phone and punched in a number, then left a message. "Work cell. I'll try her personal number." He left another message when it went straight to voicemail. Either it wasn't charged, or it was turned off.

"I'll run over to her apartment," I said.

"Good. Meantime, I'll get her shift covered."

I drove to the Hillside Apartments, located on the northwest side of Oak Lea, and pulled into a guest parking spot in front of the middle building. Mandy's squad car was parked in the back row. I gave Communications my location, got out of the car, and walked to the entrance. The outer door was unlocked, but the inner door was locked. I punched Mandy's apartment code into the buttons on the intercom panel and waited. No answer. I tried again. Still no answer. I found the manager's number on the menu and tried that one.

"Can I help you?" It was a high-pitched female voice.

"Yes, it's Sergeant Aleckson, Winnebago County. I need to see Amanda Zubinski, and she's not answering my call."

"Okay. I'll be right out."

A short, round woman in her forties peeked at me from the other side of the glass panel. She smiled then opened the door. Her age and body didn't match her voice. She took a peek outside, in the direction of Mandy's squad car.

"That's strange. She always leaves for work before this. Come in and we'll go knock on her door. I'm Meg, by the way."

"Hi, Meg."

I followed her up the steps to the second floor. I had picked Mandy up for training once, and another time when her car didn't start, but had never been inside her building. Meg took a right at the top of the stairs, walked down a few doors, and stopped in front of 207. She knocked on the door. There were no sounds on the other side.

I stepped close to the door and rapped very loudly. "Mandy, it's Corky." Still no sound.

"Have you seen her today?"

"No."

"I think we better check inside. She may have fallen and hit her head or something," I said.

As Meg turned her key in the lock, I braced myself for what we might find. Mandy hadn't seemed depressed, but what if . . . ? We stepped into the small entry by the kitchen.

"Mandy? It's Corky. Mandy, are you here?"

I looked around. It was reasonably neat. There were some dishes in the sink, but it wasn't overflowing. Meg stayed in the kitchen while I walked through the living room, past the bathroom, and into the bedroom. No Mandy.

The bed was a mess. The covers were thrown back, and both pillows had depressions in them. Mandy had a lover she was keeping secret? The uniform she had worn was lying on a chair in the corner. I lifted up her shirt. Her three badges—sheriff's star, name, and number—were still in place.

A memo pad, pen, and cuff key were in the breast pocket. Her wallet was in the back pocket of her pants. I pulled it out and looked inside. Her driver's license and sheriff's department identification were visible through plastic holders. Mandy's duty belt was at the bottom of the pile, and her service weapon rested in its holster.

Fear gripped my middle as I walked to her closet door and opened it. No Mandy. I took a look under the bed. Clear. I went into the bathroom and peeked around the drawn shower curtain. She wasn't there either. Where would she go without her wallet? Another wave of fear washed over me. There was no glaring evidence of foul play, but something was very wrong. I felt it in my bones.

I returned to the kitchen where Meg waited. My eyes darted around the room. I glanced from a calendar on the wall, to a small bulletin board with pictures tacked on it, to the key holder hanging next to it. A ring of keys dangled there. I stepped over for a closer look. The car keys were for a Saturn. Mandy's personal vehicle.

I felt Meg's eyes on me and turned around. "She's not here, and I'm wondering if you could do something for the sheriff's department?"

Her eyes widened. "If I can."

"I'd like you to talk to as many people in the building as possible, ask them if they've seen Amanda since eleven o'clock last night. She's probably with a friend, but we need to make sure she's okay. Can you do that?"

She nodded.

"Write down the names of everyone you talk to, and if anyone has seen her, give me a call. We'll come over and talk to them. And of course, if Mandy comes home, tell her to call me." I pulled a business card from my pocket, gave it to her, then withdrew my memo pad and pen. "Meg, what's your full name, date of birth, address, and phone number?" She gave me the information, and I jotted it down.

I thanked her then hurried out the door to Mandy's squad car. I looked in the windows. Nothing amiss. I spotted her Saturn a few spots down the row and jogged to it. The doors were locked and there was nothing suspicious looking, that I could see. I jogged to my car, crawled inside, and called Kenner.

"Chief Deputy, we have a problem." I summarized the apartment visit as I drove back to the sheriff's department.

"Where would she go without her wallet?" he asked.

"Something's very wrong."

When I got back to the sheriff's department, I went directly to Twardy's office. Chief Deputy Kenner and Smoke were there. All three men were standing like they were too nervous to sit.

"Come," Twardy said when he saw me.

"I checked the roster, and Zubinski went off duty at twenty-three ten last night. Her squad car is parked at her apartment, and the uniform she was wearing is in her bedroom. Her bed was unmade, but that could have been from the night before," I reported.

Kenner ran both hands through his hair. "I got her sister's number out of her file and called her. She hasn't talked to Zubinski since day before yesterday. I asked her the name of Mandy's boyfriend. She said she didn't know she had a boyfriend." Kenner looked at me. "Tell them what you saw."

"She wasn't sleeping alone."

"Only one reason I can think of to keep that a secret, especially from your sister—" Smoke said.

"He's married," Kenner finished.

Twardy pounded his fist into his hand, over and over, as he spoke. "We haven't got the human resources we need to handle all the balls we got up in the air now, and one of our own disappears, for godsakes.

"We got extra deputies on patrol, looking for any sign of Jeffrey Trippen. We got Sparrow's house staked out, waiting to arrest him as soon as he makes an appearance. We got search warrants and arrest warrants in the hopper.

"Now Amanda Zubinski, who has always been reliable and prompt, doesn't show up for work, and we're in a quandary wondering where in the hell she is."

Twardy's face was bright red. Smoke worried he would have a heart attack before it was all over. I worried he would have a stroke.

"Sheriff, should we get a warrant, send the crime lab to her apartment, see if anything turns up?" Smoke asked.

Twardy pinched the bridge of his nose while he thought. "That's a tough call. People do uncharacteristic things from time to time. If she's in love, her boyfriend may have talked her into going somewhere. And she forgot to take her wallet and lost track of time."

"There was no sign of a struggle that I could see. It just *felt* wrong," I said.

"We can't go charging in there and start tearing her place apart without any real evidence that a crime has been committed. Hard to get a warrant on that, not to mention the invasion of privacy issue."

"The sheriff's right. Corky's got the landlady doing some leg work for us. We'll see what that turns up," Kenner said.

Twardy nodded. "I'll call the Oak Lea P.D. Her apartment's in their jurisdiction. They'll help keep a watch out for her. In the meantime, we all go back to work. That's the best we can do."

There were a number of calls all evening, mostly routine. Vince Weber sent a message to my laptop asking to meet outside a gas station. We parked parallel to each other with our driver's side windows less than three feet apart.

"I have to admit, I'm pretty worried about Zubinski. I know we give each other a hard time, but I guess I like her fine," Weber confessed.

"I'm very worried. The last anyone heard from her was when she went ten-seven last night."

"And we know she made it into her apartment because her uniform was there." He tapped his steering wheel. "I get a gut ache when I think about it."

"She must have gone with whomever willingly. On my walk through, there was no furniture tipped over. Her gun was still holstered in her duty belt—"

"You leave your gun in your duty belt?"

"No, I keep it in my bed stand, unless people are over. Then I lock it in my safe."

"Yeah, I keep it on the dresser, so it's close. Kinda strange to leave it in your holster."

"Maybe she stores it there. Or she might have been in a hurry, like if she was expecting someone, and forgot."

"Like she forgot to come to work tonight? Because the squad car sitting in front of her building wasn't a good enough reminder." Weber said.

I raised my eyebrows and hitched a shoulder.

Weber shook his head. "That was kind of surprising, the sheriff's memo today saying that Jeffrey Trippen had gotten into satanic stuff and his brother thought he was planning to kill himself tonight as a sacrifice on his birthday. I mean, why?"

The sheriff would have a departmental meeting when the pending cases were settled and everything was out in the open. One—I hoped it was only one—dirty cop had forced the sheriff to work with a skeleton crew on the cult-related cases while we scrambled to learn his identity.

"I've done some studying, and it's a whole different world." I glanced at my watch. "It's an hour and a half before midnight, and we haven't found Jeffrey Trippen. I feel like we failed his brother. He feels responsible for him, yet helpless to defend and protect him."

"Sergeant, you know the guy's been living the homeless life for a while. There's hundreds of guys camping in the Twin Cities, right inside the cities, and a lot of their campsites are so well hidden no one, except them, knows they're there. Think of all the remote places Trippen could find to camp along a creek or river out here, like the one we stumbled on out in the middle of nowhere. All set up with that weird picnic table that's built to last for a hundred years."

The campsite was five miles outside of Wellspring. If Jeffrey was following along the river looking for the outdoor temple and happened upon that spot, he might think he had found it. There wasn't a pentagram, or all the other things Greg had said they used, but Jeffrey might not have thought about those things. He was a young boy the last time he was there. The picnic table was sturdy enough to support a person.

I shivered. "Vince, I just got a strange feeling. Actually, for about the hundredth time today. Ever since I was at Mandy's. Don't think I'm crazy, but I'm going to head out to that campsite to reassure myself Jeffrey Trippen isn't there. We haven't had any other leads."

"What the heck, I'll go with you."

We were about eight miles away from the spot where we had had our team exercise the week before. We decided to drive down the dirt road that led directly to the area and park some distance back so we didn't alarm Jeffrey in the event he was there. We took off, with me in the lead car. I phoned Communications to tell them our plans.

Even with the help of a nearly-full moon and my squad car spotlight, it was hard to find the road. The access was further west than I had figured, nearly in a grove of trees. Then it wound west before it turned south. Once we found the path, there was enough moonlight, so I turned off my lights. Weber followed suit. Perhaps an eighth of a mile away, at the top of a small hill, I saw flickering lights coming from the direction of the campsite.

I sent Communications a written message that we had arrived. Weber and I climbed out of our cars and closed the doors. There were voices coming from the campsite.

"Party goin' on?" he said.

"Sounds like it. I don't want to startle them, but let's walk down there and ask them if they've seen Jeff. I have his picture in my pocket."

"Okay, I'll be a good sport and humor you on this one."

We followed the path made by vehicle tires. When we got a little closer, I stopped, turned to Weber, and put my finger to my mouth in a 'shhh' gesture, then turned my radio volume down very low, just enough to hear a call. I pointed at Vince's radio. He turned it off. I moved my hand to my ear in a 'listen' gesture. He took a step forward, standing beside me.

Weber looked at me, and I read his lips by the light of the moon as he mouthed, "What the hell?"

There was a thundering male voice who spoke a sentence in a foreign language followed by a group of people who repeated what he had said. Latin? The language Smoke had thought was in Sparrow's journal entries.

I felt the color drain from my face. I turned to Weber, put my hands on his arms, pulled him close, and whispered in his ear, "I think they're chanting, in some kind of ritual."

He moved his mouth to my ear. "What do you mean ritual?"

It was my turn. "Satanic."

He pulled back a step, his hands locked on my arms and mine locked on his. His eyes were bigger than saucers.

I pulled him back to me. "Let's sneak over for a look."

He nodded, and we crept over to the tree line, hugging it as we moved as quickly and soundlessly as possible. The chanting got louder as we approached. There was a line of cars parked to the side of the path.

About ten feet from the clearing, we bent over and moved into the woods, creeping until we had a better view of the group. We stayed low and stared at the gathering.

My brain did not process what my eyes were seeing. There were a large number of people standing in a loosely-formed circle around a group of men. One of the men in the inner circle was the chant leader. His arms were extended, palms facing downward. One held a large goblet, another a wooden basin. A fourth had his hands folded around a bejeweled dagger that he rested against his waist.

Everyone was wearing black. The women were in flowing gowns, and the men had hooded robes. We had a side view of the men who stood close to the table where a woman was lying. She was covered with a white cloth and lay perfectly still. A candelabra with six flickering black candles sat on the table above her head. The moonlight and the glow from hanging, burning lamps made it look as though her copper-colored hair was highlighted with flames of fire.

Amanda Zubinski.

I grabbed for Weber's hand, but he didn't seem to feel it. He stared straight ahead, like he was in a trance. I squeezed harder, and he turned toward me. We were nose to nose.

"We need backup. *Now,*" I said into his left ear.

He gave a single nod and gestured for me to go. He moved his mouth to my ear. "Call SWAT." Weber drew his weapon.

"If that guy with the dagger moves take a head shot," I said.

My pulses were pounding so loudly in my ears I had no idea if I made any perceptible noises getting out of the woods, but prayed I didn't. Then I prayed for Mandy all the way to my squad car. I had my phone in my hand, and as soon as I was inside the vehicle I called Communications. It was twelve minutes after eleven. Jerry was still on duty.

"It's Aleckson. They've got Zubinski! We need an ambulance, the SWAT team, and every available deputy, now! At our location. SWAT doesn't need to wear all their gear. We need them. And their weapons."

I gave him as much information as I could in a minute. "Call the sheriff and chief deputy. And send the details to everyone's computers. Don't put it over the radio. Tell them the road is hard to find. It's about ten feet west of the fire number, right next to the woods. No lights, no sirens within five miles of here. And cut their headlights when they get on the path.

"Maintain silence coming in and getting out of their cars. And grab their shotguns. I'll wait a minute for ETAs, but I gotta get back, to back up Weber."

We hung up, and I heard the call go over the air, telling every deputy to immediately check the message on his or her computer. Carlson and Mason were in their squad cars and heading our way. Three on the midnight shift would be there within minutes.

I phoned Smoke. He answered on the first ring. "Weber and I are by the Raven River in Lynden Township, near Ninety-two forty-five Pequot Avenue Northwest. There's about twenty Satanists, and they're doing a ritual. It's like your nightmare, but *Zubinski's* on the altar. I'm terrified. Their hoods are up, so I can't see if one is Sparrow or not. Communications sent the details to your squad's laptop. I gotta get back to my partner and can't talk."

Smoke was breathing hard. Running. "I'm armed and out the door."

I hung up, checked that my phone was still on vibrate, and popped the button to release the twelve-gauge shotgun from its holder behind the middle console. I pulled it out, ran to Weber's car, and did the same.

I made it back to Weber in a minute. He was on one knee with his opposite foot planted on the ground in front of him, his weapon in the ready-position. His elbows were tucked into his waist, and he was set to extend his arms at a split second's notice. He didn't move his head, but his eyes darted my way. He holstered his Glock with a muffled snap and reached for the Remington. Double-ought buckshot at that range would make a big hole in a bad guy.

My hearted pounded uncontrollably as I studied the surreal scene in the clearing. The long, sharp-pointed dagger was the only visible weapon, but as far as I was concerned they all had one tucked in the pockets of their robes and gowns. One aggressive move from anyone would be his or her last. Our shotguns were loaded with five shells, and there were fifteen forty caliber bullets in each of our three Glock clips.

I heard Carlson's voice say "Ten-six" over my nearly-muted radio. Weber's eyes darted back to me. I nodded and left to meet the arriving team.

Carlson was standing by his squad car, parked behind Weber's in the lower area beneath the rise. Three other deputies arrived in the next two minutes, Norwood, Ortiz, and Levasseur. Mason pulled in a few seconds after that. As each one parked, he climbed out, eased his door shut, walked over to our forming group, and waited. They'd all remembered their shotguns.

I kept my volume low. "There's about twenty of 'em in a clearing an eighth mile ahead. Zubinski's just lying there on a table. She must be drugged. One guy has a big dagger, like the picture on the bulletin board at work. If he moves, he's dead. We need to surround them as best we can."

I stepped over to a car hood and drew an imaginary drawing with my finger. "There's a line of cars that stretches from this side of the clearing to a ways past it. Turn off your radios and phones. Move in behind the cars as far down the line as possible without being seen. If you can safely move into the trees on the other side of the clearing, do it. Weber is here." I pointed to the spot. "Mason, you're a sniper. I want you in center position, directly across from the guy with the dagger. He's facing east, standing on the far side of the table where Mandy is. Norwood, you lead. Then Ortiz, Levasseur, Mason, and Carlson. Mason, don't take your eyes or your weapon off dagger man. The rest of you keep an eye on everyone else and take appropriate action as needed."

Two sergeants, both SWAT, announced they were at the location. "Okay, you guys get into position, and I'll give the incoming sergeants the lowdown. If something happens before I get back there, move in. Carlson, you're the command leader until I tap your shoulder. Go."

Sergeants Roth and Hughes were armed with AR-15 assault rifles. I filled them in, pointing at designated spots on the car hood. "Roth, move to the far side, creep into the woods, and get as close to the clearing as possible. Hughes, you do the same on this side. I'll inform Weber then take my position next to Mason. Then we storm in."

After I let Weber in on the plan, I moved behind the cars, tapped Carlson on the shoulder, and slid in between him and Mason. Mason was two cars away. There was a better vantage point on that side with no trees to obstruct the view. The chanting had increased in intensity, and everyone's attention was focused on Mandy. She was staring at the sky. The two men standing next to her, who faced our direction, had their heads down and their hoods kept the moonlight from hitting their faces.

Before I could give the command to move in, the man raised his head, lifted the hands gripping the dagger, and took a step closer to Mandy. I recognized him, but I didn't believe it.

Deputy Devin Noris Stauder.

48

The Coven

Royce Sparrow was lying on the altar in the private temple of his Wellspring home. He prayed that Jeffrey was doing the same, wherever he was. Why had he agreed to come home, but then didn't? Perhaps their Master did not want to wait for Walpurgisnacht and had taken him already.

The clock was positioned on the wall so it would be easy for Sparrow to read. Five minutes to midnight. The time was near.

When he didn't return to work at the hospital, the staff would look through his desk and find the letter he had written to the hospital administrator. It spelled out his plans and where to find his body after his spirit had gone to its great reward.

As the last seconds ticked down, Sparrow lifted the dagger with its piercingly sharp blade to his arms' length above his chest. He aimed for his heart, but a strike anywhere in his torso would do. If he didn't die immediately, he would bleed to death eventually.

"My Lord and Master, I willingly give my body, soul, and spirit to you."

The plunge drove the sharp point into the spot he had hoped, straight through his heart.

49

"Sheriff's department, drop your weapon! One move and you're dead!" I shouted.

My vision tunneled to the deputy holding the dagger. I didn't need to see my team members to know they were moving in as fast as I was.

Time stopped.

The chanting stopped.

The group's movement stopped.

Everything stopped.

Everything except the arms of the deputy clutching the dagger.

Mason's shotgun blast exploded close to me. When the double-ought shell met its target on his chest, Stauder's body jerked back. His blood sprayed out. Splatters landed on Mandy's gown.

His arms flew up. The dagger dropped and caught somewhere in his robe. The momentum lifted his feet off the ground before gravity dropped him on his back.

The coven leader and the others were stunned.

My voice was amplified by the acoustics. "Everyone, hands on your heads where we can see them. Now! You two, with the bowl and goblet, drop those items on the ground. *Now*. And the three of you, back away from that table."

We watched each nuance of their actions as they followed my orders.

I maintained a one-arm grip on my shotgun and depressed the call button on my radio. "Six oh eight, Winnebago County. We have one perpetrator down and are holding approximately twenty others at gunpoint.

"We need the coroner and paramedics, ASAP. ETA on the ambulance?" With adrenaline pumping through me, it was difficult to talk and breathe at the same time.

Jerry answered. "The paramedics should be there. They arrived a few seconds ago."

"Tell them to drive down the path to the clearing."

I wanted to go to Mandy. She was breathing and staring, but not moving. It seemed like an hour passed before everyone in the clearing had their hands on their heads and the paramedics got there. They rushed in with a hand-held stretcher. They set it on the ground, lifted Mandy off the table onto the stretcher, picked her up, and were gone in a flash.

"Everyone, follow each one of my instructions. We have nine guns trained on you, and if we lose sight of your hands even for a second, we will assume you are going for a weapon.

"You are all under arrest for the charge of attempted murder. Keep your hands on your head and get down on your knees," I ordered.

It took a while for the few older ones to manage that.

"Now slowly raise your arms straight up, and keeping them above your head, get down and lie flat on your bellies.

Hold that position until you hear different orders. Carlson and Weber, move in and take them into custody, one at a time," I said.

Carlson handed me his shotgun, and I rested it against a car. They went over to the chant leader first. Weber kept his shotgun on the man's head while Carlson pat searched him, applied handcuffs, then got him to his feet. When he stood, I saw it was Cyril Bishop. The coven's ringleader.

"Ortiz," I called and jerked my head to the right. He walked over. "Pull your squad car up here. You'll take him in." I grabbed Carlson's shotgun and handed it to Ortiz. "Put this in your trunk for now. You got any flex cuffs in your car?"

He nodded. "I'll get 'em."

Smoke joined us, pistol in hand. He went straight to Stauder's body. Smoke turned, found my face, and shook his head. He holstered his weapon and told Carlson, "I'll take him." He walked over behind Bishop, latched onto his bicep, and walked him to the path.

Bishop's black hair was waxed and shone in the moonlight. He sneered, looked around, and said, "You will all pay eternally for this."

Smoke gave him a slight push. Ortiz was back by my side in a minute, handed me the bag of flex cuffs, then took Bishop's other arm. Smoke and Ortiz secured Bishop in the squad car.

"Levasseur." I signaled him over. "The next prisoner's yours. Give Carlson your cuffs and get your car."

When Carlson was done with number two, Smoke walked him to the path where he was met by Levasseur. Norwood took custody of the third and last of the leaders.

"Roth and Hughes, take over for Carlson and Weber."

Roth handed his assault rifle to Carlson and changed places with him. Returning weapons and handcuffs to their rightful owners would take some sorting out when it was all done.

Sheriff Twardy and Chief Deputy Kenner arrived back to back. One's exasperated-facial expression was a mirror image of the other's. They stood over Stauder's body for a drawn-out moment, but didn't say anything. There were sixteen people on the ground with nothing to do but listen to anything we said.

Twardy and Kenner looked around, taking in the details of the scene. They walked over to me. "This could go on all night," Twardy said.

"As long as it takes," Kenner said.

"I'll call Corrections, get somebody out here with their transport van. That holds six," Twardy said.

"Good. I thought we could start putting two at a time in the squad cars, but I wanted to keep the three leaders separate."

Without warning, a man stepped from the woods into the clearing. Mason was the first to yell, "Hands up!"

I blinked, thinking I was seeing things. "My God, it's Jeffrey Trippen," I said.

His head and beard had been shaved, but his little-boy-lost expression gave him away. He looked at the deputies pointing guns and the people on the ground, put his hands in the air, and started crying. "We couldn't find it. We've been looking for the temple and finally saw the lights here." It was a soft, female voice. Samantha.

I handed my shotgun to Smoke and made my way around the outer perimeter to Jeffrey. I noticed the pack on his back.

"Hello, I'm Corky, a friend of your brother Greg. He's waiting for you in Oak Lea."

He studied my face and his facial expression changed. "Greg? My brother? He said he'd never come back to Winnebago County." He spoke in a man's voice.

"I know, but he changed his mind when he heard you were in trouble. Jeffrey, let's go call him and ask him to meet us at the hospital. You can talk to him. Okay?"

He nodded.

I remembered Dr. Fischer's words. "Jeffrey, I want you to know you're safe. We are here to help you, to keep you safe. That's what we do. Keep people safe. Do you believe me?"

We looked each other in the eyes by the light of the moon and kerosene lamplight. I don't know what he saw in mine, but I saw relief in his.

"I believe you."

"I'll take your backpack, and I'll give it back later," I said.

He nodded again, but had a wary look on his face. "I didn't get here in time. I was supposed to be here for Walpurgisnacht." And his birthday.

"You got here at just the right time. So we were here to help you, keep you safe. Turn around and I'll grab your pack."

He pulled his arms out of the straps as I lifted and held the bag. It was heavy, much heavier than I had expected. I wished I could remove the other heavy burdens from his back as easily.

"Let's walk around the tree line to those cars. I'll follow you."

When we got there, I noticed Weber was keeping watch over three people who were bent over car hoods with their hands cuffed behind their backs. I handed Trippen's backpack to Smoke. He unzipped it, removed a felt box about eighteen inches long and six inches wide, and gave it to Kenner, who held it, but didn't open it.

Smoke pulled out other items: clothing, a toothbrush, a bar of soap. He took a last look inside, replaced the items, and handed it back to me.

Coroner Gordon Melberg arrived on the scene, and Twardy pointed to Stauder's body. Melberg walked over to it, crouched down, and set his bag on the ground beside him.

"Okay if I give Jeffrey a ride to the hospital to meet his brother?" I asked.

"Sure. We'll still be here when you get back," Twardy said.

When we got to my squad car, I opened the back door for Jeffrey. "Climb in, and we'll be at the hospital in about fifteen minutes." He got in without protest, and we were on our way. I radioed Communications that I was transporting one to Oak Lea Memorial then phoned Gregory Trippen. He wept when I told him Jeffrey was safe. He said he would be at the hospital when we got there.

We met Gregory in the emergency room waiting area. Tears welled in my eyes, and a sense of relief flowed through me when Gregory embraced his brother and sobbed loudly. The doctors would check Jeffrey's physical condition and take it from there. Gregory said he would call me in the morning. I told him later in the day would be better.

The nurse at the desk told me where to find Mandy. She was in the emergency room, the third curtained area down on the right. They were monitoring her condition.

"Mandy, are you awake?" I quietly asked.

She opened her eyes, turned her head to look at me, and attempted to smile. "Thank you."

I went to the bed, picked up her hand, and squeezed gently. "Mandy, that is the most scared I have ever been. Ever."

"They gave me drugs, and I could see and hear, but it was like I was paralyzed. Devin. I can't believe I let him seduce me. I was lonely. He . . ."

"He can't hurt you anymore."

"They were going to kill me. They're evil. They worship Satan. It was horrible, lying there, trying to move, thinking I was going to die. Devin was going *to kill me.*

"Then I heard you yell, and then the gunshot, and then blood flying above me, and landing on me. I knew a miracle had happened."

I thought for a second. "It was kind of a miracle we were there. Gosh, Mandy, I wish I could stay with you longer, but we've got a real cluster at the scene."

"It seemed like there were lots of people around me," she said.

"We've got everyone in custody, but not everyone's been transported." I squeezed her hand a little tighter. "Are you ready for more good news? We found Jeffrey Trippen, safe and sound. He's here, getting checked out by the docs."

"I can't believe it."

"Another miracle, I guess. Anyone call your family?" I said.

"Yeah, my sister's on her way from the cities."

"Good. I'll see you tomorrow, Mandy."

"Okay, and thanks isn't enough for what you did."

"Hey, just returning the favor." I bent down, gave her a quick hug, and hurried out.

Dr. Melberg officially pronounced Devin Stauder dead, and two men from the Anderson Funeral Home in Oak Lea were there to transport his body. Deputy Schorn had crime lab detail that week and enlisted the other deputies' help as he processed the scene. Everyone pitched in. It was three in the morning when we cleared. It would be hours before the jail had everyone booked and the reports were written.

When all the pieces of evidence were gathered, marked, and in the crime lab vehicle, we huddled together. I told them I had talked to Mandy and that her sister was with her. None of us would ever lose the horrifying image of her motionless body lying on that table. We went over and over the details, struggling to believe what we had witnessed. Devin Stauder was a Satanist. He was the dirty cop. The infiltrator. The spy. The Benedict Arnold. We repeated that a hundred times in different ways.

Todd Mason said he was feeling okay, but he knew it would hit him later. Sheriff Twardy took his shotgun, a routine procedure in officer-involved shootings. Mason would go on administrative leave after his reports were filed.

"Kenner, we don't want to wait until Monday to execute those search warrants. We'll get the judge to sign them first thing in the morning, before any family member has a chance to move anything. Sparrow wasn't one of them here tonight, but we won't wait for him to get back. We'll search his house in Wellspring while we're at it," the sheriff said.

Kenner agreed. "I'll phone the on-call judge at six."

"And schedule a debriefing as soon as possible. Monday."

Kenner nodded. "We better head back. We have a long night of writing reports ahead of us."

We went to our vehicles, climbed in, and all drove to the office.

Smoke stopped by the squad room a little after six. "We've got four teams assembled, and we're on our way to search the homes and businesses in Wellspring."

I blinked a few times. "Good luck."

Smoke was running on fumes. We all were.

It was seven when I finished dictating my reports and headed home. It had been a long time since I'd worked a sixteen-hour shift. And never a more eventful shift.

I fell into bed wondering how I'd fall asleep. The next thing I knew, my phone was ringing. Eventually the time on the digital clock came into focus. It read 2:15, but that meant nothing to me. Was it day or night?

"Hello?"

"Don't you have to get to work?"

"Smoke. Good thing you called. I was dead to the world."

"That's what I'm gonna be in about ten minutes. We did the searches and finished the reports a few minutes ago. Are you ready for this?"

I wasn't sure. "What?"

"We found Sparrow at his house in Wellspring. Dead. Looks like he spent more time there than at Saint Cloud. Had his own private altar area in the basement. Impaled himself with a dagger."

"For real?"

"For very real. If I see another jeweled dagger in my life, it will be too soon."

"Wow."

"Bishop's and Jenkins' wives and sons were part of last night's group, so that part was easy. We found the journals, and tons of other incriminating evidence, at all the scenes. They're collected and being processed by deputies as we speak. Same with Munden's.

"And we got a lot at Stauder's house, too. Turns out the deceased Detective Miles Walden was his uncle, of all things. Passed on his evil ways to his nephew. Guess we'll have to make sure he's the last of the line to get in the sheriff's department."

"So that's the connection. We were looking for someone from twenty years ago who was still with the department, but it was two of them, uncle and nephew. One then, one now. Man."

"The BCA is going to help us at the crematorium. Apparently, when people are cremated, they aren't always completely reduced to dust. Sometimes there are little bits of bones. In an ethical business, they'd make sure one guy's bones and ashes aren't mixed with another's. But who knows what they'll find at Bishop's."

As awful as that was, I hoped they would be able to learn some victims' identities through that process. It would be a lengthy process, no doubt.

"Now we know what hell on earth is," I said.

"A whole new meaning." Smoke yawned loudly. "I'll let you go so you can get ready for work. I should tell you, in the middle of it all, my friend called to say your little Queenie is weaned and ready to go."

"Seriously? Gosh, I hope they can keep her a few more days so Rebecca and Tina can go with me to pick her up. Maybe my next day off. I'll give them a call then."

50

The coven members made their court appearances on Monday. The judge ordered each to be held without bail until his or her next appearance. Three had turned out to be under-legal age and had been transported to a juvenile facility. The detectives spent days interviewing and interrogating them. Some gave information, but most did not. We had enough physical evidence and eyewitness statements to put most of them away for life.

Mandy Zubinski took an extended leave of absence to help heal her emotional scars. Everyone who had helped rescue her visited at least once. I stopped by a number of times and she was always grateful. Mason went through a debriefing, first by himself, then with the rest of us. He was Mandy's hero for life, and doing fairly well overall.

Gregory and Jeffrey Trippen had a long session with Dr. Fischer and Pastor Trondholm. They provided the names of professionals in Vermont who had stellar reputations. Gregory was committed to getting Jeffrey into a trustworthy program, and thought he might try it himself.

Gregory also realized that their mother needed to face her own demons. Knowing Sparrow was dead was a huge relief for Gregory. Jeffrey didn't seem to believe it.

We were able to locate a family member of Keith James Nutting, an early victim of the coven's satanic rituals. He was from northern Minnesota. His family had feared for his safety all those years. They were aggrieved, but finally had closure.

Crystal Planer, the young woman Sparrow had written about in his journal, seemed to have disappeared off the face of the earth.

It would be a long time before the coven members were tried, convicted, and sent to prison and things got back to a more routine level at the Winnebago County Sheriff's Department.

51

Rebecca and Tina were more excited than I was when we went to the farm to pick up my new pet. They ran around the farm, looking at the animals and playing with the puppies. We all agreed Queenie was the smallest and cutest one in the litter. Queenie was the energetic English setter I'd had my heart set on for weeks. I couldn't wait to bring her home, get to know her, and start her training.

I was sitting outside on my front step playing with Queenie, a week and a half after the traumatic mass arrest of the Wellspring coven, when Eric Stueman's car pulled into my driveway and stopped. I stood up, wondering what he was doing at my place. He got out, waved, and came over to us.

"Hi. I could say I was in the neighborhood and stopped by, but you'd know that's not true."

I waited for the real reason.

"What a cute little puppy. I didn't see him at your party." He reached down and offered his hand. Queenie started playfully gnawing at it.

"She's a her. Queenie. I just got her last week."

"Queenie." He stood and took a step closer to me. "I didn't have your cell number, and your home number's not published. Kenner said you were on days off."

"So you were in the neighborhood and stopped by."

He smiled. "I wanted to see you before this, but you know how crazy it's been with the satanic cult cases. Collinwood said the highest number they've charged on a single crime prior to this was twelve."

"So you were in the neighborhood and stopped by."

His smile broadened. "I'll come right out and say it. I'm here to ask you out on a date. How about tonight? Are you free?"

Smoke's comeback came to mind, and I paraphrased it. "No, but I'm reasonable."

Winnebago County Mysteries

<u>Murder in Winnebago County </u>follows an unlikely serial killer plaguing a rural Minnesota county. The clever murderer leaves a growing chain of apparent suicides among criminal justice professionals. As her intuition helps her draw the cases together, Winnebago County Sergeant Corinne Aleckson enlists help from Detective Elton Dawes. What Aleckson doesn't know is that the killer is keeping a close watch on her. Will she be the next target?

<u>Buried in Wolf Lake </u>When a family's golden retriever brings home the dismembered leg of a young woman, the Winnebago County Sheriff's Department launches an investigation unlike any other. Who does the leg belong to, and where is the rest of her body? Sergeant Corinne Aleckson and Detective Elton Dawes soon discover they are up against an unidentified psychopath who targets women with specific physical features. Are there other victims, and will they learn the killer's identity in time to prevent another brutal murder?

<u>The Noding Field Mystery</u> When a man's naked body is found staked out in a farmer's soybean field, Sergeant Corinne Aleckson and Detective Elton Dawes are called to the scene. The cause of death is not apparent, and the significance of why he was placed there is a mystery. As Aleckson, Dawes, and the rest of their Winnebago Sheriff's Department team gather evidence, and look for suspects and motive, they hit one dead end after another. Then an old nemesis escapes from jail and plays in the shocking end.

<u>A Death in Lionel's Woods</u> When a woman's emaciated body is found in a hunter's woods Sergeant Corinne Aleckson is coaxed back into the field to assist Detective Smoke Dawes on the case. It seems the only hope for identifying the woman lies in a photo that was buried with bags of money under her body. Aleckson and Dawes plunge into the investigation that takes them into the world of human smugglers and traffickers, unexpectedly close to home. All the while, they are working to uncover the identity of someone who is leaving Corky anonymous messages and pulling pranks at her house. A Death in Lionel's Woods is an unpredictable roller coaster ride to the electrifying end.

<u>Secret in Whitetail Lake</u> The discovery of an old Dodge Charger on the bottom of a Winnebago County lake turns into a homicide investigation when human remains are found in the car. To make matters worse, Sheriff Twardy disappears that same day, leaving everyone to wonder where he went. Sergeant Corinne Aleckson and Detective Elton Dawes probe into both mysteries, searching for answers. Little do they know they're being closely watched by the keeper of the *Secret in Whitetail Lake.*

<u>Firesetter in Blackwood Township</u> Barns are burning in Blackwood Township, and the Winnebago County Sheriff's Office realizes they have a firesetter to flush out. The investigation ramps up when a body is found in one of the barns. Meanwhile, deputies are getting disturbing deliveries. Why are they being targeted? It leaves Sergeant Corinne Aleckson and Detective Elton Dawes to wonder, what is the firesetter's message and motive?

Made in the USA
Middletown, DE
18 October 2022

12906407R00215